When the King Loses His Head

And Other Stories

Leonid Andreyev

When the King Loses His Head, and Other Stories

The present edition is a reproduction of previous publication of this classic work. Minor typographical errors may have been corrected without note; however, for an authentic reading experience the spelling, punctuation, and capitalization have been retained from the original text.

ISBN: 978-1-63637-706-3

CONTENTS

PREFACE

Leonid Andreyev was born in Orel, the capital of the Russian province of the same name, on August 21, 1871. He was ten years younger than his future patron and friend Maxim Gorki. He died on September 12, 1919, in Finland, an exile from his beloved chaos-ridden fatherland.

His father, a Russian of pure blood, by profession a surveyor, was a man of extraordinary physical vigor. He died at the early age of 42 as the result of a brain-stroke. His mother, a woman of much refinement and culture, was of Polish ancestry.

The earliest years of Andreyev's life were spent in close affiliation with the stage, through the personal acquaintance of his parents with the leading stage folks of the province.

He was a poor scholar and loved to play "hookey," preferring the great outdoors to the crowded class-room. His marks were very poor as the result. But he was a voracious reader of literature. His latter years in high school (gymnasium) were influenced by Tolstoy's works on non-resistance, by Schopenhauer, and by the first works of Maxim Gorki. The death of his father and the seeds of the pessimistic philosophy gave the inner life of the budding novelist a morose and pessimistic direction. In his teens Leonid Andreyev made three unsuccessful attempts at suicide.

It has been the fate of Leonid Andreyev to live through four distinct phases of Russian history, each of which has contributed to the shaping of his art.

In the latter eighties and the early nineties he had passed through one of the most disheartening periods in the life of the Russian people, when under the crushing heel of the despotic Tsar Alexander III all initiative and all aspirations of the mind were ruthlessly stifled. It was the period of shameful and soulless years, with miserable people, relentless persecutors, obedient slaves and a few hunted rebels.

The horror of this era of nightmare weighed heavily on the sensitive soul of young Andreyev and he attempted suicide in 1894 by shooting himself near the heart. The attempt was unsuccessful, but left behind an affliction of the heart, of which he died twenty-five years later.

In his student years (Andreyev took up the study of law in the University of Moscow) he fell under the influence of Tchekhov and of Gorki. Andreyev did not in his earlier years dream of becoming a writer. His interest in art led him to painting and his pictures were exhibited in the independent salons and much praised. His early stories were printed in the newspapers of Moscow under the nom-de-plume of James Lynch.

Andreyev's first story printed under that nom-de-plume in 1898 aroused the interest of Maxim Gorki, who sought out the future novelist and aided him greatly with advice and suggestions.

But between the two—between the singer of the people, the singer of humanity—Gorki, on the one hand, and the artist of individuality, the painter of thought, Andreyev, there is a vast difference and divergence. One is the captive of the realities of life, in which he loses himself, the other is the captive of fancies, of ever new problems of the soul, which he endeavors to illustrate by abstract schematism, but which he ultimately fails to solve.

In this phase of Russian history falls the series of Andreyev's stories in which he chastises the Russian intelligent hypochondriac and the follower of Tchekhov. Maxim Gorki is to him the personification of the joy of life and of the will to battle, which permeates the earlier writings of Andreyev.

The stormy period of the political convulsion which shook Russia in the wake of the Japanese war, evoked a number of beautiful stories and essays from Andreyev's pen, thrilled and aflame with the love of budding freedom. But even here the pessimism of Andreyev breaks through. In his charming story of the French Revolution, with which we begin this present volume, "When the King Loses His Head," when liberty is in danger, when the Twentieth, the symbol of monarchy, is in the toils of the people, here and there the crowd cries "Long Live the Twenty-First," ready to resume the badge of servitude.

In the "Abyss" Andreyev portrays the shameful fall of the young idealist, but in "The Marseillaise," the prose-poem with which we conclude the present volume, written in 1905, Andreyev pictures the apotheosis of a hero hidden behind the absurd exterior of a physical weakling. "The Marseillaise" is an overture to the stirring drama of the brief but glorious epoch of the popular risings after the Japanese war.

But the monarchic power crushed the spirit of the people. A period of unparalleled persecutions, executions and repressions followed. "The Story of the Seven that were Hanged" is characteristic of this terrible period which preceded the World War. This story is dedicated to Tolstoy, and its motto might well be "Fear not them that kill the body, but cannot kill the soul." Some of the passages of this story are so stirring that it is impossible to read them without shedding a tear.

After the fall of the Romanovs, a brief period of intoxicating sense of freedom overwhelmed Russia. It was not the time for literature. It was the time for action. But all too soon chaos ensued, and the artist dropped his art to defend outraged humanity. It was away from his country, with the whole world arrayed against Russia, and with Russia arrayed against herself, that Leonid Andreyev fell the victim of heart failure, induced, as the brief despatches from Finland state, by the shock of a bomb exploding in his vicinity.

The heroes of Andreyev's stories are "people who stand apart," solitary, lonely characters, walking among men like planets among planets, and a baneful atmosphere surrounds them. The idea of most of these stories and of most of his dramas is the conflict of the personality with fate and with the falsehood which man introduces into his fate.

He has a symbolic story named "The Wall": it is the barrier which men cannot pass. The Wall is all bloodstained; at its base crawl lepers; centuries, nations strive to climb upon it. But the wall is immobile, while ever new heaps of corpses are piled up alongside.

There are walls between the closest relatives in the stories and dramas of Andreyev. Frequently the characters depicted by him are insane. Freedom becomes an illusion, a tragic mockery of mankind.

In the story of "Father Vassili" we are told of an ill-fated parish priest. Misfortunes fall upon his head with an ominous purposeful frequency. Finally his only son is drowned. The mother takes to drink to drown her sorrow. In her insane frenzy she conceives again and bears an idiot. The new child, a little monster, brings an atmosphere of horror into the home and dominates the whole household. The drunken mother accidentally sets the home on fire and dies a victim of the conflagration. All through these misfortunes Father Vassili believes in his Maker with the depth and passion of despair. But little by little this faith and this despair pass into insanity. During a requiem mass over the body of a villager Father Vassili commands the corpse to arise. He calls upon God to sustain him and to work a miracle. He is left alone with the corpse, the worshippers having fled in terror. He inclines over the body and sees in the coffin the mocking features of his idiot child. A crash of thunder rends the sky. It seems to Father Vassili that heaven and earth are crashing into nothingness, he flees precipitately into the highway and falls dead. The utter solitude of the man, the monstrous domination of elementary powers arrayed against him, a moment of consciousness of oneness with the divine and insanity, these are the constant horrible and tragic features of Andreyev's art.

In his stories dealing with biblical characters, Judas Iscariot and Lazarus, we have horror and dreams again. Judas Iscariot and the Saviour are pictured as twins nailed to the same cross and wearing the same crown of thorns. The traitor in Andreyev's story loves Jesus the Man. There is a dread secret in the terrible eyes of Judas, as there is a wondrous secret in the beautiful eyes of Jesus. This horrible proximity of divine beauty and of monstrous hideousness presents a problem which the artist tries to solve. He makes of Judas a fanatical revolutionist, the slave of an idea who has resolved to materialize "horror and dreams" and to bring about the truth. There is in Judas that same duality which characterizes so many of Andreyev's heroes. He has two faces. He lies and dissembles. Throughout the whole story the dual personality of the Traitor is brought out with wonderful skill. In "Judas Iscariot" Andreyev contrasts Judas with Jesus. In "Lazarus" he contrasts the morose Jew, whom Jesus brought back from death into life after three days and three nights in the darkness of the tomb, with the life-loving Augustus. If in "Judas Iscariot" Judas, wise, cunning and evil, overcomes Jesus, naive, meek and trustful, in "Lazarus" it is the Roman Emperor who causes the eyes of the Jew to be pierced, but is in the end overcome himself.

"Anathema"—a play of Andreyev which in grandeur of conception equals Goethe's Faust, has for its humble hero, David Leiser, trustful, stupid, guileless, ever obedient to his heart, who reaches immortality and lives the life of immortality and light. His enemy, Anathema, who follows the cold dictates of reason, is foiled.

From Andreyev's pen we have a series of dramatic pictures, "Black Masks," "King Hunger," "Savva," "To the Stars," and others, and a number of stories, some of them in places streaked with a realism that is almost too revolting for the Anglo-Saxon ideas of propriety. Thus in "My Memoirs," he tells of an insane doctor of mathematics, who confined for life in a prison for a horrible crime sets down his experiences in a series of hypocritical diary notes, and who expatiates upon the beauties of nameless vice. In "The Darkness," the bomb throwing idealist, who hiding from the police on the eve of his deed, enters a house of ill-fame and becomes so abashed at the sight of the life of an inmate that he exclaims "It is a disgrace to be good," and kisses her hand, only to have his face slapped because the fallen woman resents his parading of goodness at her expense.

Andreyev, because of the cumulative portrayals of the weird and the horrible, has been called the Russian Edgar Allan Poe. But between Poe and Andreyev there lies a century of time and a world of space.

Poe's hero, in "The Fall of the House of Usher," is the last remnant of a feudal epoch dying in a crumbling castle, every stone of which speaks of a series of generations and of external and internal dissolution. The heroes of Andreyev are solitary men, hiding in their professorial studies, in the basements of tenement houses, in the caves of Judea. Death with Poe is mysteriously beautiful, with Andreyev it is a blighting, baneful curse. The solitude of Poe's heroes is the tragic solitude of a superman on a lonely height, the solitude of Andreyev's heroes is the solitude of little men, worn out with the futile vicissitudes of life. But the horror of life and of death makes these two great artists kin. Of the Russian authors Dostoyevsky is nearest to Andreyev. The solitude of the curse-stricken man, of the man on the brink of ruin, the morbid acuteness of his perceptions, the dominion of intellect over life, the eternal longing to overstep the boundary, the endless striving with God, the city with its garrets and basements—these are the favorite themes both of Dostoyevsky and of Andreyev.

As to style, Leonid Andreyev is a wonderful word painter, but his brush knows only somber colors. The basic background of his stories and of his dramas is a dark-grey, sometimes streaked with fiery-red. His pessimism leads him to look upon the world through dark spectacles. Duke Lorenzo is held captive by "Black Masks." He sails in a ship with "black sails." At the prow of the vessel is a "young woman in black."

The stories included in this first volume of Andreyev's works in the "Russian Authors' Library" series are: "When the King Loses his Head," "Judas Iscariot," "Lazarus," "Life of Father Vassili," "Ben-Tobith" and "Dies Irae."

ARCHIBALD J. WOLFE

WHEN THE KING LOSES HIS HEAD

PART I

There stood once in a public place a black tower with massive fortress-like walls and a few grim bastioned windows. It had been built by robber barons, but time swept them into the beyond, and the tower became partly a prison for dangerous criminals and grave offenders, and partly a residence. In the course of centuries new structures were added to it, and were buttressed against the massive walls of the tower and against one another; little by little it assumed the dimensions of a fair sized town set on a rock, with a broken skyline of chimneys, turrets and pointed roofs. When the sky gleamed green in the west there appeared, here and there, lights in the various parts of the tower. The gloomy pile assumed quaint and fanciful contours, and it somehow seemed that at its foot there stretched not an ordinary pavement, but the waves of the sea, the salty and shoreless ocean. And the picture brought to one's mind the shapes of the past, long since dead and forgotten.

An immense ancient clock, which could be seen from afar, was set in the tower. Its complicated mechanism occupied an entire story of the structure, and it was under the care of a one-eyed man who could use a magnifying glass with expert skill. This was the reason why he had become a clockmaker and had tinkered for years with small timepieces before he was given charge of the large clock. Here he felt at home and happy. Often, at odd hours, without apparent need he would enter the room where the wheels, the gears and the levers moved deliberately, and where the immense pendulum cleft the air with wide and even sweep. Having reached the limit of its travel the pendulum said:

"'Twas ever thus."

Then it sank and rose again to a new elevation and added:

"'Twill ever be, 'twas ever thus, 'twill ever be, 'twas ever thus, 'twill ever be."

These were the words with which the one-eyed clockmaker was wont to interpret the monotonous and mysterious language of the pendulum: the close contact with the large clock had made him a philosopher, as they used to say in those days.

Over the ancient city where the tower stood, and over the entire land there ruled one man, the mystic lord of the city and of the land, and his mysterious sway, the rule of one man over the

1

millions was as ancient as the city itself. He was called the King and dubbed the "Twentieth," according to the number of his predecessors of the same name, but this fact explained nothing. Just as no one knew of the early beginnings of the city, no one knew the origin of this strange dominion, and no matter how far back human memory reached the records of the hoary past presented the same mysterious picture of one man who lorded over millions. There was a silent antiquity over which the memory of man had no power, but it, too, at rare intervals, opened its lips; it dropped from its jaws a stone, a little slab marked with some characters, the fragment of a column, a brick from a wall that had crumbled into ruin—and again the mysterious characters revealed the same tale of one who had been lord over millions. Titles, names and soubriquets changed, but the image remained unchanged, as if it were immortal. The King was born and died like all men, and judging from appearance, which was that common to all men, he was a man; but when one took into account the unlimited extent of his power and might, it was easier to imagine that he was God. Especially as God had been always imagined to be like a man, and yet suffered no loss of his peculiar and incomprehensible essence. The Twentieth was the King. This meant that he had power to make a man happy or unhappy; that he could take away his fortune, his health, his liberty and his very life; at his command tens of thousands of men went forth to war, to kill and to die; in his name were wrought acts just and unjust, cruel and merciful. And his laws were no less stringent than those of God; this too enhanced his greatness in that God's laws are immutable, but he could change his at will. Distant or near, he always was higher than life; at his birth man found along with nature, cities and books—his King; dying—he left with nature, cities and books—the King.

The history of the land, oral and written, showed examples of magnanimous, just and good Kings, and though there lived people better than they, still one could understand why they might have ruled. But more frequently it happened that the King was the worst man on earth, bare of all virtues, cruel, unjust, even a madman—yet even then he remained the mysterious one who ruled over millions, and his power increased with his misdeeds. All the world hated and cursed him, but he, the one, ruled over those who hated and cursed, and this savage dominion became an enigma, and the dread of man before man was increased by the mystic terror of the unfathomable. And because of this wisdom, virtue and kindness served to weaken Kingcraft and made it a subject of strife, while tyranny, madness and malice strengthened it. And because of this the practice of beneficence and goodness was beyond the ability of even the most powerful of these mysterious lords though even the weakest of them

2

in destructiveness and evil deeds could surpass the devil and the fiends of hell. He could not give life, but he imposed death, that mysterious Anointed one of madness, death and evil; and his throne rose to greater heights, the more bones had been laid down for its foundations.

In other neighboring lands there sat also lords upon their thrones, and the origin of their dominion was lost in hoary antiquity. There were years and centuries when the mysterious lord disappeared from one of the Kingdoms, though there never was a time when the whole earth was wholly without them. Centuries passed and again, no one knows whence, there appeared in that land a throne, and again there sat thereon some mysterious one, incomprehensibly combining in himself frailty and undying power. And this mystery fascinated the people; at all times there had been among them such as loved him more than themselves, more than their wives and children, and humbly, as if from the hand of God, without murmur or pity, they received from him and in his name, death in most cruel and shameful form.

The Twentieth and his predecessors rarely showed themselves to the people, and only a few ever saw them; but they loved to scatter abroad their image, leaving it on coins, hewing it out of stone, impressing it on myriads of canvases, and adorning and perfecting it through the skill of artists. One could not take a step without seeing the face, the same simple and mysterious face, forcing itself on the mind by sheer ubiquity, conquering the imagination, and acquiring a seeming omnipresence, just as it had attained immortality. And therefore people who but faintly remembered the face of their grandfathers and could not have recognized the features of their great grandfathers, knew well the faces of their lords of a hundred, two hundred or a thousand years back. And therefore, too, no matter how plain the face of the one man who was master of millions may have been, it bore always the imprint of enigmatic and awe-inspiring mystery. So the face of the dead always seems mysterious and significant, for through the familiar and well known features one gazes upon death, the mysterious and powerful.

Thus high above life stood the King. People died, and whole generations passed from the face of the earth, but he only changed his soubriquet like a serpent shedding his skin: The Eleventh was followed by the twelfth, the fifteenth, then again came the first, the fifth, the second, and in these cold figures sounded an inevitableness like that of a swinging pendulum which marks the passing of time:

"'Twas ever thus, 'twill ever be."

PART II

And it happened that in that great country, the lord of which was the Twentieth, there occurred a revolution, a rising of the millions, as mysterious as had been the rule of the one. Something strange happened to the strong ties which had bound together the King and the people, and they began to decay noiselessly, unnoticeably, mysteriously, like a body out of which the life had departed, and in which new forces that had been in hiding somewhere commenced their work. There was the same throne, the same palace, and the same Twentieth—but his power had unaccountably passed away; and no one had noticed the hour of its passage, and all thought that it merely was ailing. The people simply lost the habit of obeying and that was all, and all at once, from out the multitude of separate trifling, unnoticed resistances, there grew up a stupendous, unconquerable movement. And as soon as the people ceased to obey, all their ancient sores were opened, and wrathfully they became conscious of hunger, injustice and oppression. And they made an uproar. And they demanded justice. And they reared a gigantic beast bristling with wrath, taking vengeance on its tamer for years of humiliation and tortures. Just as they had not held counsels to agree to obedience, they did not confer about rebelling; and straightway, from all sides there gathered a rising and made its way to the palace.

Wondering at themselves and their deeds, oblivious of the path behind them, they advanced closer and closer to the throne, fingering already its gilt carving, peeping into the royal bed-chamber and attempting to sit upon royal chairs. The King bowed and the Queen smiled, and many of the people wept with joy as they beheld the Twentieth at close range; the women stroked with cautious finger the velvet of the royal coat and the silk of the royal gown, while the men with good-natured severity amused the royal infant.

The King bowed and the pale Queen smiled, and from under the door of a neighboring apartment there crept in the black current of the blood of a nobleman, who had stabbed himself to death; he could not survive the spectacle of somebody's dirty fingers touching the royal coat, and committed suicide. And as they dispersed they shouted:

"Long live the Twentieth."

Here and there were some who frowned; but it was all so humorous that they too forgot their annoyance and gaily laughing as if at a carnival when some motley clown is crowned, they also

4

shouted, "Long live the Twentieth." And they laughed. But towards evening there was gloom in their faces and suspicion in their glances; how could they have faith in him who for a thousand years with diabolical cunning had been deceiving his good and confiding people! The palace is dark; its immense windows gleam insincerely and peer sulkily into the darkness: some scheme is being concocted there. They are conjuring the powers of darkness and calling on them for vengeance upon the people. There they loathingly cleanse the lips from traitorous kisses and bathe the royal infant who has been defiled by the touch of the people. Perhaps there is no one there. Perhaps in the immense darkened salons there is only the suicide nobleman and space—they may have disappeared. One must shout, one must call for him, if a living being still be there. "Long live the Twentieth."

A pale-grey, perplexing sky looks down upon pallid, upturned faces; the frightened clouds are scurrying over the heavens, and the immense windows gleam with a mysterious lifeless light. "Long live the Twentieth!"

The overwhelmed sentinel seems to sway in the surging crowd. He has lost his gun and is smiling; the lock upon the iron portals clatters spasmodically and feverishly; clinging to the lofty iron rods of the gate, like black and misshapen fruit are crouching bodies and outstretched hands, that look pale on top and dark below. A shaggy mass of clouds sweeps the sky and gazes down upon the scenes. Shouts. Someone has lighted a torch, and the palace windows blushed as if crimson with blood and drew nearer to the crowd. Something seemed to be creeping upon the walls and disappeared upon the roof. The lock rattled no longer. The glare of the torch revealed the railing crowded with people, and now it became again invisible. The people were moving onward.

"Long live the Twentieth!" A number of dim lights now seem to be flittering past the windows. Somebody's ugly features press closely to the pane and disappear. It is growing lighter. The torches increase in number, multiply and move up and down, like some curious dance or procession. Now the torches crowd together and incline as if saluting; the king and queen appear on the balcony. There is a blaze of light behind them, but their faces are dark, and the crowd is not sure it is really they, in person.

"Give us Light! Twentieth! Give us Light! We can not see thee!" Suddenly several torches flash to the right and to the left of them, and from a smoky cavern two flushed and trembling countenances come into view. The people in the back are yelling: "It is not they! The king has fled!" But those nearest now shout with the joy of relieved anxiety: "Long live the Twentieth!" The crimson faces

5

are now seen moving slowly up and down, now bright in the lurid glare, now vanishing in the shadow; they are bowing to the people. It is the Nineteenth, the Fourth, the Second who are bowing; bowing in the crimson mist are those mysterious creatures who had held so much enigmatic, almost divine power, and behind them are vanishing in the crimson mist of the past, murders, executions, majesty and dread. Now he must speak; the human voice is needed; when he is silent and bows with his flaming face he is terrible to look upon, like a devil conjured up from hell.

"Speak, Twentieth, speak!" A curious motion of the hand, calling for silence, a strange commanding gesture, as ancient as kingcraft itself, and a gentle unknown voice is heard dropping those ancient and curious words: "I am glad to see my good people." Is that all? And is it not enough? He is glad! The Twentieth is glad! Be not angry with us Twentieth. We love thee, Twentieth, love us, too. If you will not love us we shall come again to see you in your study where you work, in your dining-room where you eat, in your bed chamber where you sleep, and we shall compel you to love us.

"Long live the Twentieth! Long live the king! Long live our master!"

Slaves!

Who said slaves? The torches are expiring. They are departing. The dim lights are moving back into the palace, the windows are dark again, but they flush with a crimson reflection. Someone is being sought in the crowd. The crowds are hurrying, casting frightened glances behind. Had he been here or had it been a mere fancy? They ought to have touched him, fingered his garments or his face; he ought to have been made to cry out with terror or pain. They disperse in silence; the shouts of individuals are drowned in the discordant tramp of many feet; they are filled with obscure memories, presentiments and terrors. And horrible visions hover all night long over the city.

PART III

He had already attempted to flee. He had bewitched some and lulled others to sleep and had almost gained his diabolical liberty, when a faithful son of the fatherland recognized him in the disguise of a shabby domestic. Not trusting to his memory he looked on a coin which bore his image—and the bells rang out in alarm, the houses belched forth masses of pale and frightened people; it was he! Now he is in the tower, in the immense black tower with the massive walls and the small bastioned windows; and faithful sons of the people are watching him, impervious to bribery, enchantment and flattery. To drive away fear the guards drink and laugh and blow clouds of smoke right into his face, when he essays to take a walk in the prison with his devilish progeny. To prevent him from enchanting the passersby they had boarded up the lower portions of the windows and the tower gallery where he was wont to promenade, and only the wandering clouds in passing look into his face. But he is strong. He transforms the laughter of a freeman into servile tears; he sows seeds of disloyalty and treason from behind the massive walls and they penetrate into the hearts of the people like black flowers, staining the golden raiment of liberty into the likeness of a wild beast's skin. Traitors and enemies abound on all hands. Descended from their thrones other powerful and mysterious lords gather at the frontier with hordes of savage and bewitched people, matricides ready to put to death freedom, their mother. In the houses, on the streets, in the mysterious wilderness of forests and distant villages, in the proud mansions of the popular assembly, there hisses the sound of treason and glides the shadow of treachery. Woe unto the people! They are betrayed by those who had been the first to raise the banner of revolt and the traitors' wretched remains are already cast out of the dishonored sepulchres and their black blood drenches the earth. Woe unto the people! They are betrayed by those to whom they had given their hearts; betrayed by their own elect; whose faces are honest, whose tongues are uncompromisingly stern and whose pockets are full of somebody's gold.

Now the city is to be searched. It was ordered that all should be in their dwellings at mid-day; and when at the appointed hour the bells were rung, their ominous sound rolled echoing over the deserted and silent streets. Since the city's birth there had never reigned such stillness; not a soul near the fountains; the stores are closed; on the streets, from one end to the other, not a pedestrian, not a carriage to be seen. The alarmed and astonished cats wander in the shadow of the silent walls; they can not tell whether it be day or night; and so profound is the silence that it seems as if their velvety footfall were plainly audible. The measured tones of the bells pass over the streets like invisible brooms sweeping the city clean. Now the cats, too, frightened at something, have disappeared. Silence and desolation.

Suddenly on every street there appear simultaneously little

7

bands of armed people. They converse loudly and freely and stamp their feet, and although they are not many they seem to cause more noisy commotion than the whole city when it is crowded with a hundred thousand pedestrians and vehicles. Each house seems to swallow them up in succession and to belch them forth again. And as they emerge another or two more are belched forth with them, pale with malice or red with wrath. And they walked with their hands in their pockets, for in those curious days no one feared death, not even the traitors; and they entered into the dark jaws of the prison houses. Ten thousand traitors were found that day by the faithful servants of the people; they found ten thousand traitors and cast them into prison. Now the prisons were pleasant and awful to look upon; so full they were from top to bottom with disloyalty and shameful treachery. One wondered that the walls could bear the load without crumbling into dust.

That night there was a general rejoicing in the city. The houses were emptied once more and the streets were filled; endless black throngs engaged in a stupefying dance, a combination of quick and unexpected gyrations. Dancing was in progress from one end of the city to the other. Around the lamp-posts like the foaming surf that beats against the rocks, knots of merrymakers had gathered, clasping hands, their faces aglow with laughter, and wide-eyed, whirling around, now vanishing from view and ever changing in expression. From the lamp-post dangled the corpse of some executed traitor who had not succeeded in reaching the shelter of his prison. His extended legs seeking the ground, almost touched the heads of the dancers, and the corpse itself seemed to dance, yes, it seemed to be the very master of ceremonies and the ring-leader of the merriment, directing the dance.

Then they walked over to the black tower and craning their necks, shouted: "Death to the Twentieth! Death!" Cheerful lights gleamed now in the tower windows; the faithful sons of the people were watching the tyrant. Calmed and assured that he could not escape, they shouted more in a jest than seriously: "Death to the Twentieth!" And they departed, making room for other shouters. But at night horrible dreams again hovered over the city, and like poison which one has swallowed and failed to spit out, the black towers and prisons reeking with traitors and treachery, gnawed at the city's vitals.

Now they were putting the traitors to death. They had sharpened their sabres, axes and scythes; they had gathered blocks of wood and heavy stones and for forty-eight hours they worked in the prisons until they collapsed from fatigue. They slept anywhere near their bloody work, they ate and drank there. The earth refused to absorb the streams of sluggish blood; they had to cover it with heaps of straw, but that covering too was drenched and transformed into brownish refuse. Seven thousand traitors were put to death that day. Seven thousand traitors had bitten the dust in order to cleanse the city and furnish life to the newborn freedom. They marched again to see the Twentieth and held up to his view the chopped off heads and the torn out hearts of the traitors. And he saw them. Then confusion and consternation reigned in the popular assembly. They sought him who had given the order to slay and could not detect him. But someone must have given the order to slay. Was it you? Or you? Or you? But who had dared to give orders where the popular assembly alone had the right to command? Some are smiling—they seem to know something.

"Murderers!"

"No! But we have compassion with our native land, while you express pity with traitors!"

Still peace is afar off, and treachery is growing apace and multiplying; insidiously it finds its way into the very hearts of the people. Oh! the sufferings, and Oh! the bloodshed—and all in vain! Through the massive walls that mysterious sovereign still sows the seeds of treachery and enchantment. Alas for freedom! From the West comes the news of terrible dissensions, of battles, of a crazed portion of the people who had seceded and risen in arms against their mother, the Freedom. Threats are heard from the south, and from the east and the north other mysterious lords who had descended from their thrones are closing in upon the land with their savage hordes. No matter whence they come the clouds are imbued with the breath of foes and of traitors. No matter whence they blow from the north and the south, from the west and the east, the winds waft mutterings of threats and of wrath, and strike joyfully on the ear of him who is imprisoned in the tower, while they sound a funeral knell in the ears of citizens. Alas for the people! Alas for liberty! At night the moon is bright and radiant as if shining above ruins, but the sun even is lost in the mist and the black concourse of clouds, deformed, monstrous and ugly, which seem to strangle it. They attack it and strangle it and a mingled shagginess of crimson, they crash into the abyss of the west. Once for an instant the sun broke through the clouds—and how sad, awesome and frightened was that ray of light. Hurriedly tender it seemed to caress the tops of the trees, the roofs of the houses, the spires of the churches.

But in the tower the one-eyed clockmaker, who could so conveniently use the magnifying glass, walking amid his wheels and gears, his levers and ropes, and bending his head to one side

9

watches the swinging of the mighty pendulum. "'Twas ever thus—
'twill ever be. 'Twas ever thus—'twill ever be!'"

Once when he was very young the clock got out of order and
stopped for the space of two days. And it was such a terrifying
experience, as if all time had slipped into an abyss. But after the
clock had been repaired, all was well again, and now time seems to
flow between one's fingers, to ooze drop by drop, to split into little
pieces, falling an inch at a time. The immense brazen disc of the
pendulum lights up faintly as it moves and seems to swing like a ball
of gold if one looks at it with half-closed eyes. A pigeon is heard
cooing softly among the rafters. "'Twas ever thus—'twill ever be!'"
"'Twas ever thus—'twill ever be!'"

PART IV

The thousand-year-old monarchy was at last overthrown.
There was no need of the plebiscite; every man in the popular
assembly had risen to his feet, and from top to bottom it became
filled with standing men. Even that sick deputy who had been
brought in an armchair rose to his feet; supported by his friends he
straightened his limbs, crushed with paralysis, and stood erect like a
tall withered stump supported by two young and slender trees.

"The republic is accepted unanimously," someone announced
with a sonorous voice, vainly attempting to conceal its triumphant
tone.

But they all remained standing. A minute passed, then
another; already upon the public square, which was thronged with
expectant people, there had burst forth a thunderous manifestation
of joy, but in the hall there reigned a solemn stillness as in a
cathedral, and stern, majestically serious people, grown rigid in the
attitude of proud homage. Before whom are they standing? They no
longer own a King, even God, that tyrant and king of heaven, had
long since been overthrown from His celestial seat. They are paying
homage to Liberty. The aged deputy whose head had been shaking
for years with senile palsy now holds it up erect and proud. There,
with an easy gesture of his hand, he has pushed aside his friends; he
is standing alone; liberty has accomplished a miracle. These men
who had long since forgotten the art of weeping, living amid

10

tempests, riots and bloodshed, are weeping now. The cruel eyes of eagles which gazed calm and unmoved on the blood-reeking sun of the Revolution can not withstand the gentle radiance of Liberty, and they shed tears.

Silence reigns in the hall; but a tumultuous uproar is heard outside; growing in volume and intensity it loses its sharpness; it is uniform and mighty and brings to mind the roar of the limitless ocean. They are all freemen now. Free are the dying, free are those coming into the world, free are the living. The mysterious dominion of One which had held the millions in its clutches is overthrown, the black vaults of prisons have crumbled into dust—and overhead shines the cloudless and radiant sky.

"Liberty"—someone whispers softly and tenderly like the name of a sweetheart. "Liberty!" exclaims another, breathless with unutterable joy, his face aglow with intense eagerness and lofty inspiration. "Liberty!" is heard in the clanging of the iron. "Liberty!" sing the stringed instruments. "Liberty!" roars the many-voiced ocean. He is dead, the old deputy. His heart could not contain the infinite joy and it stopped, its last beat being—Liberty! The most blessed of mortals; into the mysterious shadow of the grave he will carry away an endless vision of Newborn Freedom.

They had been awaiting frenzied excesses in the city, but none took place. The breath of liberty ennobled the people, and they grew gentle and tender and chaste in their demonstrations of joy. They only gazed at one another, they caressed one another with a cautious touch of the hand; it is so sweet to caress a free creature and to look into his eyes. And no one was hanged. There was found a madman who shouted in the crowd: "Long live the Twentieth!" twirled his mustache and prepared himself for the brief struggle and the lengthy agony in the clutches of a maddened throng. And some frowned, while others, the large majority, merely wonderingly and curiously regarding the hair-brained fellow, as a crowd of sightseers might gape at some curious simian from Brazil. And they let him go.

It was late at night when they remembered the Twentieth. A crowd of citizens who refused to part with the great day decided to roam around until daybreak. By chance they bethought themselves of the Twentieth and wended their way to the tower. That black structure merged into the darkness of the sky and at the moment when the citizens approached seemed to be in the act of swallowing a little star. Some stray bright little star came close to it, flashed for a moment and disappeared in the darkness. Very close to the ground, in a lower tier of the tower, two lighted windows shone out into the darkness. There the faithful custodians kept their unceasing vigil. The clock struck the hour of two.

11

"Does he or does he not know?" inquired one of the visitors vainly attempting to make out with his glance the contours of the pile, as if endeavoring to solve its secrets. A dark silhouette now detached itself from the wall, and a dull, weary voice responded:

"He is asleep, citizen."

"Who are you, citizen? You startled me. You walk as softly as a cat!"

Other dark silhouettes now approached from various quarters and mutely confronted the newcomers.

"Why don't you answer? If you are a specter, please vanish without delay; the assembly has abolished specters."

But the stranger wearily replied: "We watch the tyrant."

"Did the commune appoint you?"

"No. We appointed ourselves. There are thirty-six of us. There had been thirty-seven, but one died; we watch the tyrant. We have lived near this wall for two months or longer. We are very weary."

"The nation thanks you. Do you know what happened to-day?"

"Yes, we heard something. We watch the tyrant."

"Have you heard that we are a republic now? That we have liberty?"

"Yes, but we watch the tyrant and we are weary."

"Let us embrace, brothers!"

Cold lips wearily touch the burning lips of the visitors.

"We are weary. He is so cunning and dangerous. Day and night we watch the doors and the windows. I watch that window; you could hardly distinguish it. So you say we have liberty? Very good. But we must go back to our posts. Be calm, citizens. He is asleep. We receive reports every half hour. He is sleeping now."

The silhouettes moved, separated themselves and vanished as if they had gone right through the walls. The gloomy old tower seemed to have grown taller, and from one of the battlements there stretched over the city a dark and shapeless cloud. It seemed as if the tower had grown out of all proportion and was stretching its hand over the city. A light flashed from the dense blackness of the wall and suddenly vanished, like a signal. The cloud now covered the whole city and reflected with a yellowish gleam the lurid glare of many fires. A drizzling rain suddenly commenced to descend. All was silent and all was restless.

Was he really sleeping?

PART V

A few more days passed in the new and delicious sensations of freedom, and again new threads of distrust and fear appeared like dark veins running through white marble. The tyrant received the news of his overthrow with suspicious calmness. How can a man be calm when deprived of a kingdom, unless he be planning something terrible? And how can the people be calm, when in their midst there lives a mysterious one having the gift of pernicious enchantment? Overthrown, he continues to be terrible; imprisoned he demonstrates at will his diabolical power which grows with distance. Thus the earth, black at close range, appears like a shining star when seen from the depths of azure space. And in his immediate surroundings his sufferings move to tears. A woman was seen to kiss the hand of the queen. A guard was observed drying his tears. An orator was heard appealing for mercy. As if even now he were not happier than thousands of people who had never seen the light? Who could warrant that on the morrow the land would not return to its ancient madness, crawling in the dust before him, begging his pardon and rearing anew his throne which it cost so much labor and pain to overthrow!

Bristling with frenzy and terror the millions are listening to the speeches in the popular assembly. Curious speeches. Terrifying words. They speak of his inviolability; they say he is sacro-sanct, that he may not be judged like others are judged, that he may not be punished like others are punished, that he may not be put to death, for he is the King. Consequently Kings still exist! And these words are spoken by those who have sworn to love the people and liberty; the words are uttered by men of tried honesty, by sworn foes of tyranny, by the sons of the people who came forth from the loins of those that were scarred by the merciless and sacrilegious rule of the Kings. Ominous blindness!

Already the majority is inclining in favor of the overthrown one; as if a dense yellow fog issuing forth from that tower had forced its way into the holy mansions of the people's mind, blinding their bright eyes strangling their newly gained freedom; thus a bride adorned with white blossoms might meet death in the hour of her bridal triumph. Dull despair creeps into the heart, and many hands convulsively stroke the trusted blade; it is better to die with Brutus than to live with Octavianus.

Final remonstrances full of deadly indignation.

"Do you wish to have one man in the land and thirty-five million animals?"

Yes, they wish it. They stand silent with downcast eyes. They are weary of fighting, weary of exercising their will, and in their lassitude, in their yawning and stretching, in their colorless cold words which, however, have a magic effect, one almost fancies the contour of a throne. Scattered exclamations, dull speeches, and the blind silence of unanimous treachery. Liberty is perishing, the luckless bride adorned with white blossoms, who has met her doom in the hour of her bridal triumph.

But hark! The sound of marching. They are coming; like the sound of dozens of gigantic drums beating a wild tattoo. Tramp! Tramp! Tramp! They come from the suburbs. Tramp! Tramp! Tramp! They march in defense of liberty. Tramp! Tramp! Tramp! Woe unto traitors! Tramp! Tramp! Tramp! Traitors, beware!

"The People ask permission to march past the assembly."

But who could stop an avalanche? Who would dare tell an earthquake, "So far and no further shalt thou go!"

The doors are thrown open. There they come from the suburbs. Their faces are the color of the earth. Their breasts are bared. An endless kaleidoscope of motley rags that serve for raiment. A triumph of impulsive, uncontrolled movements. An ominous harmony of disorder. A marching chaos. Tramp! Tramp! Tramp! Eyes flashing fire! Prongs, scythes, tridents, fenceposts. Men, women and children. Tramp! Tramp! Tramp!

"Long live the representatives of the people! Long live liberty! Death to traitors!"

The deputies smile, frown, bow amiably. They grow dizzy watching the motley procession that seems to have no end. It looks like a torrential stream rushing through a cavern. All faces begin to look alike. All shouts merge into one uniform and solid roar. The tramp of the feet resembles the patter of raindrops upon the roof, a sporific, will-subduing sound which dominates consciousness. A gigantic roof, gigantic raindrops.

Tramp! Tramp! Tramp! One hour passes, then two, then three, and still they are filing past. The torches burn with a crimson glare and emit smoke. Both openings, the one through which the people enter and the one through which they file out are like yawning jaws; and it is as if some black ribbon, gleaming with copper and iron, stretched from one door and through the other. Fanciful pictures now present themselves to the weary eye. Now it is an endless belt, now a titanic, swollen and hairy worm. Those sitting above the doors imagine themselves standing on a bridge and feel like floating away. Now and then the clear and unusually vivid realization comes to one's mind: it is the people. And pride, and

14

consciousness of the power and the thirst for great freedom such as has never been known before. A free people, what happiness!

Tramp! Tramp! Tramp! They have been marching for eight hours and still the end is not yet. From both sides, where the people enter and where they file out, rode the thunderous notes of the song of the revolution. The words can be hardly heard. Only the time, the cadences and the notes are plainly distinguished. Momentary stillness and threating shouts. "To arms, citizens! Gather into battalions! Let us go! Let us go!"

They go.

No need of a vote. Liberty is safe once more.

PART VI

Then came the fateful day of the royal judgment. The mysterious power, ancient as the world, was called upon to answer for its misdeeds to the very people it had so long held in bondage. It was called upon to answer to the world which it dishonored by the triumph of its absurdity. Stripped of its cap and bells, deprived of its gaudy throne, of its high-sounding titles and of all those queer symbols of dominion, naked it will stand before the people and will tell by whose right and authority it had exercised its rule over millions, vesting in the person of one being the power to do wrong with impunity, to rob men of their freedom, to inflict punishment and death. But the Twentieth has been judged already by the conscience of the people. No mercy will be shown him. Yet, ere he goes to his doom, let him unbosom himself, let him acquaint the people, not with his deeds, they are sufficiently well known to them, but with the thoughts, the motives and the feelings of a king. That mythical dragon who devours children and virgins, who has held the world in thrall, is now securely fettered and bound with heavy chains. He will be taken to the public square and soon the people will see his scaly trunk, his venomous fangs and the cruel jaws that exhale fierce flames.

Some plot was feared. All night long troops had marched through the tranquil streets, filling the squares and passages, fencing in the route of the royal procession with rows of gleaming bayonets, surrounding it with a wall of somber and sternly solemn faces. Above the black silhouettes of buildings and churches, that loomed sharp, square-shaped and strangely indistinct in the twilight of the early dawn, there appeared the first faint gleam of the yellow and cloudy sky, the cold sky of the city, looking as aged as the houses and, like them, covered with soot and rust. It resembled some painting hanging in a dark hall of an ancient baronial castle.

The city slept in anxious anticipation of the great and portentous day, while on the streets the citizen-soldiers moved quietly in well-formed ranks, striving to muffle the sounds of their heavy footsteps. The low-browed cannon, almost grazing the ground with their chins, rattled insolently over the roadways with the ruddy glare of a fuse on each piece of ordnance.

Orders were given in a subdued tone, almost in a whisper, as if the commanders feared to waken some light and suspicious sleeper. Whether they feared for the king and his safety, or whether they feared the king himself, no one knew. But everybody knew that there was need of preparation, need of summoning the entire strength of the people.

The morning would dawn, but slowly; massive yellow clouds, bushy and grimy as if they had been rubbed with a filthy cloth, hung over the church spires, and only as the king emerged from the tower the sun burst into radiance through a rift in the clouds. Happy augury for the people, ominous warning for the tyrant!

And thus was he taken from prison; through a narrow lane formed by two solid lines of troops there moved companies of armed soldiers—one, two, ten, you could not have counted their number. Then came the guns, rattling, rattling, rattling. Then gripped in the vice-like embrace of rifles, sabers and bayonets came the carriage, scarcely able to proceed. And again fresh guns and companies of soldiers. And all through that journey of many miles silence preceded the carriage, and was behind it and all around it. At one point in the public square there were heard a few tentative shouts, "Death to the Twentieth!" But finding no support in the crowd, the shouts subsided. Thus in the chase of a wild boar only the inexperienced dogs are heard barking, but those who will maim and be maimed are silent, gathering wrath and strength.

In the assembly there reigns an excitedly subdued hubbub of conversation. They have been expecting for some hours the coming of the tyrant, who approaches with snail-like pace; the deputies walk about the corridors in agitation, every moment changing their positions, laughing without apparent cause and animatedly gossiping about any trivial thing. But many are sitting motionless, like statues of stone, and their expression is also stone-like. Their faces are young, but the furrows thereon are deep and old, as if hewn by an ax, and their hair is rough; their eyes either ominously hidden in the cavernous depths of the skull or intently drawn forward, wide and comprehensive, as if not shaded by eyebrows, like torches burning in the gloomy recesses of a prison. There is no terror on earth which these eyes could not gaze on without a tremor. There is no cruelty, no sorrow, no spectral horror before which this glance would flinch, hardened as they had been in the furnace of the revolution. Those who were the first to launch the great movement have long since died and their ashes have been scattered abroad; they are forgotten, forgotten are their ideas, aspirations and yearnings. The onetime thunder of their speeches is like the rattle in the hands of a babe; the great freedom of which they dreamt now seems like the crib of a child with a canopy to protect it from flies and the glare of daylight. But these have grown up amid the storms and live in the tempest; they are the darling children of tumultuous days, of blood-reeking heads borne aloft on lances like pumpkins, of massive and mighty hearts made to give forth blood; of titanic orations, where a word is sharper than the dagger and an idea more pitiless than gunpowder. Obedient only to the will of the people they have summoned the specter of imperious power, and now, cold and passionless, like surgeons dissecting a corpse, like judges, like executioners, they will analyze its ghostly bluish effulgence which so awes the ignorant and the superstitious, they will dissect its spectral members, they will discover the black venom of tyranny, and they will let it pass to its doom.

Now the hubbub outside grows faint, and stillness profound and black as the heavens at night ensues; now the rattle of approaching cannon. This, too, subsides. A slight commotion near the entrance. Everybody is seated; they must be sitting when the tyrant enters. They strive to look unconcerned. Heavy tramping of troops placed in various stations about the building and a subdued clanging of arms. The last of the cannon outside conclude their noisy peregrination. Like a ring of steel they surround the buildings, their jaws pointing outward, facing the whole world—the west and the east, the north and the south. Something looking quite insignificant entered the hall. Seen from the more distant benches higher up it appeared to be a fat, undersized manikin with swift uncertain movements. Observed at close range it was seen to be a stout man of medium height, with a prominent nose that was crimson with the cold, baggy cheeks and dull little eyes, an expressive mixture of good nature, insignificance and stupidity. He turns his head, not knowing whether to bow or not, and then nods lightly; he stands in indecision, with feet spread apart, not knowing whether he may sit down or not. Not a word is heard, but there is a chair behind him, evidently intended for him, and he sits down, first unobtrusively, then more firmly, and finally assumes a majestic posture. He has evidently a severe cold, for he draws from his pocket a handkerchief and uses it with apparent enjoyment, emitting a loud and trumpet-like sound. Then he pulls himself together, pockets his handkerchief and grows majestically rigid. He is ready. Such is the Twentieth.

PART VII

They had been expecting a King, but there appeared before them a clown. They had been expecting a dragon, but there came a big-nosed bourgeois with a handkerchief and a bad cold. It was funny, and curious and a little uncanny. Had not someone substituted a pretender in his place? "It is I, the King," says the Twentieth.

Yes, it is he, indeed. How funny he is! Think of him for a King! The people smiled, shrugged their shoulders and could hardly refrain from laughter. They exchanged mocking smiles and salutes and seemed to inquire in the language of signs: "Well, what do you think of Him?" The deputies were very serious and pale. Undoubtedly the feeling of responsibility oppressed them. But the people were merry in a quiet way. How had they managed to make their way into the assembly hall? How does water trickle through a hole? They had penetrated through some broken windows, they had almost slipped through the keyholes. Hundreds of ragged and phantastically attired but extremely courteous and affable strangers. Crowding a deputy they solicitously inquired: "Hope I am not in your way, citizen?" They were very polite. Like quaint birds, they clung in dark rows to the window sills, obstructing the light and seemed to be signalling something to the people in the square outside. It was apparently something funny.

But the deputies are serious, very serious and even pale. They fix their eager eyes like magnifying lenses upon the Twentieth, gazing upon him long and intently, and turn away frowning. Some have closed their eyes altogether. They loathe the sight of the tyrant. "Citizen deputy," exclaims with delighted awe one of the courteous strangers; "see how the tyrant's eyes are glowing." Without raising his drooping eyelids the deputy replies, "Yes!"

18

"How well nourished he looks."

"Yes."

"But you are not very talkative, citizen!"

Silence again. There below the Twentieth is already mumbling his speech. He can not understand of what he could be accused. He had always loved the people and the people loved him; and he still loved the people in spite of all insults. If the people think a Republic would suit them better, let them have a republic. He has nothing against it.

"But why then did you summon other tyrants?"

"I did not summon them; they came of their own accord."

This answer is false. Documents had been found in a secret drawer establishing the fact of the negotiations. But he insists, clumsily and stupidly, like any ordinary rascal caught cheating. He even looks offended. As a matter of fact he has always had the best interests of the people at heart. No, he has not been cruel; he always pardoned whomever he could pardon. No, he has not ruined the land by his extravagance, he only used for himself as much as an ordinary plain citizen might. He had never been a profligate or a wastrel. He is a lover of Greek and Latin classical literature and of cabinet making. All the furniture in his study is the work of his hands. So much is correct. To look at him, he certainly had the appearance of a plain citizen; there are multitudes of stout fellows like him with noses that emit trumpet-like sounds; they may be met a-plenty on the riverside of a holiday, fishing. Insignificant funny men with big noses. But he had been a King! What could it mean? Then anybody could be a King!

A gorilla might become an absolute ruler over men! And a golden throne might be reared for it to sit on! And divine honor might be paid to it, and it might lay dawn the laws of life for the people. A hoary gorilla, a pitiful survival of the forest!

The brief autumn day is drawing to a close, and the people begin to express impatience. Why bother so long with the tyrant? What, is there some new treachery being hatched? In the twilight of an ante-chamber two deputies meet. They scrutinize one another and exchange a glance of mutual recognition. Then they walk together, for some reason avoiding contact with their bodies.

"But where is the tyrant?" suddenly exclaims one of them and grasps the shoulder of his companion, "Tell me, where is the tyrant?"

"I don't know. I feel too ashamed to enter the hall."

"Horrible thought! Is insignificance the secret of tyranny? Are nonentities our real tyrants?"

"I don't know, but I am ashamed."

The little ante-chamber was quiet, but from all sides, from the assembly hall and from the public square outside, there was heard a dull roaring. Each individual perhaps spoke in low tones, but altogether the result was an elemental turmoil like the roaring of the distant ocean. A ruddy glare seemed to be flitting over the walls, evidently men outside were lighting their torches. Then not afar off was heard the measured tramping of feet and the subdued rattle of arms. They were relieving the watches. Whom are they watching? What is the use?

"Drive him out of the country!" "No. The people will not permit it. He must be killed." "But that would be another wrong."

The ruddy spots seem now climbing up and down along the walls, and spectral shadows make their appearance, now creeping, now leaping; as if the bloody days of the past and of the present were passing in review in an endless procession through the visions of a dreamer. The turmoil outside grows more boisterous; one can almost discern individual shouts. "For the first time in my life, to-day a feeling of dread has seized my heart."

"Likewise of despair, and of shame."

"Yes, and of despair! Let me have your hand, brother. How cold it is. Here in the face of unknown perils and in the hour of a great humiliation, let us swear that we will not betray freedom. We shall perish. I felt it to-day. But perishing let us shout, "Liberty, liberty, brothers!" Let us shout it so loud that a world of slaves shall quake with fear. Clasp my hand tighter, brother."

It was still now; here and there crimson spots flared up along the walls, while the misty shadows moved with swiftness, but the abyss below roared and thundered with increasing fury, as if a dreadful and mighty hurricane had come sweeping onward from the north and the south, from the west and the east, and had stirred the multitude with its terror. Fragments of songs and howls and one word as if sketched in stupendous jagged black outlines in the chaos of sounds:

"Death! Death to the Tyrant!"

The two deputies were standing lost in a reverie. Time passed on, but still they stood there, unmoved in the maddened chase of shadow shapes and smoke, and it seemed as if they had been standing there for ages. Thousands of spectral years surrounded them with the mighty and majestic silence of eternity, while the shadows whirled on frenziedly, and the shouts rose and fell beating against the window like windswept breakers. At times the weird and mysterious rhythm of the surf could be discerned in the turmoil and the thunderous roar of the breaking waves. "Death! Death to the tyrant!" At last they stirred from the spot.

"Well let us go in there!" "Let us go in! Fool that I was! I had thought that this day would end the fight with tyranny." "The fight is just commencing. Let us go in!"

They passed through dark corridors and dawn marble stairways, through chilly and silent halls that are as damp as cellars. Suddenly a gleam of light, a wave of heated air like the breath of a furnace, a hubbub of voices like a hundred caged parrots talking against time. Then another doorway and at their feet there opens an immense chasm, littered with heads, semi-dark and filled with smoke. Reddish tongues of candles stifling for want of fresh air. Someone is speaking somewhere. Thunderous applause. The speech is apparently ended. At the very bottom of the abyss, between two flickering lights is the small figure of the Twentieth. He is wiping the perspiration from his forehead with a handkerchief, bends low over the table and reads something with an indistinct mumbling voice. He is reading his speech of defense. How hot he feels! Ho, Twentieth! Remember that you are king. Raise your voice ennoble the ax and the executioner! No! He mumbles on, tragically serious in his stupidity.

PART VIII

Many watched the execution of the king from the roofs, but even the roofs were not sufficient to accommodate the sight-seers and many did not succeed after all in seeing how kings are executed. But the high and narrow houses, with the queer coiffure of mobile creatures instead of roofs seemed to have become endowed with life, and their opened windows resembled black, winking eyes. Behind the houses rose church spires and towers, some pointed and others blunt, and at first glance they looked the same as usual, but on closer observation they appeared to be dotted with dark transverse lines which seemed to be swaying to and fro; they, too, were crowded with people. Nothing could be seen from so great a height, but they looked on just the same. Seen from the roofs of houses the scaffold seemed as small as a child's plaything, something like a toy barrow with broken handles. The few persons who stood apart from the sight-seers and in the immediate neighborhood of the scaffold, the only few persons who stood by

21

themselves (the rest of the people having been merged into a dense mass of black), those few persons standing by themselves oddly resembled tiny black ants walking erect. Everything seemed to be on a level, and yet they laboriously and slowly ascended invisible steps. And it seemed strange that right beside one, upon the neighboring roofs, there stood people with large heads, mouths and noses. The drums beat loudly. A little black coach drove up to the scaffold. For quite a little while nothing could be discerned. Then a little group separated itself from the mass and very slowly ascended some invisible steps. Then the group dispersed, leaving in the center a tiny looking individual. The drums beat again and one's heart stood still. Suddenly the tattoo came to an end hoarsely and brokenly. All was still. The tiny lone figure raised its hand, dropped it and raised it again. It is evidently speaking, but not a word is heard. What is it saying? What is it saying? Suddenly the drums broke into a tattoo, scattering abroad their martial beats, and rending the air into myriads of particles which hindered one from seeing. Commotion on the scaffold. The little figure has vanished. He is being executed. The drums beat again and all of a sudden, hoarsely and brokenly, cease from their tumult. On the spot where the Twentieth had stood just a moment before there is a new little figure with extended hand. And in that hand there is seen something tiny, that is light on one side and dark on the other, like a pin head dyed in two colors. It is the head of the King. At last! The coffin, with the body and the head of the King, was rushed off somewhere, and the conveyance that bore it away drove off at a breakneck speed, crushing the people in its path. It was feared that the frenzied populace would not spare even the remains of the tyrant. But the people were terrible indeed. Imbued with the ancient slavish fear they could not bring themselves to believe that it had really taken place, that the inviolable sacrosanct and potent sovereign had placed his head under the ax of the executioner: desperately and blindly they besieged the scaffold; eyes very often play tricks on one and the ears deceive. They must touch the scaffold with their hands, they must breathe in the odor of royal blood, steep their arms in it up to the elbows. They fought, scrambled, fell and screamed. There something soft, like a bundle of rags, rolls under the feet of the crowd. It is the body of one crushed to death. Then another and another. Having fought their way to the heap of ruins which remained of the scaffold, with feverish hands they broke off fragments of it, scraping them off with their nails; they demolished the scaffold greedily, blindly grabbing heavy beams, and after a step or two fell under the burden. And the crowd closed in over the heads of the fallen while the beams rose to the surface, floated along as if borne on some current, and diving again it showed for a moment its jagged edge and then disappeared. Some found a little pool of blood that the thirsting ground had not yet drained and that had not yet been trampled under foot, and they dipped into it their handkerchiefs and their raiment. Many smeared the blood on their lips and imprinted some mysterious signs on their foreheads, anointing themselves with the blood of the King to the new reign of freedom. They were intoxicated with savage delight. Unaccompanied by song or speech they whirled in a breathless dance; ran about raising aloft their bloodstained rags, and scattered over the city, shouting, roaring and laughing incontinently and strangely. Some attempted to sing, but songs were too slow, too harmonious and rhythmical, and they again resumed their wild laughing and shouting. They started toward the national assembly intending to thank the deputies for ridding the land of the tyrant, but on the way they were deflected from their goal by the pursuit of a traitor who shouted: "The King is dead, long live the King! Long live the Twenty-first!" And then they dispersed—after having hanged someone.

Many of those who secretly continued to be loyal to the King could not bear the thought of his execution and lost their minds; many others, though they were cowards, committed suicide. Until the very last moment they waited for something, hoped for something, and had faith in the efficacy of their prayers. But when the execution had taken place they were seized with despair. Some grimly and sullenly, others in sacrilegious frenzy pierced their hearts with daggers. And there were some who ran out into the street with a savage thirst for martyrdom, and facing the avalanche of the people shouted madly, "Long live the Twenty-first!" and they perished.

The day was drawing to a close and the night was breaking upon the city, the stern and truthful night which has no eyes for that which is visible. The city was yet bright with the glare of street lights, but the river under the bridge was as black as liquid soot, and only in the distance, where it curved, and where the last pale cold gleams of sunset were dying away, it shone dimly like the cold reflection of polished metal. Two men stood on the bridge, leaning against its masonry, and peered into the dark and mysterious depth of the river.

"Do you believe that freedom really came to-day?" asked one of the twain in a low tone of voice, for the city was yet bright with many lights, while the river below stretched away, wrapped in blackness.

"Look, a corpse is floating there," exclaimed the other, and he spoke in a low tone of voice, for the corpse was very near and its broad blue face was turned upward.

"There are many of them floating in the river these days. They are floating down to the sea."

"I have not much faith in their liberty. They are too happy over the death of the Insignificant One."

From the city where the lights were yet burning the breeze wafted sounds of voices, of laughter and of songs. Merrymaking was still in progress.

"Dominion must be destroyed yet," said the first.

"The slaves must be destroyed. There is no such thing as dominion; slavery alone exists. There goes another corpse. And still another. How many there are of them. Where do they come from? They appear so suddenly from under the bridge!"

"But the people love liberty."

"No. They merely fear the whip. When they shall learn to love liberty they will become free."

"Let us go hence. The sight of these corpses nauseates me."

And as they turned to depart, while the lights were yet shining in the city and the river was as black as liquid soot, they beheld something massive and somber, that seemed begotten of darkness and light. From the east, where the river lost itself in the maze of gloom-enveloped meadows, and where the darkness was a stir like a thing of life, there rose something immense, shapeless and blind. It rose and stopped motionless, and though it had no eyes it looked, and though it had no hands, it extended them over the city, and though it was a dead thing, it lived and breathed. The sight was awe inspiring.

"That is the fog rising over the river," said the first.

"No, that is a cloud," said the second.

It was both a fog and a cloud.

"It seems to be looking." It was.

"It seems to be listening." It was.

"It is coming toward us." No, it remained motionless. It remained motionless, immense, shapeless and blind; upon its weird excrescences shone with a ruddy glow the reflected gleaming of the city's lights, and below, at its foot, the black river lost itself in the embrace of gloom enveloped meadows, and the darkness was a stir like a thing of life. Swaying sullenly upon the waves corpses floated into the darkness and lost themselves in the gloom, and new corpses took their places, swaying dumbly and sullenly and disappeared— countless corpses, silent, thinking their own thoughts, black and cold as the water that was carrying them hence. And in that lofty

24

tower from where early that morning the King had been taken to his doom, the one-eyed clockmaker was fast asleep right under the great pendulum. That day he had been very pleased with the stillness that reigned in his tower. He even had burst into song, that one-eyed clockmaker. Yes, he had been singing; and he walked about affectionately among his wheels and levers until dark. He felt the guy ropes, sat on the rungs of his ladders, swinging his feet and purring, and would not look at the pendulum, pretending that he was cross. But then he looked at it sideways and laughed out loudly, and the pendulum answered him with joyous peals. It kept on swinging, smiling all over its brazen face and roaring; "'Twas ever thus! 'Twill ever be! 'Twas ever thus! 'Twill ever be!"

"Come now! Come now!" urged the one-eyed clockmaker, splitting his sides with laughter. "'Twas ever thus! 'Twill ever be!" And when it had grown quite dark the one-eyed hermit sought rest beneath the swinging pendulum and was soon asleep. But the pendulum did not sleep, and kept on swinging all night long above his head, wafting strange dreams to the sleeper.

(THE END)

JUDAS ISCARIOT

CHAPTER I

Jesus Christ had been frequently warned that Judas of Kerioth was a man of ill repute, a man against whom one should be on guard. Some of the disciples of Jesus who had been to Judea knew him well personally, others had heard a great deal of him, and there was none to say a good word concerning him. And if the good condemned him saying that Judas was covetous, treacherous, given to hypocrisy and falsehood, evil men also, when questioned about him, denounced him in the most opprobrious terms. "He always sows dissensions among us" they would say spitting contemptuously at the mere mention of his name; "he has thoughts of his own, and creeps into a house softly like a scorpion, but goes out with noise." Even thieves have friends, robbers have comrades, and liars have wives to whom they speak the truth, but Judas mocks alike the thieves and the honest, though he is a skillful thief himself, and in appearance he is the most ill-favored among the inhabitants of Judea. "No, he is not of us this Judas of Kerioth", the evil would say to the surprise of those good people who saw but little difference between them and other vicious men in Judea.

It was rumored also that Judas had years back forsaken his wife, and that the poor woman, hungry and wretched, was vainly striving to eke out her sustenance from the three rocks that formed the patrimony of Judas, while he wandered aimlessly for many years among the nations, reaching in his travels the sea, and even another sea that was further still, lying, cutting apish grimaces and keenly searching for something with his thievish eye, only to depart suddenly, leaving in his wake unpleasantness and dissension,— curious, cunning and wicked like a one-eyed demon. He had no children, and this again showed that Judas was an evil man, and that God desired no progeny from him.

None of the disciples had noticed the occasion on which this red-haired and repulsive Judean first came near the Christ. But he had been going their way for some time already, unabashed, mingling in their conversations, rendering them small services, bowing, smiling, ingratiating himself. There were moments when he seemed to fit into the general scheme, deceiving the wearied scrutiny, but often he obtruded himself on the eye and the ear, offending both as something incredibly repulsive, false and

26

loathsome. Then they would drive him away with stern rebuke, and for a time he would be lost somewhere on the road, merely to reappear unobserved, servile, flattering and cunning like a one-eyed demon. And there was no doubt to some of His disciples that in his desire to come near Jesus there was hidden some mysterious object, some evil and calculating design.

But Jesus did not heed their counsel; their voice of warning did not touch His ear. With that spirit of radiant contradiction which irrepressibly drew Him to the rejected and the unloved, He resolutely received Judas and included him even in the circle of His chosen ones. The disciples were agitated and murmured among themselves, but He sat still, His face turned to the setting sun, and listened pensively,—perhaps to them and perhaps to something entirely different. For ten days not a breath of wind had stirred the atmosphere, and the same diaphanous air, stationary, immobile, keen of scent and perception hung over the earth. And it seemed as though it had preserved in its diaphanous depth all that had been shouted and sung during these days by man, beast or bird,—the tears, the sobs and the merry songs, the prayers and the curses; and these glassy transfixed sounds seemed to burden and satiate it with invisible life. And once more the sun was setting. Its flaming orb was heavily rolling down the firmament, setting it ablaze with its dying radiance, and all on earth that was turned toward it: the swarthy face of Jesus, the walls of houses and the foliage of trees reflected obediently that distant and weirdly pensive light. The white wall was no longer white now, nor did the crimson city on the crimson hill appear white to the eye.

And now came Judas.

He came humbly bowing, bending his back, cautiously and anxiously stretching out his misshapen large head, and looking just like those who knew had pictured him. He was gaunt, well built, in stature almost as tall as Jesus, who was slightly bent from the habit of thinking while He walked. And he seemed to be sufficiently vigorous, though for some reason he pretended to be ailing and frail, and his voice was changeable: now manly and strong, now shrill like the voice of an old woman scolding her husband, thin and grating on the ear. And often the listener wished to draw the words of Judas out of his ears like some vile insect. His stubbly red hair failed to conceal the strange and unusual form of his skull: it seemed cleft from the back by a double blow of the sword and patched together. It was plainly divided into four parts, and its appearance inspired mistrust and even awe. Such a skull does not bode peace and concord; such a skull leaves in its wake the noise of bloody and cruel conflicts. The face of Judas, too, was double: one

27

side, with its black, keen, observing eye was living, mobile, ready to gather into a multitude of irregular wrinkles. The other side was free from wrinkles, deathly smooth, flat and rigid; and though in size it was equal to the other, it seemed immense because of the wide-open, sightless eye. Covered with an opaque film it never closed night or day, facing alike the light and the darkness; but its vigilant and cunning mate was so close that one was loth to credit its entire blindness. When in fear or excitement Judas happened to close his seeing eye and shake his head, it rolled with the motion of the head and gazed silently and intently. Even altogether unobserving persons realized when they looked on the Iscariot that such a man could bring no good; but Jesus took him up and even seated him at His side, at His very side!

John, the beloved disciple, moved away loathingly, while the others, loving their Teacher, looked on the ground with disapproval. But Judas sat down, and, moving his head to the left and to the right, immediately commenced to complain with a thin voice of various ailments, how his breast pained at night, how he was apt to lose breath when walking uphill or grow dizzy at the edge of the precipice, hardly restraining a stupid desire to cast himself into the abyss. And many other things he invented impiously, evidently failing to grasp that sickness comes to man not by chance but is born from a failure to shape his acts in accord with the commands of the Eternal. He rubbed his chest with his palm and coughed hypocritically, this Judas of Kerioth, amid general silence and downcast glances.

John, avoiding the Teacher's glance, whispered to Simon Peter:—"Art thou not tired of this falsehood? I cannot bear it longer and I shall go hence."

Peter looked at Jesus, and meeting His glance, swiftly rose to his feet. "Wait!" he said to his friend.

Once more he glanced at Jesus and then, impetuously, like a rock dislodged from the mountain side, he gained the side of Judas Iscariot and loudly greeted him with a wide and unmistakable cordiality:—"Now you are with us, Judas!" Then he amiably slapped the newcomer's curved back, and not seeing the Teacher, though feeling His glance, he added with that loud voice of his which dispelled all objections as water displaces air:

"Your bad looks do not matter. We get uglier creatures into our nets and they turn out the best to eat. And it is not for us, fishers for the Lord, to throw away our haul because the fish is ugly and one-eyed. I saw once in Tyre an octopus caught by the fishermen there and was scared enough to run. They laughed at me, who am a fisherman from Tiberias, and gave me a taste of it. And I asked for another helping, it was so fine. Dost Thou remember, Teacher, I told Thee of it and Thou didst laugh? And thou, too, Judas, resemblest an octopus, at least one half of thee does."

And he laughed loudly, pleased with his jest. When Peter spoke, his words sounded firm and solid as though he were nailing them down with a hammer. When Peter moved or did anything he made a noise that was heard afar off and evoked a response from the dullest objects: the stone floor groaned under his feet, the doors trembled and banged, and the very air was thrilled. In the mountain fastnesses his voice woke an angry echo, and in the morning, while they fished, it rolled sonorously over the somnolently glistening waters and beguiled the first timid rays of the sun into a responsive smile. And perhaps that was why they loved Peter so: while upon the faces of others there rested yet the shadows of the night, his massive head and bare bosom and freely swinging arms glowed already in the radiance of the rising sun.

The words of Peter, approved by the Teacher, dispelled the embarrassment of the disciples. But some of them, who had been to the seashore and had seen the octopus, were disquieted by the simile which Peter had so frivolously applied to the new disciple. They remembered the monster's immense eyes, the multitude of its greedy tentacles, its pretended calm at the very moment it was ready to embrace and to crush the victim and to suck out its life, without a single wink of its great big eyes.

What was that? Jesus was silent, Jesus smiled; He was watching them with a kindly smile while Peter spoke of the octopus,—and one after the other the confused disciples approached Judas, addressing him cordially, but they walked away quickly and in embarrassment.

And only John, the Son of Zebedee, remained obstinately silent; and Thomas too was ruminating over the incident and apparently could not make up his mind to say anything. He intently watched Christ and Judas who were seated together, and this strange proximity of divine beauty and monstrous hideousness, of the Man with the gentle glance and the Octopus with the immense, immobile lack-lustre, greedy eyes—oppressed his mind like an unfathomable mystery. He strained and wrinkled his straight and smooth forehead, half closing his eyes in an effort to see better, but his exertion had only the effect of making it appear that Judas had really eight restlessly shuffling tentacles. But that was an error. Thomas realized this and gazed again with obstinate effort.

But Judas little by little grew bolder: he stretched out his arms, which he had held cramped at the elbows, relaxed the muscles that had kept his jaws in a state of rigidity and cautiously proceeded to exhibit his redhaired skull. It was in the plain view of all, but it seemed to Judas that it had been deeply and impenetrably hidden from sight by some invisible, opaque and cunningly devised film. And as one emerging from the grave, he first felt the rays of light touching his strangely shaped skull and then his sight met the eyes of the onlookers. He paused and suddenly revealed his entire face. But nothing happened. Peter had gone somewhere on an errand. Jesus sat musing and leaned His head upon His arm, softly swinging His sunburnt foot. The disciples were conversing quietly and only Thomas was attentively and seriously scrutinizing him like a conscientious tailor taking his customer's measure. Judas smiled, but Thomas did not respond, though he apparently took the smile into account, like everything else, and continued his scrutiny. But a disquieting sensation annoyed the left side of Judas' face and he turned around: from a dark corner John was looking upon him with his cold and beautiful eyes, handsome, pure, without a spot on his snowwhite conscience. Walking apparently like other people, but with the inward feeling of slinking away like a chastised dog, Judas approached him and said:

"Why art thou silent, John? Thy words are like golden fruit in transparent silver vessels. Give some of it unto Judas who is so poor."

John gazed at the immobile and wide-open eye and did not utter a word. And he saw Judas creep away, linger an instant irresolutely and disappear in the darkness of the open doorway.

It was the time of the full moon and many took the opportunity for a walk. Jesus, too, went forth with the others, and Judas watched the departing figures from the low roof on which he had spread his bed. In the moonlight each figure had on airy and deliberate aspect and seemed to float, with its black shadow in the rear. Suddenly the man would vanish in the gloom and then his voice would be heard. But when the people emerged again into the moonlight, they seemed silent like the white walls, like the black shadows, like that transparently hazy and moonlit night.

Most people were sleeping already when Judas heard the gentle voice of the homecoming Christ. And all had grown still in the house and about him. The cock crew; somewhere an ass, disturbed in his slumber, brayed in a loud and injured tone, and ungraciously stopped again after a few protests. But Judas slept not; he was listening intently from his hiding place. The moon illumined one half of his face and its radiance cast a queer reflection in the large and open eye, as if mirroring itself on a lake of ice.

Suddenly, as if remembering something, he coughed several times in quick succession, and rubbed with his palm his hairy and vigorous breast: someone might be awake and listening to the thoughts of Judas.

CHAPTER II

Little by little the disciples became accustomed to Judas and ceased to notice his ugliness. Jesus turned over to him the treasure chest, and with it the household cares: his task was now to purchase the necessary food and raiment, to distribute alms, and to prepare a lodging place during their wanderings. All this he accomplished skillfully and in a very short time he succeeded in gaining the goodwill of some of the disciples who observed the pains he was taking. Judas, indeed, lied incessantly, but they had become used to this also, for they failed to find any evil deed in the wake of his lying, and it added a peculiar piquancy to his tales making life appear like some absurd, and at times terrible legend.

From Judas' tales it seemed as though he knew all men, and each man whom he knew had at one time or another in his life committed an evil deed, perhaps a crime. Good people in his opinion were those who knew well how to hide their actions and thoughts; but if one were to embrace them, to set them at ease with caresses and, to closely question them, he felt sure evil and falsehood would ooze from them like poison from a suppurating wound. He readily agreed that he too was wont to lie now and then, but affirmed with an oath that others lied even more, and that if there was one person in the world foully imposed upon and ill-used that person was Judas. Many people had deceived him, and more than once and in divers ways. Thus a certain steward who had charge of a nobleman's treasure had confessed to Judas that for ten years he had coveted the possession of the treasure entrusted to him, but feared his master and his conscience. And Judas believed him, but lo! suddenly he stole the treasure and deceived Judas. And again Judas believed him, but he as unexpectedly returned the stolen goods to his master—and again deceived Judas. And everybody was deceiving him—even the animals. If he petted a dog, it would snap at his fingers; if he beat it with a rod it licked his hand and looked into his eyes with a filial expression. He killed such a dog once, buried the animal deep in the ground and lay a heavy

31

stone on the burial spot, but who knows? perhaps because he had killed it, it became endowed with a more abundant life and was no longer resting in its grave but merrily running about with other dogs.

Every one laughed at Judas' tales, and he himself smiled pleasantly, winking his live and mocking eye, and smilingly confessed again that he had lied a little: that he had never killed such a dog, but promised to find it and surely kill it, for he hated to be deceived. And they laughed still more at such words.

But sometimes in his tales he exceeded the limits of probability and verisimilitude and ascribed to people tendencies such as are foreign even to beasts and accused them of simply incredible crimes. And as he mentioned in such connection names of the most respected people, some were indignant at the slander, while others jestingly inquired:

"But thy father and mother, Judas, were they not good people?"

Judas winked his eye, smiled and shrugged his shoulders. And as he shook his head his congealed wide open eye shook in its orbit and gazed dumbly:

"And who was my father? Perhaps the man who chastised me when I was a child, perhaps the devil, or a goat or a rooster. Can Judas know with whom his mother shared her couch? Judas has many fathers. Of whom speak you?"

But at this the ire of all was aroused, for they greatly honored their parents, and Matthew, thoroughly versed in the Scriptures, sternly repeated the words of Solomon:

"He who speaks ill of his father and his mother, his lamp will be extinguished in utter darkness."

And John of Zebedee inquired contemptuously: "And how about us? What evil wilt thou say about us, Judas of Kerioth?"

But he, with pretended fear, threw up his hands, cringing and whining like a beggar vainly praying alms from a passer-by:

"Ah! Wouldst thou tempt poor Judas? Mock poor Judas, deceive poor guileless Judas?"

While one side of his face was distorted in apish grimaces, the other seemed serious and stern and the never-closed eye peered mutely and vaguely into space. Above all others, and most loudly, Simon Peter was wont to laugh at his jests. But once it happened that with a sudden frown he paused and hastily took Judas aside, almost dragging him by his sleeve:

"And Jesus? What thinkest thou of Jesus?" he inquired in a loud whisper bending over him. "But no jesting now, I pray thee."

Judas looked up with hatred:

"And what thinkest thou?"

"I think that He is the Son of the living God."

"Then why askest thou? What could Judas say whose father is a goat?"

"But dost thou love Him? It seems that thou lovest no one."

And with the same odd malice-reeking manner the Iscariot snapped out:

"I do."

After this conversation Peter for a day or two loudly referred to Judas as his friend the octopus, while the other clumsily and wrathfully sought to escape from him into some obscure nook where he would sit and sulk, while his white never-closed eye gleamed ominously in the dark.

Thomas alone regarded Judas' tales with seriousness. He was incapable of understanding jests, pretensions and lies, plays of words and of thoughts, and in everything sought the substantial and positive. All stories of Judas concerning evil people and their deeds he interrupted with brief business-like questions:

"Can you prove it? Who heard this? And who else was present? What was his name?"

Judas shrilly protested that he himself had heard and seen it all, but the obstinate Thomas persisted in questioning him calmly and methodically until Judas confessed that he had lied or until he invented a more plausible falsehood over which Thomas would pore for some time. Then discovering the deception he immediately returned and quietly exposed the liar. Judas on the whole aroused in him an intense curiosity, which brought about a queer sort of a friendship between them, noisy, full of laughter and vituperation on the one hand, and characterized by calm and insistent inquisitiveness on the other. At times Judas felt an irresistible contempt for his unimaginative friend and piercing him with a poignant glance he would inquire with irritation and almost pleadingly:

"What else dost thou want? I have told thee all, all."

"I want thee to explain to me how a goat could be thy father," insisted Thomas phlegmatically and waited for an answer. Once after listening to such a query Judas relapsed into silence and scanned the inquirer from head to foot in amazement. He saw a man of erect and lanky stature, of grey countenance, transparently clear straightforward eyes, two massive folds starting at the nose and losing themselves in the evenly trimmed rough beard, and observed with conviction:

"How stupid thou art Thomas! What seest thou in thy dreams? A tree, a wall, an ass?"

And Thomas blushed in confusion, finding no answer. But just as Judas' living and unsteady eye was about to close in sleep, he suddenly exclaimed (they both now slept on the roof):

"Thou art wrong, Judas. I do see evil dreams sometimes. How sayest thou, is a man responsible for his dreams?"

"And who else sees them but the man himself?"

Thomas softly sighed and lapsed into musing. Judas smiled contemptuously, tightly shutting his thievish eyes and calmly yielded himself up to his rebellious dreams, monstrous visions, and mad imaginings which rent to pieces his illshaped skull.

When in the wanderings of Jesus through Judea the pilgrims approached a village, the Iscariot was in the habit of relating evil things concerning the inhabitants thereof and predicting calamities. But it generally happened that the people whom he denounced met Christ and His friends joyously, surrounded them with attentions, and the treasure chest of Judas grew so heavy that he could hardly carry it.

And when he was twitted with his mistake he shrugged his shoulders in resignation and said:

"Yes, yes. Judas thought they were wicked and they are good. They believed quickly and gave us money. And again they deceived Judas, poor trusting Judas of Kerioth."

But once having departed from a village where they had been cordially received Thomas and Judas had a violent dispute, and in order to settle it they chanced to turn back. A day later they caught up with Jesus and the disciples. Thomas looked confused and saddened, but Judas bore himself triumphantly, as if waiting for the others to come and congratulate him. Coming near the Teacher, Thomas announced:

"Judas was right, Lord. Those were stupid and wicked people. Thy seed fell upon rocky ground."

And then he related what had happened. Soon after Jesus and His disciples had gone an old woman discovered the loss of a kid and accused the strangers of the theft. The villagers argued with her, but she obstinately insisted that nobody else could have stolen it but Jesus. Many believed her and talked of pursuing the strangers. But soon the kid was found (it had become entangled in the bushes). The villagers, however, decided that Jesus was after all a deceiver and perhaps a thief.

"Indeed?" said Peter, distending his nostrils. "Lord, say the word and I shall return to those fools."

But Jesus, who had kept silence all this time, glanced at him sternly, and Peter stopped and hid himself behind the backs of others. And no one else spoke of the incident, as if nothing had

34

happened, as if he, Judas, had proved to be in the wrong. Vainly he strove to show himself from every point of view, laboring to impart to his twofold predatory, birdlike beaked face an appearance of modesty. No one looked on him, except to cast a casual, very unfriendly and even contemptuous glance.

And from that day the attitude of Jesus towards him strangely changed. Until then it had somehow seemed as though Judas never spoke directly to Jesus, and as though Jesus never addressed him directly, but still the Teacher had frequently looked at him with a kindly glance, smiling at some of his conceits, and if he missed him for any length of time he was wont to inquire: "And where is Judas?" But now he looked on Judas without noticing him, though as heretofore His glance sought him out, and even more persistently than formerly, whenever He began to speak to His disciples or to the people—but He either turned His back to Judas as He sat down or cast His words at him over His shoulder or else appeared not to notice him at all. And whatever He said, though it may have been one thing to-day or another the next, though it were the same thing that Judas himself had in his mind, it seemed as though He always spoke against Judas. And unto all He was a tender and beautiful flower, the fragrant Rose of Lebanon, but for Judas He had only sharp thorns—as though Judas had no heart, as though he had no eyes or nostrils, as though he were not better able than all others to appreciate the beauty of tender and thornless rose leaves.

"Thomas, lovest thou the yellow Rose of Lebanon that has a swarthy face and eyes like a hind?" he once asked of his friend and Thomas indifferently replied:

"The Rose? Yes, its odor is agreeable to me, but I have never heard that roses had swarthy faces or eyes like hinds!"

"How? Dost thou not even know that the many-armed cactus which yesterday rent thy garment has only one red flower and only one eye?"

But Thomas was ignorant of this also, though the day before a cactus had actually gripped a portion of his garment and rent it into shreds. He knew nothing this Thomas, though he inquired about everything and gazed so straightforwardly with his clear and transparent eyes through which one could see as through a Phoenician glass the wall behind him and the plodding ass hitched to it.

Before long another incident occurred when Judas again proved to have been correct. In a certain Judean village which he had severely criticised and sought to have left out of the itinerary, Christ was received with much hostility and after He had preached and denounced the hypocrites, the populace was aroused to a wild remonstrance and thought of stoning Him and His disciples.

The opponents were numerous and they would have surely succeeded in carrying out their design if it had not been for Judas of Kerioth. Seized with a mad fear for Jesus, as though perceiving already the drops of crimson on His white robe, Judas blindly and frenziedly cast himself against the mob, menacing, screaming, pleading, and lying, and thus gave Jesus and His disciples an opportunity to escape. Amazingly agile, as though scurrying on dozens of feet, ludicrous and terrible in his frenzied pleading, he rushed madly before the crowd and fascinated it with some strange spell. He screamed that the Nazarene was not at all possessed of the devil, that He was a mere deceiver, a thief, a lover of money, like all of His disciples, like he, Judas, himself,—he shook the money chest in their faces, distorted his features and pleaded with them casting himself to the ground. And gradually the wrath of the mob turned into laughter and disgust and the arms that had held the stones sank to their sides.

"Unworthy, unworthy they are to die of an honest man's hand," exclaimed some, while others musingly gazed after the speedily vanished Judas.

And again Judas expected congratulations, praises, and thanks, and made a show of his rent garments and falsely claimed that he had been beaten, but again he was inconceivably deceived. Filled with wrath Jesus walked ahead taking large steps and silent, and even John and Peter dared not approach him, while the others coming across Judas, with his rent garments, his face aglow with excitement and triumph though still a little pale with recent fright, drove him away with curt and angry remarks. As if he had not saved them, as if he had not saved their teacher whom they loved so much.

"Dost thou wish to see a pack of fools?" he remarked to Thomas who musingly plodded by his side. "Look how they walk along the roadway, like a herd of sheep, raising the dust. And thou, clever Thomas, art dragging along behind; and I, noble and beautiful Judas, am also trudging in the rear like a filthy slave not fit to walk by the side of his master."

"Why callest thou thyself beautiful?" inquired the surprised Thomas.

"Because I am handsome," replied Judas with conviction and began to relate to him, with many additions, how he had deceived the enemies of Jesus and laughed at them and their stones.

"But thou didst lie!" remarked Thomas.

"Of course I lied," agreed the Iscariot in a matter-of-fact tone. "I gave them what they asked and they returned to me what I needed. And what is a lie, my clever Thomas? Would not the death of Jesus have been the greater lie?"

"Thou didst wrong. Now I know that thy father was the devil. He taught thee this, Judas."

The Iscariots cheek blanched and seemed to overshadow Thomas, as though a white cloud had descended and hidden the roadway and Jesus. With a lithe movement Judas suddenly seized Thomas and pressed him to himself with a grip so tight that he could not move and whispered into his ear:

"Good. The devil taught me? Good, Thomas, good. And I saved Jesus, didn't I? Then the devil loves Jesus, then the devil needs Jesus and Truth? Good, good Thomas. But my father was not the devil, he was a goat. Mayhap the goat needs Jesus? Hey? And you, do you not want Him? Do you not want the Truth?"

Angered and slightly frightened Thomas with an effort released himself from Judas' slimy embrace and walked ahead swiftly, but soon slowed down in order to ponder over what had just happened.

But Judas plodded on quietly in the rear, falling back little by little. The wanderers had merged into one motley group in the distance and it was impossible to tell accurately which of the little figures was Jesus. Now even the tiny figure of Thomas changed into a grey dot, and suddenly they were all lost to sight behind a turn in the road; glancing around Judas turned aside from the roadway and with mighty leaps descended into the depths of a rocky ravine. His robe inflated from his swift and impetuous flight and his arms stretched upward as though he soared on wings. There on a steep decline he slipped and rapidly rolled down in a grey heap, his flesh torn by the shaggy rock, and leaped again to his feet angrily shaking his fist at the mountain.

"You too, curse you!"

And suddenly forsaking his swiftness of movement for a sullen and concentrated deliberateness he chose a spot near a large rock and slowly seated himself. He turned around as if in search of a comfortable position, pressed the palms of his hands close together against the grey rock and heavily leaned his head upon them. Thus he sat for an hour or two without stirring, deceiving the birds, motionless and grey like the rock itself. Before him, behind him and around him rose the steep sides of the ravine cutting with their sharp outline into the azure sky; and everywhere rose immense stones, rooted into the ground, as if there had passed over the place a shower of rocks and its heavy drops had grown transfixed in neverending thought. The wild and deserted ravine resembled an overturned decapitated skull and each rock therein seemed a congealed thought, and there were many of them, and they all were brooding heavy, limitless, stubborn thoughts.

There a deceived scorpion hobbled amicably past Judas on his rickety legs; Judas glanced at him without lifting his head from the stone, and again his eyes stopped rigidly fixed on some object, both motionless, both covered with an odd and whitish film, both seemingly blind and dreadfully seeing. Then from the ground, from the rocks, from the crevices began to rise the calm gloom of night; it enshrouded the motionless Judas and swiftly crept upwards to the luminously pallid sky. The night was advancing with its thoughts and dreams.

That night Judas failed to return to the lodging, and the disciples torn from their thoughts by cares for food and drink murmured at his negligence.

CHAPTER III

Once about noon time, Jesus and his disciples were ascending a rocky and mountainous path barren of shade, and as they had been over five hours on the road Jesus commenced to complain of weariness. The disciples stopped and Peter with his friend John spread their mantles and those of other disciples on the ground and fastened them overhead on two protruding rocks and thus prepared a sort of a tent for Jesus. And he reclined in that tent, resting from the heat of the sun, while they sought to divert Him with merry talk and jests. But seeing that speech wearied Him they withdrew a short distance and engaged in various occupations, being themselves but little sensitive to heat and fatigue. Some searched the mountainside for edible roots among the rocks, and brought them to Jesus, others ascended higher and higher. John had found a pretty blue lizard among the stones and bore it tenderly to Jesus, with a gentle smile; the lizard gazed with its protruding mysterious eyes into His eyes and then swiftly glided with its cold little body over His warm hand and rapidly bore away somewhere its tender and trembling tail.

Peter, caring little for such diversions, amused himself in company with Philip by detaching large stones from the mountainside and rolling them down in a contest of strength. Attracted by their loud laughter, little by little the others gathered around them and took part in the game. Straining every muscle each tore from the glen a hoary moss-covered stone, lifted it high overhead with both arms and dropped it down the incline. It struck heavily with a short, blunt contact and seemed to stop for an instant, as if in thought, then irresolutely it took the first leap, and each time it touched the earth it gathered from it speed and strength, grew light, ferocious, all-crushing. Then it leaped no longer, but flew with flashing teeth, and the air with a whizzing noise made way for the compact rotund missile. Now it reached the edge of the ravine; with a smooth final movement the stone flew up a little distance into the air, and rolled below, clumsy, heavy and circular, towards the bottom of the invisible abyss.

"Now then one more!" cried Peter. His white teeth glistened through his black beard and mustache, his powerful breast and arms were bared and the old angry stones, dully wondering at the strength that cast them, one after the other submissively passed into the abyss. Even frail John threw little pebbles, and Jesus smiling gently watched their game. "Well, Judas, why dost thou not take part in the game, it is apparently so diverting?" asked Thomas having found his queer friend motionless behind a large grey rock.

"My breast pains and they have not called me."

"Is there any need to call thee? Well, I call thee. Come. Look how large are the stones that Peter is casting down."

Judas glanced sideways at him and for the first time Thomas dimly realized that Judas of Kerioth had two faces. But hardly had he grasped the idea when Judas remarked in his wonted tone, ingratiating and at the same time sneering:

"Is there any one stronger than Peter? When he shouts all the asses in Jerusalem think their Messias has come and respond. Hast thou ever heard their braying?"

Smiling amicably and bashfully covering his breast that was covered with curly red hair Judas entered the circle of the players. And as they all felt merry they received him with glad shouts and hilarious jests and even John indulgently smiled when Judas, groaning and simulating great strain detached an immense stone. But now he easily raised it and cast it down. His blind wide-open eye shifted and fixed itself rigidly on Peter, while the other, cunning and happy twinkled with suppressed merriment.

"Well, you throw another one," broke in Peter in an offended tone.

And then one after another they raised and dropped gigantic stones, and in surprise the disciples watched them. Peter would throw a large stone, but Judas a still larger one. Peter, with a frown, wrathfully turned a fragment of the rock and reeling raised it and dropped it into the depths. Judas, still smiling, searched with a glance for a still larger fragment, caressingly dug into it with his lean long fingers, clung to it, swayed with it and with blanching cheek sent it down into the abyss. Having dropped his stone, Peter fell back and thus watched its flight, while Judas bent forward, leaned over the abyss and spread out his long and creepy arms as though he meant to fly after the stone. Finally both of them, first Peter and then Judas, seized a grey stone and were unable to raise it, neither one nor the other. Flushed with his effort Peter resolutely approached Jesus and loudly exclaimed:

"Lord, I do not want Judas to be stronger than I. Help me to raise that stone and cast it down."

And Jesus softly made some reply. Peter dissatisfied shrugged his broad shoulders, but dared no rejoinder and returned with the following words:

"He said: 'And who shall help the Iscariot?'"

But glancing at Judas, who with bated breath and tightly clenched teeth still clung to the stubborn stone, Peter burst out in a laugh:

"Look at the sick man! Look at our poor ailing Judas."

And Judas himself laughed, being so unexpectedly exposed in a lie, and the others laughed also; even Thomas suffered a smile to slip past his straight, shaggy mustache.

With merry and friendly speech they started again on their way, and Peter, having made full peace with the victor, now and again nudged his ribs with his fists and laughed loudly.

"The sick man!"

Everyone praised Judas, everyone acknowledged him victor, everyone conversed with him cordially, but Jesus—Jesus even this time failed to praise Judas. Silently He walked on ahead, gnawing at a blade of grass, and little by little the disciples ceased their laughter and joined Jesus. Soon it happened that they walked all in one group ahead, but Judas, the victor Judas, the strong Judas, trudged along in the rear swallowing dust.

They paused, and Jesus laying one hand on Peter's shoulder pointed with the other into the distance, where already in the mist had appeared Jerusalem; and the big broad back of Peter carefully couched His fine sunburnt hand.

For the night's lodging they stopped in Bethany, in the house of Lazarus. And when they all gathered to converse, Judas thought it a good time to recall his victory over Peter. The disciples, however, had little to say and were unusually silent. The images of the journey just completed, the sun, the rocks, the grass, Christ reposing in the tent, floated softly through their minds, exhaling a gentle pensiveness, generating dimly sweet dreams of some eternal motion under the sun. The wearied body rested sweetly, musing of something mysteriously beautiful and great—and not one remembered Judas.

Judas went out. Then he returned. Jesus was speaking and his disciples listened in silence. Motionless as a statue, Mary sat at His feet and with head thrown back gazed into His face. John had come close to the Teacher and strove to touch the hem of His garment with his hand, but so as not to disturb him. And having touched it he sat breathlessly still. And Peter breathed hard and loud, echoing the words of Jesus with his breath.

The Iscariot stopped at the threshold and contemptuously passed his glance over those assembled, concentrating its flames upon Jesus. And as he gazed, all around him grew dim and was lost in gloom and silence; Jesus only, with uplifted hand, was radiant. But now He too seemed to rise in the air, seemed to melt and His substance seemed to change into luminous mist such as hangs over the lake when the moon goes down; and His soft-spoken words sounded somewhere afar off and gentle. And gazing deeper into this wavering vision, drinking in with his ears the tender melody of those distant and spectral words, Judas gripped his whole soul with claws of iron and silently in its unfathomable gloom commenced to rear something stupendous. Slowly in the dense darkness, he raised immense mountainous masses, piling them up one upon another, and raised others and piled them up again; and something was growing in the darkness, expanding voicelessly, spreading its outlines. Now he felt his head transformed into a vast dome, and in its impenetrable gloom there grew and grew something stupendous, and someone wrought therein, raising mountainlike masses, piling them up one upon another and raising up new ones ... And gently there sounded somewhere distant and spectral words.

Thus he stood, blocking the doorway, towering tall and dark, while Jesus spoke, and Peter's loud breathing same in unison with His words. But suddenly Jesus ceased—with an abruptly incomplete sound, and Peter, like one awakened out of a trance, triumphantly exclaimed:

"Lord, Thou knowest the words of Eternal Life!"

But Jesus was gazing somewhere in silence. And when they followed his glance they saw Judas in the doorway rigid, open-mouthed and with staring eyes. And not knowing what it was about, they laughed. But Matthew, learned in the Scriptures, touched Judas' shoulder and remarked in Solomon's words:

"He who has a gentle look will be shown mercy, but he who is met in the gate will oppress others."

Judas shuddered and even uttered a faint hoarse cry of fear, and all of his body—eyes, arms and legs seemed to flee in different directions. So a beast might look when suddenly facing the eyes of man. Jesus walked straight against Judas, seemingly bearing some word on His lips, and he walked past Judas through the door which was now open and free.

Long after midnight Thomas, becoming worried, approached Judas' sleeping place and bending over him inquired:

"Thou weepest, Judas?"

"No, go away, Thomas."

"Then why groanest thou and gnashest thy teeth? Art thou ill?"

Judas was silent for a space of time, and then from his lips poured forth one after another heavy words, throbbing with yearning and wrath.

"Why does He not love me? Why does He love them? Am I not more beautiful, am I not better, am I not stronger than they? Did I not save His life while the others were running away cringing like cowardly curs?"

"My poor friend, thou art not entirely in the right. Thou are not at all beautiful and thy tongue is as disagreeable as thy face. Thou art forever lying and speaking ill of others. How dost thou expect that Jesus should love thee?"

But Judas heard him not and continued: "Why is He with those who do not love Him, instead of with Judas? John brought Him a lizard, I would have brought Him a venomous snake. Peter cast stones, I would have turned the mountain around for Him. But what is a snake? Draw its tooth and it will cling about thy neck like a necklace. What is a mountain which one can dig with his hands and trample under foot? I would have given Him Judas, daring, beautiful Judas. But now He will perish and Judas will perish with Him."

"Thou sayest strange things, Judas."

"The withered fig tree which is to be hewn down! Why, that is I, He said it of me! Why does He not hew? He dare not, Thomas. I know Him. He fears Judas! He hides before the daring, the beautiful Judas! He loves the fools, the traitors, the liars! Thou art a liar, Thomas, hast thou heard me?"

Thomas was greatly surprised, and thought of protesting, but he decided that Judas was merely brawling, and contented himself by shaking his head. But Judas' agony increased: he moaned, gnashed his teeth, and one could hear his huge body shifting restlessly under the blanket.

"What is it that pains Judas so? Who has set fire to his body?

He gives his son unto the dogs, he yields his daughter into the hands of robbers for defilement. But is not the heart of Judas tender? Go away, Thomas, go away, thou fool. Leave Judas alone, strong, daring, beautiful Judas."

CHAPTER IV

Judas purloined a few pieces of silver and the theft was discovered by Thomas who had chanced to note the exact sum of money given him. It was thought likely that he had stolen on previous occasions, and the indignation of the disciples knew no bounds. Bristling with wrath Peter seized Judas by the neck and half dragged him to Jesus. The pale and frightened culprit offered no resistance.

"Teacher, look. Our jester! Just look at him, the thief. Thou trustest him, but he steals our money. The rogue! If thou wilt but say the word, I shall...."

But Jesus was silent. Peter looked up curiously scanning the Teacher's expression, and with flushed face relaxed his hold on Judas. The latter smoothed his garments with a sheepish mien and assumed the downcast appearance of a penitent sinner.

"What do you think of that!" growled Peter, and walked out of the room banging the door. Everybody was annoyed, and the disciples declared that on no account would they remain together with Judas. John, however, with a sudden inspiration quietly slipped into the room whence through the open doorway was now heard the gentle and apparently cordial voice of Jesus.

When John returned, his face was pale and his eyes were red with recent tears.

"The Teacher says ... The Teacher says that Judas may take all the money he likes."

Peter laughed angrily. Swiftly and reproachfully John glanced at the impetuous disciple, and suddenly, all aglow, his tears mingling with his wrath, his joy mingling with his tears, he exclaimed with a ringing voice:

"And none shall keep count of the money which Judas receives. He is our brother and all the money is his as well as ours, and if he needs much let him take much, telling no one nor taking

43

counsel with any. Judas is our brother and you have deeply offended against him," thus sayeth our Teacher. "Shame on us, brethren!"

In the doorway stood Judas, pale and with a sickly smile. John with a quick movement approached him and kissed him thrice on the cheek. And after him, exchanging glances and awkwardly, came the others, James, Philip, and the rest. After each kiss Judas wiped his mouth, though he received the kiss with a resounding smack as if the sound afforded him much pleasure. The last to kiss him was Peter.

"We are all fools, Judas. We are all blind. One alone is seeing, One alone is wise. May I kiss thee?"

"Why not? Kiss," assented Judas.

Peter cordially kissed him and whispered into his ear:

"And I almost choked thee. The others were gentler, but I seized thee by the throat. Did it pain thee?"

"A little."

"I shall go to Him and tell Him. I was even angry with Him," gloomily remarked Peter striving to open the door without noise.

"And how about thee, Thomas?" sternly inquired John who was watching the actions of the disciples.

"I don't know yet. I must think."

And Thomas thought long, almost the whole day.

The disciples had gone about their business, and somewhere behind the wall Peter shouted loudly and merrily, but Thomas was still thinking. Pie would have finished sooner, but Judas, whose mocking glance persistently pursued his movement, disturbed him. Now and then the Iscariot inquired with a mock curiosity:

"Well, how is it Thomas? How art thou progressing?"

Then Judas brought his treasure chest and loudly jingling his coins he commenced to count them, pretending to ignore the presence of Thomas.

"Twenty one, twenty two, twenty three. Look, Thomas, another false coin. What great rogues people are, they even offer false money unto God. Twenty four. And then they will say Judas had stolen it. Twenty five. Twenty six...."

Thomas resolutely advanced to him, (it was already towards evening) and said:

"He was right, Judas. Let me kiss thee."

"Indeed? Twenty nine. Thirty. But it is all in vain. I shall steal again. Thirty one...."

"How canst thou steal if there is no more thine or anybody else's? Thou wilt take what thou needest, brother."

"And didst thou require all this time merely to repeat His words? Thou doest not value time, Thomas?"

"I fear thou mockest me, brother."

"And think, dost thou act correctly in repeating His words? It was He who had spoken, and they were His words, not thine. It was He who had kissed me, but you defiled my mouth. I can still feel your moist lips creeping over my face. How disgusting that was, Thomas! Thirty eight. Thirty nine. Forty pieces of silver. Dost thou want to count it over?"

"But He is our Teacher. How should we not repeat His words?"

"Has Judas no longer a neck to drag him by? Is he now naked so that ye cannot seize him? The Teacher will leave the house, Judas may accidentally steal three coins, and will ye not again seize him by the neck?"

"We know now, Judas. We understand."

"But have not all disciples a poor memory? And do not the disciples deceive their teachers? The Teacher lifts the rod, the disciples cry: 'We know the lesson!' The teacher lies down to sleep and the disciples inquire: 'Is not this what our teacher taught us?' And here this morning thou didst call me thief, but now callest thou me brother. What wilt thou call me on the morrow?"

Judas laughed, and picking up with one arm the heavy and jingling money chest he continued:

"When the wind blows strongly it raises the dust and the stupid people see the dust and say: 'Behold, the wind bloweth.' But it is only dust, my good Thomas, the refuse of asses, trodden under foot. There it strikes a wall and is now humbly lying at its foot, but the wind is flying further, the wind is flying further, my good Thomas."

Judas pointed in illustration over the wall and laughed again:

"I am glad that thou art merry, Judas," replied Thomas. "Pity it is that in thy merriment there is so much malice."

"How should not a man be merry who has been kissed so much and who is so useful? If I had not stolen three pieces of silver, how should John have known the exaltation of joy? Is it not pleasurable to be a hook whereupon John hangs his mouldy virtue to dry and thou thy moth-eaten wisdom?"

"I think it is best for me to go."

"But I am merely joking. I am jesting, Thomas. I merely wished to know if thou didst really long to kiss the old and repulsive Judas who had stolen three pieces of silver and given the money to a sinful woman."

"A sinful woman?" echoed Thomas in surprise. "And didst thou tell our Teacher this also?"

"There, doubting again, Thomas! Yes, to a sinful woman. But if thou only knew what a miserable woman she was. She must have gone without food two days."

"Knowest that this circumstance for a certainty?" inquired Thomas in confusion.

"Of course. I had been with her two days myself and saw that she had eaten nothing, for she merely drank wine, red wine. And she reeled with exhaustion and I fell with her."

Thomas leaped to his feet and walking a short distance away, turned and remarked to Judas.

"Apparently Satan has entered thy body."

And as he departed he heard the heavy money chest jingle mournfully through the gloom in the hands of Judas ... And it seemed as though Judas were laughing.

But the very next day Thomas had to admit that he had been mistaken in Judas: so gentle, simple and at the same time serious had become the Iscariot. He cut no more grimaces, refrained from malicious jesting, no longer cringed before people or insulted them, but attended to his household tasks quietly and unobtrusively. He was as agile as ever: as though he had not two legs like the rest of the people, but dozens of them. Now, however, he scurried about noiselessly, without squealing and screaming or the hyena laugh that had characterized his previous activity. And when Jesus now commenced to speak he sat down in a corner with folded hands and his large eyes assumed such a gentle expression that everybody noticed it. And he ceased to speak evil of people, keeping silence in preference, so that even the stern Matthew found it proper to praise him, which he did in the words of Solomon: "The fool speaketh scornfully of his neighbor, but the wise man is silent," and he raised his finger as if recalling the former proneness of Judas to speak evil. And the others also noted this change in Judas and rejoiced over it. Only Jesus still viewed him with the same look of estrangement although He in no manner expressed His disfavor. And John himself, towards whom, as the beloved disciple of Jesus and his protector, Judas now manifested a most deferential demeanor, even John's attitude towards him was softened and he occasionally held converse with him.

"How thinkest thou, Judas," said he once condescendingly, "which of us twain, Peter or I, will be nearest to Christ in His heavenly kingdom?"

Judas thought for a moment and replied:

"I think thou wilt."

"And Peter thinks he will," smiled John.

"No. Peter's shouting would scatter the angels. Hearest thou him? Of course, he will dispute with thee and will strive to come first and occupy the place, for he claims that he too loves Jesus. But he is growing old, while thou art young. He is slow, while thou art fleetfooted and thou wilt be the first to enter with Christ. Am I not right?"

"Yes. I shall never leave Jesus' side," assented John.

That same day Simon Peter addressed the very same question to Judas. But fearing that his loud voice would be heard by others he led Judas to the furthest corner of the house.

"Well how thinkest thou?" he inquired anxiously. "Thou art wise. Even the Teacher praises thy wisdom. Thou wilt tell me the truth."

"Thou, of course," the Iscariot replied without hesitation. And Peter indignantly exclaimed:

"I told him so."

"But, of course, even there he will try to dispute the first place with thee."

"Of course he will."

"But what can he do if he find the place already occupied by thee? Thou wilt not leave Him alone. Did he not call thee a Rock?"

Peter laid his hand on Judas' shoulder and fervently exclaimed:

"I tell thee, Judas, thou art the wisest among us. Pity thou art so malevolent and sneering. The Teacher does not like it. And thou couldst be a beloved disciple no less than John. But even unto thee I shall not yield my place by the side of Jesus, neither here on earth nor over there. Hearest thou me?" And he raised his hand with a threatening gesture.

Thus Judas sought to please both, the while he was harboring thoughts of his own. And remaining the same modest, quiet and unobtrusive Judas, he strove to say something agreeable to all.

Thus he said to Thomas: "The fool believeth every word, but the man of wisdom takes heed of his ways." But to Matthew who loved to eat and drink and was ashamed of this weakness he cited the words of Solomon.

"The righteous shall eat his fill, but the seed of the lawless is in want."

But such pleasant words he spoke rarely, which lent to them a special value. Now he remained silent for long periods and listened attentively to others, though he kept thinking thoughts of his own. Judas in his musing mood had a disagreeable and ludicrous, and at the same time a disconcerting appearance. While his cunning live

47

eye was mobile he appeared to be genuine and gentle, but when both of his eyes assumed that fixed and rigid look, and the skin on his forehead gathered into queer wrinkles and folds, one received the disquieting impression that within that skull there swarmed very peculiar thoughts, utterly strange, quite peculiar thoughts that had no language of their own and they enveloped the cogitating Iscariot with a shroud of mystery so disturbing that the beholder longed to have him break the silence quickly, to stir a little or even to lie. For even a lie uttered by a human tongue seemed truth and light in the face of this hopelessly mute and unresponsive silence.

"Lost in thought again, Judas?" rang out the sonorous voice of Peter, suddenly breaking through the dull silence of the Iscariot's musing. "What art thou thinking of?"

"Of many things," replied the Iscariot with a quiet smile. And observing the unpleasant effect of his silence upon the others, he began more and more frequently to separate himself from the disciples, taking lonely walks or spending hours alone on the flat roof of the house. More than once Thomas collided on the roof with a grey bundle out of which suddenly disentangled themselves the ungainly limbs of Judas and was startled by the well known mocking accents of the Iscariot's voice.

Only once again the man of Kerioth oddly and abruptly recalled to the memory of the disciples the Judas of former days, and this occurred during the dispute concerning the first place in the Kingdom of heaven. In the presence of the Teacher, Peter and John hotly and with mutual recriminations defended their claims to the place nearest to Jesus. They enumerated their merits, compared the degree of their love of Jesus, shouted angrily and even abused one another incontinently,—Peter, all flushed with wrath and thundering, John pale and still, with trembling hands and stinging words. Their dispute was fast becoming unseemly and the Teacher was commencing to frown, when Peter chanced to look up at Judas and laughed out exultingly. John also glanced at Judas and smiled contentedly. Each remembered what the wise Iscariot had told him. With the foretaste of certain triumph they both summoned Judas to be their judge, and Peter cried out: "Hey, thou wise Judas. Tell us who will be first and nearest to Jesus, he or I?"

But Judas was silent. He breathed heavily and fixed his gaze longingly, questioningly, on the deep and calm eyes of Jesus.

"Yes," condescendingly agreed John, "tell him who will be the first and nearest to Jesus."

With his glance still fixed on Christ, Judas rose slowly to his feet and replied calmly and gravely:

"I."

Jesus slowly dropped his eyes, while the Iscariot, beating his breast with a bony finger sternly and solemnly repeated:

"I! I shall be near Jesus."

And with these words he went out leaving the disciples dumbfounded by this insolent outbreak. Only Peter, as if suddenly recollecting something, whispered to Thomas in an unexpectedly quiet tone:

"This is then what he is thinking about. Didst thou hear him?"

CHAPTER V

It was just about this time that Judas Iscariot took his first decisive step towards betrayal: he paid a secret visit to the high priest Annas. He was received very sternly, but this did not disconcert him and he demanded a prolonged private interview. Left alone with the stern ascetic old man who eyed him contemptuously from under his bushy eyebrows, he told him that he, Judas, was a pious man who had become a disciple of Jesus of Nazareth with the sole aim of exposing the deceiver and of betraying him into the hands of the law.

"And who is He, this Nazarene?" slightingly inquired Annas, as if he had heard the name of Jesus for the first time.

Judas for his part pretended to take this strange ignorance of the high priest at its face value and reported to him at length concerning the sermons of Jesus, His wonders, His hatred of the Pharisees and the Temple, the violations of the Law by Him, and His desire to snatch the power from the hands of the ecclesiastics and to establish His own kingdom. And so skillfully did he mingle truth with falsehood that Annas glanced at him more attentively, while he indolently observed:

"Are there so few deceivers and madmen in Judea?"

"No. But He is a dangerous man," hotly replied Judas. "He violates the Law. And it is better for one man to perish than for the whole people."

Annas nodded approvingly.

"But He has, methinks, many disciples."

"Yes, many."

"And they probably love Him devotedly?"

"They say that they love Him; that they love Him more than themselves."

"But if we should want to seize Him, would they not take His part? Will there be no uprising?"

Judas laughed long and bitterly.

"They? They are cowardly curs who run as soon as a man stoops to pick up a stone. They!"

"Are they so bad?" coldly inquired Annas.

"And do the bad flee from the good? Do not rather! the good flee before the bad? Ha! They are good and therefore they will run. They are good and therefore they will hide themselves. They are good and therefore they will only appear when Jesus is ready for burial. And they will bury Him themselves, do thou but put Him to death."

"But do they not love Him? Thou saidst so."

"Their Teacher they love always, but more in death than living. As long as the Teacher lives He is apt to examine the pupils, and woe then unto the latter. But when the Teacher is dead, they become teachers in their turn, and woe then unto others! Ha!"

Annas looked searchingly at the traitor, and his shriveled lips wrinkled slightly: it was a sign that Annas was smiling.

"They have injured thee. I see it."

"Can anything remain a secret to thy insight, O wise Annas? Thou hast penetrated the very heart of Judas. Yes, they injured poor Judas. They said that I had stolen three pieces of silver, as if Judas were not the most honest man in Israel."

And for a long time they spoke of Jesus, of His disciples, and of His pernicious influence on the people of Israel. But the cautious and cunning high priest Annas did not give his final answer on this occasion. He had been watching Jesus for a long time and had long since sealed the fate of the prophet of Galilee in the secret councils of his relatives and friends, the chiefs and the Sadducees. But he distrusted Judas who had been reported to him as an evil and double-dealing man. He did not attach much faith to his frivolous remarks on the cowardice of the disciples and the people. Annas had entire confidence in his own might, but he feared bloodshed, he feared to stir up a tumultuous uprising into which the stiff-necked and volatile people of Jerusalem could be so easily harangued; he feared finally the sternly repressive interference of Roman authorities. Fanned by resistance, fructified by the crimson blood of the people which endows with life all whereon it falls, the heresy might spread all the more rapidly and engulf Annas himself, his rule and his friends. And when the Iscariot sought admission for the second time, Annas was perturbed and refused to receive him. But a third and a fourth time the Iscariot called, insistent as the wind that knocks day and night against the closed door and breathes through the fissures.

"I see that wise Annas has some apprehensions," said Judas when finally admitted to the High Priest.

"I am strong enough to fear nothing," haughtily replied Annas, and the Iscariot made a servile obeisance. "What wouldst thou?"

"I want to betray unto you the Nazarene."

"We do not want Him."

Judas bowed low and lingered humbly, fixing his eye upon the high priest.

"Go."

"But I must come again. Is it not so, venerable Annas?"

"Thou wilt not be admitted. Go."

But again and again Judas of Kerioth knocked at the high priest's portal and was once more admitted into the presence of the aged Annas. Shriveled and angry, oppressed with thought, he regarded the betrayer in silence and seemed to be counting the hairs on his illshaped head. Judas also was silent, as if, for his part, counting the hairs in the silvery thin beard of the high priest.

"Well, thou art here again?" haughtily ejaculated the irritated high priest, as though spuing the words on his visitor's head.

"I want to betray unto you the Nazarene."

They both lapsed into silence, scanning intently one another's features, the Iscariot gazing calmly, but a feeling of subdued malevolence, dry and cold like the morning frost in the winter time, was beginning to gnaw at the heart of Annas.

"And what askest thou for thy Jesus?"

"And what will ye give?"

With a feeling of quiet elation Annas insultingly retorted:

"You are a band of rascals, all of you. Thirty pieces of silver, that is all we will give for Him."

And his heart was filled with delighted gratification as he observed how Judas' whole body was set agog by this announcement. The Iscariot turned and scurried about, agile and swift, as if he had not two but a dozen legs.

"For Jesus? Thirty pieces of silver?" cried Judas in a tone of wild amazement that rejoiced the heart of Annas. "For Jesus of Nazareth? You would buy Jesus for thirty pieces of silver? And you think that Jesus can be sold unto you for thirty pieces of silver?"

Judas swiftly turned to the wall and laughed into its smooth and whited face, waving wildly arms.

"Hearest thou? Thirty pieces of silver! For Jesus!"

With quiet enjoyment Annas indifferently replied: "If thou wilt not have it, go. We shall find some man who will sell more cheaply."

And like sellers of old raiment who shout and swear and scold, fighting over the price of some worthless garment, they commenced their monstrous and frenzied haggling.

Thrilled with a strange ecstasy Judas ran about twisting his limbs and shouting, and enumerating on the fingers of his hand the merits of Him whom he was betraying.

"And that He is good and heals the sick, is that nothing? Is that worth nothing in your estimation? Hey? No? Tell me like an honest man?"

"If thou," interposed the high priest whose cold disfavor was rapidly fanned into violent wrath by the taunting words of Judas,—but the later interrupted him unabashed.

"And that He is youthful and beautiful like the narcissus of Sharon, like the lily of the valley? Hey? Is that nothing? Perhaps you will say that He is aged and worthless?"

"If thou," still strove to cry Annas, but his senile voice was drowned in the storm of Judas' protests.

"Thirty pieces of silver! That makes hardly an obolus for a drop of blood. Less than half an obolus for a tear. Quarter an obolus for a groan. And the cries of pain! and convulsions! What is the stopping of His heart? And the closing of His eyes? Is that all for naught?" screamed the Iscariot towering over the high priest, encircling him with the frenzied whirlwind of his gestures and words.

"For all! For all!" replied the breathless high priest.

"And how much will you earn on the deal? Hey? Would you rob poor Judas? Tear the piece of bread out of his children's mouths? I shall go out into the market place and shout: 'Annas has robbed poor Judas. Help!'"

Wearied and dizzy, Annas in futile frenzy stamped the floor with his soft slipper and waved him away: "Begone! Begone!"

But Judas suddenly made a humble obeisance and spread out his arms: "And if so, why art thou angry with poor Judas who is seeking the good of his children? Thou too hast children, fine, handsome young men."

"We shall get another.... We shall get another.... Begone!"

"And did I say that I would not give in? Do I not believe thee that another may come and give up Jesus unto you for fifteen oboli? For two oboli? For one obolus?"

Then with another low obeisance, and with ingratiating words, Judas submissively agreed to accept the money offered him.

With a trembling and wrinkled hand Annas, now silent and flushed with excitement, gave him the money. He sat with averted face and in silence, biting his lips and waited until Judas had tested every silver coin between his teeth. Now and then Annas looked around and then, as quickly turned his glance to the ceiling and again bit his lips.

"There are so many false coins about now," calmly explained Judas. "This is money offered up by pious people for the Temple," remarked Annas looking around hastily and still more quickly turning to Judas the back of his bald head which was now crimson with anger.

"But can pious people distinguish false coins from the genuine? Only rogues can do this."

Judas did not take home the money received from the high priest, but going beyond the city he buried it beneath a stone. And he returned with slow, heavy and cautious steps, like a wounded animal creeping to its lair after a cruel and mortal combat. But Judas had no lair of his own to which he might creep, though there was a house and in that house he saw Jesus. Tired, emaciated, worn out with his incessant war against the Pharisees who daily surrounded Him in the Temple like a wall of white, shining, learned foreheads, He was seated, leaning against the wall and was apparently fast asleep. Through the open window entered the restless echoes of the city, behind the wall was heard the knocking of Peter who was making a new table for the common meal and sang a Galilean ditty as he worked. He heard nothing and slept soundly and firmly, and this was He who had been bought for thirty pieces of silver.

Advancing noisclessly, Judas with the gentle care of a mother fearing to awaken her ailing babe, with the amazement of a dumb brute that has crept from its lair and lingers in fascination before some pretty white flower, Judas touched His soft hair and precipitately withdrew his hand. He touched it again and as noiselessly crept out.

"Lord!" he exclaimed. "Lord!"

And going to a deserted spot he wept there a long time, writhing, twisting his limbs, scratching his breast with his nails and biting his shoulders. Suddenly he ceased to weep, to moan and to gnash his teeth and lapsed into deep thought, turning his moist face to one side in the attitude of listening. And thus he stood for a long time, immobile, determined and a stranger to all like his very fate.

With a calm love and tender solicitude Judas surrounded the doomed Jesus during these last days of His brief life. Coy and timorous like a maiden in her first love, strangely intuitive and keen of perception, he divined the slightest unexpressed wish of Jesus, penetrated into the hidden depths of His feelings, His fleeting instants of yearning, His heavy moments of weariness. And no matter where the foot of Jesus stepped it rested on something soft, no matter where He turned His glance it met something pleasant. Formerly Judas had held in disfavor Mary Magdalene and the other women who were near Jesus, playing rude jokes at their expense and causing them much annoyance. Now he became their friend, their ludicrous and awkward confederate. With a profound interest he discussed with them the little intimate and beloved traits of Jesus, quizzing them insistently for a long time concerning one and the same thing. With a great show of secrecy he thrust coins into their hands, and they bought ointments, the precious and fragrant myrrh so beloved of Jesus, and anointed His feet. Haggling desperately he bought expensive wine for Jesus and then growled when Peter drank it all with the indifference of a man to whom only quantity matters. In that rocky country surrounding Jerusalem and almost bare of trees and flowers, he managed to obtain fresh spring flowers and green herbs, and offered them to Jesus through the mediation of these same women. For the first time in his life he fetched in his arms little children, finding them somewhere in the neighboring homesteads or in the highways, and forcedly caressed them to keep them from weeping. And it frequently happened that there crawled on the knees of Jesus, while he sat in deep thought, a tiny, curly haired little fellow with a soiled little nose, and insistently sought His caress. And while the two rejoiced in one another, Judas sternly walked a short distance off with the air of a jailer who has admitted a butterfly into the cell of his prisoner and then with a show of asperity grumbles about the disorder.

In the evenings, when darkness and fear stood guard at the door, the Iscariot artfully contrived to bring into the conversation Galilee, a land unknown to him but dear to Jesus, with its peaceful lakes and green shores. And he worried the clumsy Peter until stifled memories awoke in his heart and before his eyes and ears appeared vivid pictures and sounds of the beautiful life of Galilee. Avidly attentive and with mouth half-opened like a child's, with the twinkling of anticipated laughter in His eyes, Jesus listened to Peter's impetuous, ringing and merry speech, and at times He so loudly laughed at his conceits that the disciple had to stop his recital for minutes at a time. But better even than Peter's was the speech of John. There was nothing ludicrous, nothing unexpectedly grotesque in his words, but his descriptions were so thoughtful, unusual and beautiful that tears appeared in the eyes of Jesus, and Judas nudged

54

Mary Magdalene, whispering triumphantly into her ears: "How he speaks! Listen!"

"I am listening."

"But listen still better. You women never listen well."

And when they all dispersed to seek their bedsides, Jesus kissed John with a tender gratitude and cordially patted the shoulder of Peter.

Without envy, with a contemptuous indulgence, Judas witnessed these caresses. What signified all these tales, these kisses, these sighs, compared with that knowledge which he had, he, Judas of Kerioth, redhaired, repulsive Judas, born amid the rocks.

CHAPTER VI

Betraying Jesus with one hand, Judas took great pains to destroy his own plans with the other. He did not attempt to dissuade Jesus from embarking on that last perilous journey to Jerusalem, as did the women, he even inclined to side with the relatives of Jesus and with those of his disciples who considered the victory over Jerusalem indispensable to the complete triumph of the cause. But he stubbornly and insistently warned them of its dangers and depicted in vivid colors the formidable hostility of the Pharisees, their readiness to commit any crime and their unflinching determination either openly or privily to slay the prophet of Galilee.

Daily and hourly he spoke of it and there was not a believer whom Judas failed to admonish shaking his uplifted finger impressively and severely:

"Jesus must be guarded! Jesus must be guarded! Jesus must be protected when the time comes."

Whether it was the boundless faith of the disciples in the marvelous power of their Teacher, or the consciousness of the righteousness of their cause or sheer blindness, Judas' anxious words were met with a smile, and his endless warnings elicited even murmurs of remonstrance.

Judas managed to obtain somewhere a couple of swords, but only Peter was pleased with his foresight, and only Peter praised Jesus and the swords, while the others remarked disapprovingly:

"Are the warriors to gird ourselves with swords. And is Jesus a general and not a prophet?"

"But if they will want to slay Him?"

"They will not dare when they see that the whole people is following Him."

"But if they should dare after all? What then?"

And John scornfully retorted:

"One might think, Judas, that thou alone lovest the Teacher."

And, greedily clinging to these words, taking no offence, Judas began to question them eagerly, fervently, with a solemn impressiveness:

"But do ye love Him? Truly?"

And each believer who came to see Jesus he repeatedly questioned:

"And dost thou love Him? Dost thou love Him truly?"

And all answered saying that they truly loved Him. He frequently drew Thomas into conversation and warningly raising his bony forefinger crowned with a long and untidy finger nail he significantly admonished him:

"Look to it, Thomas. A terrible time is approaching. Are ye prepared? Why didst thou not take the sword which I brought?"

And Thomas sententiously replied:

"We are men unaccustomed to the use of arms. And if we take up the struggle with the Roman soldiers we shall all be slain. Besides didst thou not bring only two swords? What can be done with two swords?"

"We can get others. And we might take them away from the soldiers," said Judas with a show of impatience, and even Thomas, the serious, smiled through his shaggy beard.

"Judas, Judas! What thoughts be these? And where didst thou procure these swords? For they resemble the swords of the Roman soldiers."

"I stole them. I might have stolen more, but I heard voices and fled."

Thomas answered reproachfully and sadly:

"There again thou didst wrong. Why stealest thou, Judas?"

"But nothing is another's property."

"Good, but the warriors may be questioned to-morrow 'Where are your swords?' and not finding them they may suffer punishment innocently."

And later, after the death of Jesus, the disciples remembered these words of Judas and concluded that he had purposed to destroy them together with their Teacher by luring them into an

56

unequal and fatal combat. And once more they cursed the hateful name of Judas of Kerioth, the Traitor.

And Judas, after such conversation, sought out the women in his anger and complained to them tearfully. And the women heard him eagerly. There was in his love to Jesus something feminine and tender and it brought him nearer to the women, making him simple, intelligible and even good-looking in their eyes, though there still remained a certain air of superiority in his attitude towards them.

"Be these men?" he bitterly denounced the disciples, turning confidingly his blind and immobile eye towards Mary, "No they are not men. They have not an obolus' worth of blood in their veins."

"Thou art forever speaking evil of people," replied Mary.

"Am I ever speaking evil of people?" exclaimed Judas in surprise. "Well, I may sometimes say something evil of them, but could they not be just a trifle better? Ah Mary, stupid Mary, why art thou not a man to carry a sword?"

"I fear I could not lift it, it is so heavy," smiled Mary.

"Thou wilt wield it, if men prove too evil to draw a sword. Didst thou give unto Jesus the lily which I found this morn in the hills? I rose at dawn to seek it and the sun was so red to-day, Mary. Was He glad? Did He smile?"

"Yes, He was very glad. He said that it was fragrant with the odors of Galilee."

"Of course, thou didst not tell Him Judas had gotten it, Judas of Kerioth?"

"Thou badest me not to tell."

"Truly, truly", sighed Judas. "But thou mightest have mentioned it inadvertently, women are so prone to talk. Then thou didst not tell it Him by any chance? Thou wast so firm? Yes, yes, Mary, thou art a good woman. Thou knowest I have a wife somewhere. I should like to see her now: perhaps she was not a bad woman. I do not know. She used to say: 'Judas is a liar. Judas, son of Simon, is wicked!' And I left her. But it may be that she is a good woman. What thinkest thou?"

"How can I know, who have never seen her?"

"Truly, truly, Mary. And what thinkest thou, thirty pieces of silver ... is it a large sum of money?"

"I think it is not so much."

"Truly, truly. And what didst thou earn when thou wast a sinner? Five pieces of silver or ten? Wast thou high in price?"

Mary Magdalene blushed and dropped her head till her luxuriant golden hair hid her entire face leaving merely the rounded white chin visible:

"How mean art thou, Judas. I seek to forget it, but thou remindest me."

"No, Mary, thou shouldest not forget it. Why? Let others forget that thou wast a sinner, but thou forget not. It is meet that others forget it, but why shouldest thou?"

"I lived in sin."

"Let him fear who has committed no sin. But he who has committed sin, why should he fear? Do the dead fear death and not the living? No, the dead mock the living and their fear of death."

Thus cordially talking they sat together for hours, he, well on in years, gaunt hideous to behold, with illshaped head and weirdly disproportioned face, she youthful, coy, gentle, fascinated with life as though with some legend or strange dream.

But the time passed heedlessly and the thirty pieces of silver were reposing under the stone, and the terrible day of betrayal was approaching inexorably. Already Jesus had entered Jerusalem riding on the foal of an ass, and the people had acclaimed Him, spreading their garments in His path, with cries of triumphant welcome:

"Hosannah, Hosannah! Blessed be He that cometh in the name of the Lord."

And so great was the jubilation, and so irrepressible was the love that strove heavenward in these welcoming shouts that Jesus wept and His disciples proudly exclaimed:

"Is this not the Son of God who is with us?"

And they also cried out in triumph:

"Hosannah! Hosannah! Blessed be He that cometh in the name of the Lord."

And that night for a long time they remained awake thinking over the solemn and triumphant entry, and Peter was like unto a madman; he was as one possessed by the demon of merriment and pride. He shouted loudly, drowning the speech of others with his leonine roar, he laughed uproariously, flinging his laughter at the heads of others like large rolling boulders, he embraced John, and James and even kissed Judas. And he boisterously admitted that he had harbored fears concerning Jesus, but now feared no longer, for he saw the love the people bore for Him. The Iscariot's unsteady eye strayed from face to face in amazement. He mused for a while, listened and looked around again, and then led Thomas aside. Then, as if impaling him against the wall with his piercing glance he questioned him with wonderment and fear not unmixed with some dim hopefulness:

"Thomas, and if He is right? If it be He that has the rock beneath His feet, and I merely shifting sand? What then?"

58

"Of whom art thou speaking?" inquired Thomas.

"What will Judas of Kerioth do then? Then I shall have to strangle Him myself to bring out the Truth. Who is playing Judas false, ye or Judas himself? Who is deceiving Judas? Who?"

"I cannot understand thee, Judas. Thou speakest in riddles. Who is deceiving Judas? Who is right?"

And shaking his head Judas repeated like an echo:

"Who is deceiving Judas? Who is right?"

And still more surprised was Thomas, and he felt even worried when during the night there rang out the loud and almost joyous voice of Judas:

"Then there will be no Judas of Kerioth. Then there will be no Jesus. There will be only.... Thomas, stupid Thomas! Didst thou ever wish to seize this earth of ours and raise it in thy hands? And then perhaps to drop it?"

"That were impossible, what sayest thou Judas?"

"That is possible," replied the Iscariot with conviction. "And we shall seize it some day and lift it up in our hands while thou art asleep, stupid Thomas. Sleep. I am merry, Thomas. When thou sleepest, the flutes of Galilee play in thy nostrils, Thomas. Sleep."

But already the believers had scattered throughout Jerusalem and disappeared within their houses, behind walls, and the faces of the people who still walked abroad were now inscrutable. The rejoicing had ceased Already dim rumors of peril crept out of some crevices. Peter was gloomily trying the edge of the sword given him by Judas, and ever sadder and sterner grew the face of the Teacher. Time was swiftly passing and inexorably approached the dread day of the Betrayal. Now also the Last Supper was over, pregnant with sadness and dim fears, and the vague words of Jesus of someone who would betray Him had been spoken.

"Knowest thou who will betray Him?" inquired Thomas gazing at Judas with his straight and limpid, almost transparent eyes.

"Yes, I know," replied Judas, sternly and resolutely. "Thou, Thomas, wilt betray Him. But He does not believe Himself what He is saying. It is time. It is time. Why does He not call to His side Judas, the strong and the beautiful?"

And time, the inexorable, was now measured no longer by days but by fast fleeting hours. And it was even, and the stillness of even, and lengthy shadows gathered over the earth, the first piercing arrows of the impending night of great conflict, when a sad and solemn voice sounded through the darkness. It was Judas who spoke:

"Thou knowest where I am going, Lord? I am going to betray Thee into the hands of Thine enemies."

And there was a long silence, and the stillness of even and piercing black shadows.

"Thou art silent, Lord? Thou commandest me to go?"

And silence again.

"Bid me stay. But Thou canst not? Or darest not? Or wilt not?"

And again silence, immense as the eyes of Eternity.

"But Thou knowest that I love Thee. Thou knowest all. Why lookest Thou thus upon Judas? Great is the secret of Thy beautiful eyes, but is mine the less? Bid me stay.... But Thou art silent. Thou art ever silent? Lord, Lord, why in anguish and with yearning have I sought Thee always, sought Thee all my life and found Thee? Make Thou me free. Lift from me the burden; it is greater than mountains of lead. Hearest Thou not the bosom of Judas of Kerioth groaning beneath it?"

And final silence, unfathomable as the last glance of Eternity.

"I go."

And the stillness of even was not broken, it cried not out nor wept, nor faintly echoed the fine and glassy air—so still was the sound of his departing steps. They sounded and were lost. And the stillness of even relapsed into musing, it stretched its lengthening shadows, and blushed darkly, then suddenly sighed with the yearning rustle of stirring foliage; it sighed and was still, lost in the embrace of Night.

Other sounds now invaded the air, rapping, tapping, knocking: as if someone had opened a cornucopia of vivid sonorous noises and they were dropping upon the earth, not singly or in twos, but in heaps. And drowning them all, echoing against the trees, the shadows and the wall, enveloping the speaker himself roared the resolute and lordly voice of Peter: he swore that he would never leave his Teacher.

"Lord!" he cried, longingly, wrathfully. "Lord! With Thee I am ready to go to prison and even unto death."

And softly, like the faint echo of someone's departed steps, the merciless answer sounded:

"I say unto thee, Peter, that ere the cock crow thrice to-day thou wilt have denied me thrice."

CHAPTER VII

The moon had already risen when Jesus started towards Mount Olivet where he was wont of late to pass his nights. But He lagged strangely, and His disciples, who were ready to proceed, urged Him on. Then He suddenly spoke:

"He who has a sack let him take it, likewise a staff. And He who has none, let him sell his raiment and buy a sword. For I say unto you that this day it shall happen unto me as even was written: he was counted among the transgressors!"

The disciples were amazed and exchanged confused glances.

But Peter replied:

"Lord! Here are two swords."

He glanced searchingly into their kindly faces, dropped His head and gently replied:

"It is enough."

Loudly echoed the steps of the wanderers through the narrow streets and the disciples were terrified at the sounds of their own steps. Their black shadows lengthened upon the white moon-illuminated walls and they were terrified at the sight of their own shadows. Thus silently they passed through the sleeping city. Now they passed out of the gates of Jerusalem and in a deep cleft among the hills that were filled with mysterious and immobile shadows the brook of Kedron met their gaze. Now everything terrified them. The soft gurgling and the splashing of the water against the stones sounded to them like voices of people lying in ambush. The shapeless fanciful shadows of rocks and trees obstructing their way worried them, and the motionless stillness of the night appeared to them endowed with life and movement. But as they ascended and neared the garden of Gethsemane where they had spent so many nights in security and peace they gradually gained courage. Now and then they cast a backward glance at the sleeping city now reposing white in the light of the moon and discussed their recent fright; and those who walked in the rear heard an occasional fragment of the Teacher's words. He was telling them that they would all forsake Him.

They stopped in the very outskirts of the garden. Most of the disciples regained right there and with subdued voices commenced to make preparations for sleep, spreading their mantles in the transparent lacework of shadows and moonlight. But Jesus, torn with disquietude, with four of His nearest disciples plunged further into the depths of the garden. There they sat down on the ground that had not yet grown cold from the heat of the day, and while Jesus observed silence, Peter and John lazily exchanged meaningless remarks. Yawning with weariness they spoke of the chilly night and remarked how dear the meat was in Jerusalem, while fish was not to be had at all. They were guessing at the number of worshippers that would gather in Jerusalem during the holidays, and Peter, stretching his words into a prolonged yawn, affirmed that they would amount to twenty thousand, while John, and his brother Tames indolently claimed that the number would not exceed ten thousand. Suddenly Jesus quickly rose to His feet.

"My soul is sorrowful even unto death. Tarry ye here and watch a while," He said and with swift steps He retired into the grove where He was lost in the impenetrable maze of light and shadows.

"Where did He go?" wondered John raising himself on his elbow. Peter turned his head in the direction of the departed Teacher and wearily answered:

"I don't know." And once more loudly yawning he reclined on his back and lay still. The others too had quieted down by this time and the vigorous sleep of healthy fatigue chained their stolid figures. Through his heavy sleep Peter dimly saw something white bending over him and seemed to hear some voice that sounded afar off and died leaving no trace in his dulled consciousness:

"Simon Peter, sleepest thou?"

And once more he was fast asleep, and again some still voice reached his ear and died away leaving no trace:

"Could ye not watch with me one brief hour?"

"Lord, if Thou knewest how sleepy I am," he thought in half slumber, but it seemed to him as if he had said it aloud. And again he slept and a long time passed when suddenly there stood beside him the form of Jesus and a sonorous waking voice roused him and the others:

"Are ye still sleeping and resting? It is finished. The hour has come for the Son of Man to be betrayed into the hands of sinners."

The disciples leaped to their feet, picking up their mantles in confusion and shivering with the chill of sudden awaking. Through the maze of trees, illuminating them with the lurid light of their torches, with heavy tramping of feet and loud noise, and the crack of breaking twigs, a crowd of warriors and temple attendants was seen approaching. And from the other side the rest of the disciples came running, trembling with the cold, with terrified, sleepy faces, failing to realize what had occurred and anxiously inquiring:

"What is this? Who are these with torches?"

Thomas, pale, with his beard awry, with chatting teeth, remarked to Peter:

"Apparently these men are after us."

Now the crowd of warriors surrounded them and the smoking unsteady glare of the torches had chased the quiet and serene radiance of the moon somewhere into the heights over the treetops. At the head of the warriors was Judas of Kerioth; scurrying hither and thither and keenly rolling his seeing eye he searched for Jesus. At last he found Him, and resting for a moment his glance on the tall and slender form for the Master he hurriedly whispered to the attendants: "He whom I shall kiss the same is the man. Take Him and lead Him carefully. But be careful, do you hear me?"

Then hurriedly moving toward Jesus, who awaited him in silence, he plunged like a dagger a steady and piercing glance into His calm, dark eyes.

"Rejoice, Rabbi," he exclaimed loudly, imbuing the words of common salutation with a strange and terrible significance.

But Jesus was silent, and the disciples gazed awestricken upon the Traitor, unable to fathom how the soul of Man could contain so much wickedness. With a hasty look the Iscariot measured their confused ranks, noted the tremor that threatened to change into the abject palsy of terror, noted their pallor, the meaningless smiles, the nerveless movements of arms that seemed to be gripped with iron clamps at the shoulder; and his heart was set aflame with bitter anguish not unlike the agony which had oppressed Jesus a short time since. His soul transformed into a hundred ringing and sobbing chords, he rushed forward to Jesus and tenderly kissed His windchilled cheek, so softly, so tenderly, with such agony of love and yearning that were Jesus a flower upheld by a slender stem, that kiss would not have shaken from it one pearl of dew or dislodged one tender leaf.

"Judas," said Jesus, and the lightning of His glance bared the monstrous mass of forbidding shadows that were the soul of the Iscariot, but did not reveal its boundless depths. "Judas! With a kiss betrayest thou the Son of Man?"

And He saw that hideous chaos quivering, stirring and agog through and through. Speechless and stern as Death in his haughty majesty stood Judas of Kerioth and all of his being within him groaned, thundered and wailed with a myriad of stormy and fiery voices: "Yes! With a kiss of love we betray Thee. With a kiss of love we betray Thee unto mockery, torture and death. With a voice of love we summon torturers from their dark lairs, and rear a cross. And high above the gloom of the earth upon the cross we raise up love crucified by love!"

Thus stood Judas, wordless and cold as death, and the cry of his soul was met by the cries and the tumult that encircled Jesus. With the rude indecision of armed force, with the awkwardness of a dimly grasped purpose the soldiers had already seized Him by the hand and were dragging Him somewhere, mistaking their own aimlessness for resistance, their own terror for their victim's mockery and scorn. Like a herd of frightened lambs the disciples had huddled together, offering no resistance, though impeding everybody including themselves; and only a few had any thought of going or acting for themselves, apart from the rest. Surrounded on every side, Peter, son of Simon, with an effort, as if having lost all strength, drew the sword from its sheath and weakly dropped it with a glancing blow upon the head of one of the servants,—but failed to harm him in the least. And observing this Jesus commanded him to drop the useless weapon. With a faint rattle the sword fell to the ground, a piece of metal so manifestly bereft of its power to pierce and to injure that none troubled to pick it up. Thus it lay in the mud and many days later some children found it in the same spot and made it their plaything.

The soldiers were dispersing the disciples and the latter again huddled together stupidly getting into the soldiers' way, and this continued until the soldiers were seized with a contemptuous wrath. There one of them with a frown walked up to the shouting John, while another roughly brushed aside the arm of Thomas who had placed it upon his shoulder in an endeavor to argue with him, and in his turn shook threateningly a powerful balled fist before a pair of very straight-looking and transparent eyes. And John ran, as also did Thomas and James; and all the disciples, as many as were there, forsaking Jesus, ran helter-skelter to save themselves. Losing their mantles, running into the trees, stumbling against stones and falling they fled into the mountains, driven by terror and in the stillness of the moonlit night the ground resounded under their fugitive feet. Some unknown, who had evidently just risen from sleep, for he was covered with only a blanket, excitedly scurried to and fro in the crowd of warriors and servitors. But as they tried to seize him he cried out in fear and started to run, like the others, leaving his raiment in the hands of the soldiers. Thus perfectly nude, he ran with desperate leaps and his naked body gleamed oddly in the moonlight.

When Jesus was led away Peter emerged from his hiding place behind the trees and from a distance followed his Teacher. And seeing ahead of him another man who walked in silence, he thought it was John and softly called to him:

"John, is it thou?"

64

"Ah, thou Peter?" replied the other stopping, and Peter recognized the Betrayer's voice. "Why then Peter didst thou not flee with the others?"

Peter stopped and loathingly replied:

"Get thee behind me, Satan."

Judas laughed and paying no more attention to Peter walked on towards the place where gleamed the smoking torches and the rattle of arms mingled with the tramp of feet. Peter followed him cautiously and thus almost together they entered the court of the high priest's house and joined a crowd of servants warming themselves at the fire. Judas was sullenly warming his bony hands over the logs when he heard somewhere in the rear the loud voice of Peter:

"No, I don't know Him."

But someone evidently insisted that he was a disciple of Jesus, for even more loudly Peter repeated:

"But no and no, I don't know whereof ye are speaking."

Without looking around and smiling involuntarily Judas nodded his head affirmingly and murmured:

"Just so, Peter. Yield to none thy place at the side of Jesus."

And he did not see how the terror-stricken Peter departed from the court in order not to be caught again. And from that evening until the very death of Jesus Judas never saw near Him any of His disciples: and in that multitude there were only these two, inseparable unto death, strangely bound together by fellow-suffering,—He who was betrayed unto mockery and torture and he who had betrayed Him. From one chalice of suffering they drank like brothers, the Betrayed and the the Traitor, and the fiery liquid seared alike the pure and the impure lips.

Gazing fixedly at the fire which beguiled the eye into a sensation of heat, holding over it his lanky and shivering hands, all tangled into a maze of arms and legs, trembling shadows and fitful light, the Iscariot groaned pitifully and hoarsely:

"How cold! My God, how cold!"

Thus in the night time, when the fisher folk have set out in their boats leaving ashore a smouldering campfire some strange denizen of the deep may come forth from the bowels of the sea and creeping to the fire gaze on it fixedly and wildly, stretching its limbs towards the flames and groan pitifully and hoarsely:

"How cold! Oh, my God, how cold!"

Suddenly behind his back the Iscariot heard a tumult of loud voices, cries, the sound of rude laughter, full of the familiar, sleepily-greedy malice, and the thud of sharp, quick, blows raining on a living body. He turned around, pierced through and through with agonized pain, aching in every limb and in every bone—they were beating Jesus.

It has come then.

He saw the soldiers lead Jesus into the guard-house. The night was passing, the fires were going out, ashes began to cover them, and from the guard-house there came still the noise of hoarse shouts, laughter and oaths. They were beating Jesus. As one who has lost his way the Iscariot scurried about the empty court, stopping himself suddenly on a run, raising his head and starting off again, stumbling in surprise against the campfires and the walls. Then he glued his face to the walls of the guard-house, to the cracks in the door, to the windows and greedily watched what was going in within. He saw a stuffy, crowded, dirty little room, like all the guard-houses in the world, with a floor that had been diligently spat on and with walls that were greasy and stained as if hundreds of filthy people had walked or slept upon them. And he saw the Man who was being beaten. They smote Him on the face and on the head, they flung Him from one to another across the room like a sack. And because He did not cry out or resist after minutes of strained observation it actually appeared as though it were not a living being but some limp manikin without bones or blood that was thrown about. And the figure bent over oddly, just like a manikin, and when in falling it struck the floor with its head the impression of the contact was not like that of some hard object striking another, but as of some thing soft and incapable of pain. And after watching it long it seemed like some weird and interminable game, something that almost amounted to an illusion. After one vigorous blow the man or the manikin smoothly dropped on the knees of a soldier. He pushed it away and it turned and fell on the next man's knees, and so on. Shouts of wild laughter greeted this game and Judas also smiled—as if some powerful hand with fingers of steel had torn open his mouth. The lips of Judas had played him false this time.

The night seemed to drag and the campfires still smouldered. Judas fell back from the wall and slowly trudged over to one of the fires, stirred up the coals, revived the flames, and though now he did not feel cold, he held over it his slightly trembling hands. And longingly he murmured:

"Ah, it hurts, little son, it hurts, child, child, child. It pains, very, very much."

Then he walked over to the window that gleamed yellow from the dim lantern within the bars and once more he commenced to watch the chastisement of Jesus. Once before the very eyes of Judas flitted the vision of His dark face, now disfigured and encircled in a maze of tangled hair. There someone's hand seized this hair, felled the Man and methodically turning the head from side to side began to wipe with His face the filthy floor. Under the very window a soldier slept opening his wide-open mouth wherein two rows of teeth gleamed white and shiny. Now somebody's broad back with a fat bare neck shut out the view from the window and nothing more could be seen. And suddenly all grew still.

"What is it? Why are they silent? What if they have comprehended?"

Instantly the head of Judas was filled with the roaring, shouting and tumult of a thousand frenzied thoughts. What if they have realized? What if they have comprehended that this was—the very best among men. This is so plain, so simple. What is going on there now? Are they kneeling before Him, weeping softly, kissing His feet? There He will emerge in an instant, and behind Him will come forth in abject submission the others; how He will come forth and draw near to Judas, the conqueror, the Son of Man, the Lord of Truth, God....

Who is deceiving Judas? Who is right?

But no. Shouts and uproar again. They are beating Him again. They have not comprehended. They have not realized and they are beating Him with greater violence, more cruelly. And the fires are burning low, being covered with ashes, and the smoke over them is as transparently blue as the air, and the sky is as light as the moon. It is the dawn of day.

"What is day?" asked Judas.

Now everything is ablaze, everything glows, everything has grown young, and the smoke above is no longer blue but pink. The sun is rising.

"What is the sun?" asketh Judas.

CHAPTER VIII

They pointed him out with their fingers, and some contemptuously, while others with hatred and terror added:

"See, this is Judas, the Traitor."

This was the beginning of his shameful infamy to which he condemned himself for all ages. Thousands of years will pass, nation will succeed nation, and still the words will be heard in the air, uttered with contempt and dread by the good and the evil:

"Judas, the Traitor! Judas, the Traitor!"

But he listened with indifference to the words spoken concerning him, absorbed in a feeling of a supreme curiosity. From the very morn that Jesus was led out of the guard-house after His chastisement Judas followed Him, his heart strangely free from longing, pain or joy. It was only filled with the unconquerable craving to see and to hear all. Though he had not slept all night he felt as though walking on air; where the people would not let him pass he elbowed his way forward and with agility gained a point of vantage. During the examination of Jesus by Kaiaphas he held his hand to his ear so as not to lose a word and nodded his head approvingly, whispering:

"That's so. That's so. Hearest Thou this, Jesus?"

But he was not free—he was like a fly tied to a thread: buzzing it flies hither and thither but not for an instant the pliant and obstinate thread releases it. Thoughts that seemed hewed out of stone weighed down his head and he could not shake them off. He knew not what thoughts these were, he feared to stir them up, but he felt their presence constantly. And at times they threatened to overwhelm him, almost crushing him with their incredible weight as though the roof of some rocky vault slowly and terribly subsided over his head. Then he held his hand to his heart and shook himself as though shivering with the cold, and his glance straying to another and still another spot as Jesus was led out from the presence of Kaiaphas, he met His wearied glance at quite close quarters, and without rendering account to himself of his action, he nodded his head a few times with a show of friendliness and murmured:

"I am here, sonny, I am here." Then he wrathfully shoved aside some gaping countryman who stood in his way. Now they were moving, an immense and noisy throng, on to Pilate, for the last examination and trial, and with the same insupportable curiosity Judas eagerly and swiftly scanned the faces of the people. Many were entirely unknown to him; Judas had never seen them before; but some there were who had shouted "Hosannah!" to Jesus, and with every step the number of such seemed to increase.

"Just so!" flashed through the mind of Judas. He reeled like a drunken man. "It is all finished. Now they will shout: He is ours! He is our Jesus! What are ye doing? And everyone will see it...."

But the believers walked in silence, with forced smiles on their faces, pretending that all this did not concern them in the least. Others discussed something in subdued tones, but in the tumult and commotion, in the uproar of frenzied shouts of Christ's enemies, their timid voices were drowned without leaving a trace. And again he felt relieved. Suddenly Judas noticed Thomas, who was cautiously proceeding not afar off, and with a sudden resolve he rushed forward intending to speak to him. Seeing the Traitor, Thomas was frightened and sought to escape, but in a narrow and dirty lane, between two walls, Judas caught up with him:

"Thomas! Wait!"

Thomas stopped and solemnly holding up both hands exclaimed:

"Depart from me, Satan."

With a gesture of impatience the Iscariot replied:

"How stupid thou art, Thomas! I thought that thou hadst more sense than the others. Satan! Satan! This must be proved."

Dropping his hands, Thomas inquired in surprise:

"But didst thou not betray the Teacher? I saw with my own eyes that thou broughtest the soldiers. Didst thou not point out Jesus unto them? If this is not betrayal, what is a betrayal?"

"Something else, something else," hastily interposed Judas. "Listen. There are many of you here. It behooves you to meet and to demand loudly: 'Give unto us Jesus. He is ours.' They will not refuse you, they will not dare. They will understand themselves...."

"What art thou saying!" replied Thomas shaking his head. "Didst thou not see the number of armed soldiers and servants of the temple? And, besides, a court has not been held yet, and we must not interfere with the court. Will not the court understand that Jesus is innocent and will not the judges immediately order Him released?"

"Dost thou think so too?" musingly inquired Judas. "Thomas, Thomas, but if this be the truth? What then? Who is right? Who deceived Judas?"

"We argued all night and we decided that the judges simply could not condemn the Innocent one. But if they should...."

"Well?" urged the Iscariot.

"... then they are not true judges. And they will fare ill some day when they give account to the real Judge...."

"The real Judge! Is there a real one?" laughed Judas.

"And the brethren have all cursed thee, but as thou sayest that thou art not a Traitor, I think thou oughtest to be judged...."

Without waiting to hear the end Judas abruptly turned on his heels and rushed off in pursuit if the departing multitude. But he slowed down and walked deliberately, realizing that a crowd never proceeds very fast and that by walking apart one can always catch up with it.

When Pilate led Jesus out of his palace and placed Him in full view of the people, Judas, pinned to a column by the heavy backs of some soldiers, frenziedly twisted his head in order to see something between two shining helmets. He suddenly realized that now all was over indeed. The sun shone high over the heads of the multitude and under its very rays stood Jesus, bloodstained, pale, with a crown of thorns the sharp points of which had pierced His brow. He stood at the very edge of the elevation, visible from His head to His small sunbrowned feet, and so calmly expectant He was, so radiant in His sinlessness and purity that only a blind man unable to see the very sun could fail to see it, only a madman could fail to realize it. And the people were silent, so silent that Judas heard the breathing of the soldier in front of him, and the scraping of his belt as he took each breath.

"That's it. It is all over. They will now understand," thought Judas; and suddenly some strange sensation not unlike the blinding joy of falling from an infinite altitude into the gaping abyss of blue stopped his heart.

Contemptuously stretching his lip down to his clean-shaven, rotund chin, Pilate flings at the people dry curt words as one might cast bones at a horde of hungry hounds to cheat their thirst for fresh blood and living quivering flesh.

"Ye have brought unto me this Man as a corrupter of the people. I have examined Him before you and have found the Man guilty of nothing whereof ye accuse Him.."

Judas closed his eyes. He was waiting.

And the whole people began to shout, scream and howl with a thousand bestial and human voices:

"Death unto Him! Crucify Him! Crucify Him!"

And now, as if deriding their own souls, as if craving to taste to the dregs in one moment all the infinity of fall, frenzy and shame, these very people screaming and howling demand:

"Release unto us Barabbas. But Him crucify! Crucify!"

But the Roman has not yet spoken his final word. His haughty clean-shaven face is twitching with loathing and wrath. He understands.. He has comprehended. There He is speaking softly to the servants of the temple, but his voice is drowned in the uproar of the multitude. What is he saying? Does he command them to take up their swords and to fall upon the madmen?

"Bring me water!"

Water? What kind of water? What for?

There he is washing his hands ... why is he washing his white, clean ringcovered hands? And now he cries out angrily raising his hands in the face of the amazed people:

"I am innocent of the blood of this righteous man. See ye to it."

The water is still dripping from these white fingers down on

70

the marble slabs of the floor, but some white mass is already limply groveling at the feet of Pilate, someone's burning and sharp lips are kissing his weakly resisting hand, clinging to it like a leech, sucking at it, drawing the blood to the surface and almost biting it. With loathing and dread he looks down and sees a gigantic and writhing body, a wild face that looks as though it had been split in twain, two eyes so strangely unlike one another, as though not one creature but a multitude lay clutching at his feet and hands. And he hears a fervent and broken whisper:

"Thou art wise! Thou art noble! Thou art wise!"

And this savage face seems to glow with such truly satanic joy that Pilate cannot repress a cry as he repels him with his foot, and Judas falls down to the ground. And lying on the flagstones, like an overturned devil, he still stretches out his hand towards Pilate and shouts as one infatuated:

"Thou art wise! Thou art noble! Thou art wise!"

Then he swiftly leaps to his feet and flees accompanied by the laughter of the soldiers. All is not yet over. When they see the cross, when they see the nails, they may comprehend then.... What then? Passingly he notices Thomas, breathless and pale, and for some reason nods to him assuringly. Then he catches up with Jesus on the way to the execution. The path is hard; the little stones roll from under one's feet; Judas suddenly realizes that he is tired. He concentrates his mind on finding a good foothold, and as he looks about he sees Mary Magdalene weeping, he sees a multitude of weeping women, with dishevelled hair, red eyes, distorted lips, all the infinite grief of the feminine soul given over unto despair. Suddenly he revives and taking advantage of an opportune moment, he rushes forward to Jesus:

"I am with Thee," he whispers hurriedly.

The soldiers drive him away with stinging blows of their whips, and writhing to escape the leash, gnashing his teeth at the soldiers, he hurriedly explains:

"I am with Thee. Thither. Understandest Thou? Thither!"

Wiping the blood from his face he shakes his fist at the soldier who turns around and points him out to his comrades. He looks about for some reason in search of Thomas, but finds neither him nor any of the other disciples in the accompanying crowd. Again he feels weary and heavily shuffles his feet, carefully scanning the sharp little crumbling stones underfoot.

. . . . When the hammer was raised to nail the left hand of Jesus to the tree Judas shut his eyes and for an eternity neither breathed, nor saw, nor lived, only listened. But now iron struck iron with a gnashing sound, and blow after blow followed blunt, brief,

71

low. One could hear the sharp nail entering the soft wood distending its particles.

One hand. It is not yet too late.

Another hand. It is not yet too late.

One foot, another. Is really all over? Irresolutely he opens his eyes and sees the cross rise unsteadily and take root in the ditch. He sees how the hands of Jesus convulse under the strain, extend agonizingly, how the wounds spread and suddenly the collapsing abdomen sinks below the ribs. The arms stretch and stretch and grow thin and white, they twist at the shoulders, the wounds under the nails redden and expand; they threaten to tear in an instant.. But, they stop. All motion has stopped. Only the ribs move lightly, raised by His deep quick breathing.

On the very brow of the Earth rises the cross and on it hangs Jesus crucified. The terror and the dreams of Judas are accomplished—he rises from his knees (he had been kneeling for some reason) and looks around coldly. Thus may look some stern conqueror having purposed in his heart to visit ruin and death upon all as he takes one last look on the wealthy vanquished city, still living and noisy, but already spectral beneath the cold hand of death. And suddenly as clearly as his terrible triumph the Iscariot sees its ominous frailty. What if they realize? It is not yet too late. Jesus is still living. There He gazes with his beckoning, yearning eyes....

What can keep from tearing the thin veil that covers the eyes of the people, so thin that it almost is not? What if they suddenly comprehend? What if they move in one immense throng of men, women and children, silent, without shouting, and overwhelm the soldiers, drowning them in their own blood, root out the accursed cross and the hands of the survivors raise aloft upon the brow of the Earth the released Jesus? Hosannah! Hosannah!

Hosannah? No. Let Judas lie down on the ground, let him lie down and bare his teeth like a dog and watch and wait until they all rise. But what has happened to time? Now it stops and one longs to kick it onward, to lash it like a lazy ass, now it rushes on madly downhill, cutting off one's breath, and one vainly seeks to steady oneself. There Mary Magdalene is weeping. There weeps the mother of Jesus. Let them weep. As if her tears meant anything, for that matter the tears of all the mothers, all the women in the universe!

"What are tears?" asks Judas and frenziedly pushes onward the disobliging time, pummels it with his fists, curses it like a slave. It is someone else's, that is why it does not obey. If it were Judas! but it belongs to all these who are weeping, laughing, gossiping as if

72

they were in the marketplace. It belongs to the sun, it belongs to the cross and to the heart of Jesus who is dying so slowly.

What a miserable heart is that of Judas. He is holding it with his hands but it shouts Hosannah! so loudly that all will soon hear it. He presses it tightly to the ground, and it shouts Hosannah! Hosannah! like a poltroon scattering sacred mysteries in the street.

Suddenly a loud broken cry.. Dull shouts, a hurried commotion around the cross. What is it? Have they comprehended?

No, Jesus is dying. And can this be? Yes, Jesus is dying. The pale arms are limp, but the face, the breast and the legs are quivering with short convulsions. And can this be? Yes, He is dying. The breath comes less frequently. Now it has stopped. No, another sigh, Jesus is still upon earth. And still another? No ... No ... No ... Jesus is dead.

It is finished. Hosannah! Hosannah!

The terror and the dreams are accomplished. Who will snatch the victory from the Iscariot's hands? It is finished. Let all nations, as many as there be, flock to Golgotha and cry out with their millions of throats: Hosannah! Hosannah! let them pour out seas of blood and tears at its foot,—they will only find a shameful cross and a dead Jesus.

Calmly and coldly Judas scrutinizes the figure of the Dead, resting his glance an instant upon the cheek on which but the night before he had impressed his farewell kiss, and then deliberately walks away. Now the whole earth belongs to him, and he walks firmly like a commander, like a king, like He who in this universe is so infinitely and serenely alone. He notes the mother of Jesus and addresses her sternly:

"Weepest thou, mother? Weep, weep, and a long time will weep with thee all the mothers of earth. Until we shall return together with Jesus and destroy death."

What is he saying? Is he mad or merely mocking? But he seems serious and his face is solemn, and his eyes no longer scurry about with insane haste. There he stops and with a cold scrutiny views the earth, so changed and small. How little it now is, and he feels the whole of the orb beneath his feet. He looks at the little hills gently blushing under the last rays of the sun, and he feels the mountains beneath his feet. He gazes on the sky gaping wide with its azure mouth, he gazes on the round little sun futilely striving to burn and to blind, and he feels the sky and the sun beneath his heel. Infinitely and serenely alone he has proudly sensed the impotence of all the powers that are at work in the world and has cast them all down into the abyss.

And he walks on with calm and masterful steps. And the time moves neither ahead of him nor in the rear: obediently with its invisible mass it keeps pace with him.

It is finished.

CHAPTER IX

Like an old hypocrite, coughing, smiling ingratiatingly, bowing profusely, Judas of Kerioth, the Traitor, appeared before the Sanhedrim. It was on the day following the murder of Jesus, towards noon. They were all there, His judges and murderers, the aged Annas with his sons, those accurate and repulsive copies of their father, and Kaiaphas, his son-in-law, wormeaten with ambition, and other members of the Sanhedrim, who had stolen their names from the memory of the people, wealthy and renowned Sadducees, proud of their power and their knowledge of the law. They received the Traitor in silence and their haughty faces remained unmoved as if nothing had entered the room. And even the very least among them, a nonentity utterly ignored by the others, raised to the ceiling his birdlike features and looked as if nothing had entered. Judas bowed, bowed and bowed, but they maintained their silence: as if not a human being had entered, but some unclean and unnoticeable insect had crept into their midst. But Judas of Kerioth was not a man to feel embarrassed: they were silent, but he kept on bowing and thought that if he had to keep on bowing until night he would do so.

At last the impatient Kaiaphas inquired:

"What dost thou want?"

Judas bowed once more and modestly replied:

"It is I, Judas of Kerioth, who betrayed unto you Jesus of Nazareth."

"Well, what now? Thou hast received thy reward. Go," commanded Annas, but Judas kept on bowing as if he had not heard the command. And glancing at him Kaiaphas inquired of Annas:

"How much was he given?"

"Thirty pieces of silver."

Kaiaphas smiled and even the senile Annas smiled also. A

74

merry smile flitted over all the haughty faces: and he of the birdlike countenance even laughed. Paling perceptibly Judas broke in:

"Quite so. Quite so. Of course, a very small sum, but is Judas dissatisfied? Does Judas cry out that he was robbed? He is content. Did he not aid a sacred cause? A sacred cause, to be sure. Do not the wisest of men listen now to Judas of Kerioth and think: 'He is one of us, Judas of Kerioth, he is our brother, our friend, Judas of Kerioth, the Traitor.' Does not Annas long to kneel before Judas and kiss his hand? Only Judas will not suffer it, for he is a coward, he fears that Annas might bite."

Kaiaphas commanded:

"Drive this dog away. Why is he barking here?"

"Go hence. We have no time to listen to thy babbling," indifferently remarked Annas.

Judas straightened up and shut his eyes. That hypocrisy which he had so lightly borne all his life he felt now as an insupportable burden, and with one movement of his eyelids he cast it off. And when he looked up again at Annas his glance was frank and straight and dreadful in its naked truthfulness. But they paid no attention even to this.

"Wouldst thou be driven out with rods?" shouted Kaiaphas.

Suffocating with the burden of terrible words which he sought to lift higher and higher as if to cast them down upon the heads of the judges Judas hoarsely inquired:

"And do ye know who He was, He whom ye yesterday condemned and crucified?"

"We know. Go."

With one word he will now tear that thin veil that clouds their eyes, and the whole earth will shake with the impact of the merciless truth. They had souls—and they will lose them. They had life—and they will be deprived of it. Light had been before their eyes—and eternal gloom and terror will engulf them.

And these are the words that rend the speaker's throat:

"He was not a deceiver. He was innocent and pure. Hear ye? Judas cheated you. Judas betrayed unto you an Innocent One."

He waited and heard the indifferent senile quaver of Annas: "And is that all thou wouldst tell us?"

"Perhaps ye have not comprehended me?" Judas replied with dignity, all color fading from his cheeks. "Judas deceived you. You have killed an Innocent One."

One of the judges, a man with a birdlike face, smiled, but Annas was unmoved. Annas was bored, Annas yawned. And Kaiaphas joined him in a yawn and wearily remarked: "I was told of the great mind of Judas of Kerioth. But he is a fool, and a great bore as well as a fool."

"What?" cried Judas shaken through and through with a desperate rage. "And are ye wise? Judas has deceived you, do you hear me? Not Him did he betray, but you, ye wise ones, you, ye strong ones, he betrayed unto shameful death which shall not end in eternity. Thirty pieces of silver! Yes. Yes. That is the price of your own blood, blood that is filthy as the swill which the women cast out from the gates of their houses. Oh Annas, Annas, aged, grey-bearded, stupid Annas, choking with law, why didst thou not give another piece of silver, another obolus? For at that price thou wilt be rated forever!"

"Begone!" shouted Kaiaphas trembling with wrath. But Annas stopped him with a gesture and as stolidly asked Judas:

"Is this all now?"

"If I shall go into the desert and cry out to the wild beasts: 'Beasts of the desert, have ye heard the price they have put on their Jesus?' What will the wild beasts do? They will creep out of their lairs, they will howl with wrath; they will forget the fear of man and they will rush here to devour you. If I tell unto the sea: 'O sea, knowest thou the price they have put upon their Jesus?' If I shall tell unto the mountains: 'Ye mountains, know ye the price they have placed upon their Jesus?' The sea and the mountains will leave their places appointed unto them since eternity and rush towards you and fall upon your heads."

"Would not Judas like to become a prophet? He speaks so loudly," remarked he of the birdlike face mockingly and ingratiatingly peering into the eyes of Kaiaphas.

"To-day I saw a pallid sun. It looked down in terror upon this earth inquiring: 'Where, O where is man?' I saw to-day a scorpion. He sat upon a rock and laughing inquired: 'Where, O where is man?' I drew nearer and glanced into his eyes. And he laughed and repeated: 'Where, O where is man?' Where, oh, where is man? Tell me, I do not see. Has Judas become blind, poor Judas of Kerioth?"

And the Iscariot wept loudly. And in that moment he resembled a madman. Kaiaphas turned away contemptuously, but Annas thought awhile and remarked: "I see, Judas, that thou didst really receive but a small reward, and this evidently agitates thee. Here is more money, take it and give unto thy children."

He threw something that jingled abruptly. And hardly had that sound died when another oddly resembling it succeeded: it was Judas casting handfuls of silver coins and oboli into the faces of the high priest and the judges, returning his reward for Jesus. In a crazy shower the coins flew about, striking the faces of the judges, the

76

tables and scattering on the floor. Some of the judges sought to shield themselves with the palms of their hands, others leaping from their seats shouted and cursed. Judas aiming at Annas threw the last coin for which he had fished a long time with his trembling hand, and wrathfully spitting upon the floor walked out.

"Well. Well," he growled passing swiftly through lanes and scaring little children. "Methinks thou didst weep, Judas, hey? Is Kaiaphas really right in calling Judas of Kerioth a stupid fool? He who weepeth in the day of the great vengeance is not worthy of it, knowest thou this, Judas? Do not let thine eyes get the best of thee, do not let thy heart play false. Do not put out the flames with thy tears, Judas of Kerioth."

The disciples of Jesus sat sadly and silently anxiously listening to the sounds outside. There was still danger that the vengeance of the foes of Jesus would not content itself with His death, and they all expected the intrusion of soldiers and perhaps further executions. Near John, who as the favorite disciple of Jesus felt the death of the Teacher most, sat Mary Magdalene and Matthew, gently comforted him. Mary, whose face was swollen with weeping softly stroked his luxuriant wavy hair, while Matthew instructively quoted the words of Solomon:

"He that is longsuffering is better than the mighty, and he that ruleth his heart than he that taketh a city."

At that moment loudly banging the door Judas Iscariot entered the room. They leaped to their feet in terror and for an instant failed to recognize the newcomer, but when they observed his hateful countenance and the redhaired illshaped head they raised an uproar. Peter lifted up his hands and cried out:

"Begone, Traitor, begone lest I kill thee."

But scanning the face and the eyes of the Traitor they lapsed into silence, whispering with awe:

"Leave him. Leave him. Satan has entered his body."

Taking advantage of the silence Judas exclaimed:

"Rejoice, rejoice, ye eyes of Judas the Iscariot. Ye have just seen the coldblooded murderers, and now ye behold the cowardly traitors. Where is Jesus? I ask of you, where is Jesus?"

There was something commanding in the hoarse voice of the Iscariot and Thomas meekly replied:

"Thou knowest, Judas, that our Teacher was crucified yesterday."

"How did you suffer it? Where was your love? Thou, beloved disciple, thou, O Rock, where were ye when they crucified your friend upon the tree?"

"But what could we do, judge thyself?" replied Thomas shrugging his shoulders.

"Thou askest this, Thomas? Well, well," replied Judas craning his head and suddenly he broke out with vehemence: "He who loves asks not what to do. He goes and does all. He weeps, he snaps, he strangles his foe, he breaks his limbs. He who loves! When thy son is drowning, goest thou into the marketplace and askest the passer-by: 'What am I to do? My son is drowning. Dost thou not leap into the water and drown with the son together? He who loves!"

Peter sullenly replied to the frenzied harangue of Judas:

"I unsheathed the sword but He himself bade me put it up."

"He bade thee? And thou didst obey?" laughed the Iscariot. "Peter, Peter, was it meet to obey Him? Does He understand aught of men and of fighting?"

"He who disobeys Him will go down to the Gehenna of fire."

"Then why didst thou not go? Why didst thou not go, Peter? Gehenna of fire, indeed, what is Gehenna? And why didst thou not go? Why hast thou a soul if thou darest not throw it into the fire at will?"

"Silence, He himself desired this sacrifice," exclaimed John rising to his feet. "And His sacrifice was beautiful."

"Is there a beautiful sacrifice? What sayest thou, beloved disciple? Where there is a sacrifice, there is the slayer and the betrayer also. Sacrifice is suffering for one and shame for the others. Traitors, traitors, what have ye done with this earth? They are gazing upon this earth from above and from below with derision, saying: 'Look at this earth, on it they crucified Jesus.' And they spit upon it even as I do."

Judas spat wrathfully.

"He took upon Himself the sins of all mankind. His sacrifice is beautiful," insisted John.

"Nay, but ye upon yourselves have taken all sin. Beloved disciple! Will there not spring up from thee a race of traitors, a brood of little-souled liars? Ye blinded men, what have ye done with this earth? Ye compassed about to destroy it. You will soon kiss the cross whereon ye crucified Jesus. Yes, indeed, you will kiss the cross, Judas promises you that."

"Judas, do riot blaspheme," roared Peter flushing. "How could we kill all his foes? There were so many of them."

"And thou, Peter," angrily retorted John. "Dost thou not see that he is possessed of Satan. Get thee hence, tempter. Thou art full of lies. The Teacher commanded not to slay."

"But did He forbid you to die? Why are ye living whereas He is dead? Why do your legs walk, your tongues utter folly, your eyes

78

wink, whereas He is dead, immovable, voiceless? How dare thy cheeks be red, John, whereas His are pale? How darest thou shout, Peter, whereas He is silent? What ye should have done, ye ask of Judas? And Judas replies to you, beautiful, daring Judas of Kerioth: ye should have died. Ye should have fallen on the way, clutching the soldiers' swords and hands. Ye should have drowned them in a sea of your own blood; ye should have died, died. His very Father should have called out with dread if ye all had entered."

Judas paused, raised his hand, and suddenly noticed on the table the remains of a meal. And with a queer amazement, curiously, as if he were looking at food for the first time, he closely scrutinized it and slowly inquired: "What is this? Ye have eaten? Perhaps slept also?"

"I have slept," curtly replied Peter, dropping his head, scenting already in Judas' manner a tone of command. "I have slept and eaten."

Thomas resolutely and firmly interposed: "This is all wrong, Judas. Think: if we had all died, who would have been left to tell about Jesus? Who would carry the teachings of Jesus to the people, if all of us had died, John and Peter and I?"

"And what is truth in the lips of traitors? Does it not turn to falsehood? Thomas, Thomas, dost thou not understand that thou art now a watchman at the grave of dead truth? The watchman falleth asleep, a thief cometh and carrieth away the truth—tell me where is the truth? Be thou accursed, Thomas! Fruitless and beggarly wilt thou be forever, and ye are accursed with Him."

"Be thou thyself accursed, Satan," retorted John, and his words were repeated by James and Matthew and all the other disciples. Peter alone was silent.

"I go to Him!" said Judas raising aloft his masterful hand. "Who will follow the Iscariot to Jesus?"

"I! I! I am with thee," cried Peter rising. But John and the others stopped him with terror, saying: "Madman, dost thou forget that he betrayed our Teacher into the hands of His enemies?"

Peter smote his breast with his fist and wept bitterly.

"Whither shall I go, Lord? O Lord, whither?"

Long ago, during his solitary rambles, Judas had picked out the spot whereon he intended to kill himself after the death of Jesus. It was on the side of the mountain, high over Jerusalem, and only one tree was growing there, twisted all out of shape, knocked about by the wind which tore at it from all sides and half-withered. One of its gnarled and leafbare branches it stretched cut over Jerusalem as though blessing the city or perhaps threatening it, and this one Judas selected whereon to fasten his noose. But the path to

79

the tree was long and difficult, and Judas of Kerioth was very tired. Still the same sharp little stones rolled from under his feet as if dragging him back, and the mountain was high, windswept and gloomy. And Judas sat down for a rest several times, breathing heavily, while from the back through the crevices there swept over him the chilling breath of the mountain.

"Thou too, accursed hill," contemptuously muttered Judas and breathing heavily he shook his benumbed head wherein all thoughts had turned to stone. Then suddenly he raised it, opening wide his chilled eyes and wrathfully growled:

"No, they are too bad altogether for Judas. Hearest thou, Jesus? Now wilt thou believe me? I am coming. Meet me kindly, for I am weary. I am very weary. Then together, with a brother's embrace, we shall return to this earth. Is it well?"

And again opening wide his eyes he murmured:

"But perhaps even there thou wilt be angry with Judas of Kerioth? And perhaps thou wilt not believe? And peradventure, thou wilt send me to hell? Well, what then? I shall go to hell. And in the flames of thy hell I shall forge the iron to wreck thy heaven. Well? Wilt thou believe me then? Wilt thou then go back with me to this earth, O Jesus?"

Finally Judas reached the top of the mountain and the gnarled tree and here the wind commenced to torture him. But when Judas had chided it it began to whistle soft and low; the wind started off in another direction and was bidding him farewell.

"Well, well. But those others are curs," responded Judas making a noose. And as the rope might play him false and break he hung it over the abyss,—if it did break he would still find his death upon the rocks. And before pushing himself away from the edge and hanging himself over the precipice, Judas once more carefully admonished Jesus:

"But Thou meet me kindly, for I am very weary, Jesus."

And he leaped. The rope stretched to its limit, but sustained the weight. The neck of Judas grew thin, while his hands and legs folded and hung down limply as if wet. He died. Thus within two days, one after the other, departed from this earth Jesus of Nazareth and Judas of Kerioth, the Traitor.

All night like some hideous fruit the body of Judas swung over Jerusalem; and the wind turned his face now towards the city now to the desert. But whichever way his death-marred face turned, its red and bloodshot eyes, both of which were now alike, like brothers, resolutely gazed upon the sky. Towards morning some observant one noticed Judas suspended over the city and cried out in terror. Men came and took him down, but learning his identity threw him into a deep ravine where they cast the carcases of horses, dogs, cats and other carrion.

That same night all believers learned of the terrible death of the Traitor, and the next day all Jerusalem knew it. Rocky Judea heard it, and green-clad Galilee too; and from one sea even to another more distant one the news of the death of the Traitor was carried. Not swifter nor slower than the passing of time, but step by step with it, the message spread; and as there is no end to time there will be no end to the stories of Judas' betrayal and his terrible death. And all—the good and the bad alike—will curse his shameful memory, and among all nations, as many as there are or will ever be, he will remain alone in his cruel fate—Judas of Kerioth, the Traitor.

LAZARUS

CHAPTER I

When Lazarus emerged from the grave wherein for the space of three days and three nights he had dwelt under the mysterious dominion of death, and returned living to his abode, the ominous peculiarities which later made his very name a thing of dread remained for a long time unnoticed.

Rejoicing in his return to life, his friends and neighbors overwhelmed him with caresses and they satisfied their eager interest by ministering to him and caring for his food, his drink and his raiment. They clothed him in rich attire, bright with the hues of hope and merriment, and when he sat among them once more, arrayed like the bridegroom in his wedding garments, and ate and drank once more, they wept for joy and summoned the neighbors to view him, who had so miraculously risen from the dead. The neighbors came and rejoiced; strangers too came from distant cities and villages and in accents of tumultuous praise voiced their homage to the miracle—the house of Mary and Martha hummed like a beehive.

All that seemed novel in the features of Lazarus and in his demeanor they explained as natural traces of his serious illness and the shock through which he had passed. It was manifest that the destructive effect of Death upon the corpse had been merely arrested by the miraculuous power, but not altogether undone. And what the hand of Death had already accomplished upon the face and the body of Lazarus was like an artist's unfinished sketch covered by a thin film. A deep earthy bluish pallor rested on the temples of Lazarus, below his eyes and on his hollow cheeks; his lanky fingers were of the same earthy blue and his nails, which had grown long during his sojourn in the grave had turned livid. Here and there, on the lips and elsewhere, his skin, swollen in the grave, had cracked open and was covered by a fine reddish film that glistened like transparent slime. And he had grown very fat. His body, inflated in the grave, retained that ominous obesity beneath which one scents the putrid sap of dissolution. But the cadaverous and fetid odor which had permeated the burial robes of Lazarus, and seemingly his very body, soon disappeared completely; in the course of weeks even the bluish tint of his hands and of his countenance faded, and time also smoothed out the reddish blisters though they never vanished altogether. Such was the appearance of Lazarus as he faced the world in this his second life. To those who had seen him buried it seemed perfectly natural.

The manner of Lazarus also had undergone a change, but this circumstance surprised no one and failed to attract due attention. Until his death Lazarus had always been care free and merry. He had loved laughter and harmless jests. It was this agreeable and merry disposition, free from malice and gloom, that had made him so well beloved by the Teacher. But now he was grave and silent. He neither jested himself nor responded with an approving smile to the jests of others: and the words which he uttered on rare occasions were the simplest, most commonplace and indispensable words, as bare of a profounder meaning as the sounds with which animals express pain or pleasure, thirst and hunger. Such words a man may speak all his life and none would ever learn what grieved or pleased him in the depths of his soul.

Thus he sat with the face of a corpse over which for the space of three days the hand of death had held sway in the gloom of the grave,—arrayed in solemn wedding garments that glistened with ruddy gold and blood-red crimson; dull and silent, ominously transformed and uncanny, but still undiscovered in his new character, he sat at the festive board among his banqueting friends and neighbors. Now tenderly, now tempestuously the waves of rejoicing surged around him; fervently affectionate glances feasted upon his face that was still numb, with the chill of the grave; the warm hand of a friend caressed his blue tipped leaden fingers. The music played. They had summoned musicians to play merry tunes: the cymbal, the pipe, the lute and the timbrel. And it sounded like the humming of bees, like the chirping of crickets, like the singing of birds, this rejoicing in the house of Mary and Martha.

CHAPTER II

A reckless one lifted the veil. A reckless one, with one breath of a fleeting word, destroyed the sweet dreams and revealed the truth in its hideous nakedness. The thought was not yet clear in the questioner's head when his lips, parting in a smile inquired:

"Why don't you tell us, Lazarus, what was There?"

And they all paused, amazed at the query, as though they had just realized that Lazarus had been dead three days, and they glanced up curiously awaiting the answer. But Lazarus was silent.

"Will you not tell us?" questioned the curious one "Was is so dreadful There?"

And again the thought failed to keep pace with the words: if it had kept abreast with them the question would not have been put, for it gripped in the next instant the questioner's own heart with fear unutterable. And they were all perturbed, they waited eagerly for the reply of Lazarus; but he was dumb, looking cold and stern and downcast. And then they noted anew, as though for the first time, the dreadful bluish pallor of his countenance and his hideous obesity; his livid hand still reposed on the table as though forgotten there. All eyes were fixed on that hand in a strange fascination as though expecting that it might give the craved reply. The musicians had still been playing, but lo! now the silence reached them too, like a rivulet which reaches and quenches the scattered coals, and smothered were the sounds of merriment. The pipes were mute; the high-sounding cymbal and the melodious timbrel were silent; with the sound of a breaking chord, as though song itself were dying, tremulously, brokenly groaned the lute; and all was still.

"Thou wilt not?" repeated the questioner unable to repress his prating tongue. Silence reigned and the bluish hand reposed on the table and did not stir. Then it moved a little, and all heaved a sigh of relief and lifted their eyes: Lazarus, the risen, was gazing straight into their faces with a glance that took in all,—stolid and gruesome.

This was on the third day after he had emerged from his grave. Since then many had tested the pernicious power of his gaze, but neither those whom it wrecked forever, nor those who in the primal sources of life that are as mysterious as death itself found force to resist, could ever explain the nature of that dreadful, that invisible something which reposed in the depths of his black pupils. Lazarus looked into the world calmly and frankly without seeking to hide anything, without any thought of revealing anything; his gaze was as cold as the glance of one infinitely indifferent to all things living. Many thoughtless people jostled him in the street failing to recognize him, and only later learned the identity of that quiet corpulent man the edge of whose gaudy and festive apparel had brushed against them. The sun shone as brightly as ever, the fountains murmured their song, and the native sky remained as cloudless and azure as before, but those who had fallen under the sway of that mysterious glance neither felt the glow of the sun, nor heard the fountain nor recognized the sky. Some of these wept bitterly, others tore their hair in despair and madly called to their friends for help, but mostly it happened that they began to die, languidly, without a struggle, drooping for many weary years, pining away under the eyes of their friends, fading, withering, listless like a tree drying up silently on rocky ground. And the first, who cried and stormed, came sometimes back to life, but the others—never.

"Then thou wilt not tell us, Lazarus, what thou hast seen There?" for the third time repeated the insistent inquirer. But now his voice was dull and weary, and deathly grey languor looked from his eyes. And the same deathly dull languor hid the faces of the others like a veil of dust: they exchanged glances of dreary wonderment as though at a loss to grasp why they had met around the richly laden table. The conversation lagged. The guests began to feel vaguely that it was time to go home, but they were too weak to overcome the viscous and paralyzing listlessness that had robbed their muscles of strength, and they kept their seats, each for himself, isolated like dimly flickering lights scattered about the field in the darkness of night.

But the musicians were paid to play, and once more they took up their instruments and the air was filled with the sounds of music: but the notes, both merry and mournful, sounded mechanical and forced. The same familiar melody was unrolled before the ears of the guests, but the latter listened in wonderment: they could not understand why people found it necessary or amusing to have others pull at tightly drawn strings or whistle with inflated cheeks through thin reeds to produce the oddly discordant noises.

"How badly they play!" someone said.

The musicians felt hurt and departed. One after another the guests left too, for the night had already fallen. And when the calm of night surrounded them, and they had begun to breathe at ease there rose before each one of them the image of Lazarus: the blue cadaverous face, the wedding garments, gaudy and sumptuous, and the frigid stare in the depths of which had congealed the Horrible. As though, turned to stone they stood in different corners, and darkness enveloped them; and in that darkness more and more vividly burned the dreadful vision of him who for three days and for three nights had been under the mysterious spell of Death. Three days he had been dead; three times the sun rose and set, and he was dead; the children played, the brooks coursed babbling over the stones, the biting dust swept over the highway,—but he was dead. And now he was again among the living—touching them, looking at them—LOOKING at them! and from the black orbs of his pupils, as through a dark glass, there gazed upon the people the inscrutable Beyond.

CHAPTER III

No one took care of Lazarus; he had retained no neighbors or friends, and the great desert which enchained the Holy City had encroached to the very threshold of his dwelling. And it entered his house, made itself broad on his couch, like a spouse, and quenched the fire in his hearth. One after the other his sisters, Mary and Martha, forsook him; for a long time Martha had loathed to leave him, not knowing who would feed him and comfort him; she wept and prayed.

But one night when the wind swept over the desert and whistled through the tops of the cypress trees bending them over the roof of his hut, she quietly dressed and quietly went out into the darkness. Lazarus might have heard the slamming door, he might have heard it banging against the doorposts as it failed to shut tightly. But he did not rise, he did not step out, he did not investigate. And all through the night until the morn the cypress trees rustled overhead, and the door piteously knocked against the posts letting in the cold, the greedy, the insistent desert.

He was shunned as a leper, and as a leper they almost forced him to wear a bell around his neck in order to warn the people of his approach, but someone, with blanching cheek, suggested how dreadful it would be to hear the bell of Lazarus in the dead of night outside the windows,—and with blanching cheeks the people agreed with him.

And as he did nothing for himself, he would probably have starved had not his neighbors, impelled by a strange fear, saved some food for him. Children carried it to him. They did not fear him, neither did they mock him, as, with innocent cruelty, they often laugh at unfortunate beings. They were indifferent to him, and Lazarus evinced the same indifference toward them. Given over to the ravages of time and the encroachments of the desert, his house was falling to wreck and ruin, and his flock of goats, bleating and hungry, had a long time since scattered among his neighbors. His wedding garments too had grown old. Just as he had donned them on that happy day when the musicians played he had worn them ever since, without change, as though unable to see the difference between the new and the old, the torn and the whole. The bright colors had faded and paled; the wicked dogs of the city and the sharp thorns of the desert had rent the delicate fabric into shreds.

In the day time when the merciless sun consumed all that was living, and the very scorpions sought refuge under the stones writing with a frenzied desire to sting he sat unmoved beneath the burning rays, holding aloft his blue streaked face and shaggy wild beard.

While yet the people stopped to talk to him, someone once inquired:

"Poor Lazarus, it evidently pleases thee to sit and look upon the sun?" and he replied:

"Yes. It pleases me."

So severe must have been the cold of those three days in the grave, so dense its gloom, that there was not any heat nor any light upon earth strong enough to warm Lazarus, bright enough to illumine the darkness of his eyes,—thus thought the curious as they departed sighing.

And when the sun's luridly crimson disc descended to earth Lazarus retired into the desert and walked straight towards the sun as though striving to catch up with it. Always he walked straight towards the sun, and those who tried to follow him in order to learn what he did at night in the desert had indelibly impressed on their memory the black silhouette of a tall and corpulent man against the crimson back-ground of the mighty orb. The night with its terrors drove them back, and they never learned what Lazarus was doing in the desert, but the image of the black shadow on a crimson background burned itself on their brain and refused to leave them. Like an animal frenziedly rubbing its eyes to remove a cinder they stupidly rubbed their eyes, but the impression left by Lazarus was not to be blotted out, and death alone granted oblivion.

But there were people afar off who had never seen Lazarus, having merely heard rumors of him. These with a daring curiosity that is stronger than fear and feeds on fear, with a secret sneer in their hearts, ventured to approach him as he basked in the sun, and engaged in conversation with him. By this time the appearance of Lazarus had somewhat changed for the better, and he no longer looked so terrifying. And in the first moment they snapped their fingers and thought disapprovingly of the folly of the inhabitants of the Holy City. And when their short conversation was over, they wended their way home, but their appearance was such that the inhabitants of the Holy City at once recognized them saying:

"There goes another madman upon whom Lazarus has cast his glance," and they paused raising their hands with compassion.

Brave warriors came rattling their arms, men who knew no fear; with laughter and songs came happy hearted youths; careworn traders, jingling their coins, ran in for a moment; and the haughty temple attendants left their staffs at the door of Lazarus,—but none returned the same as he had come. The same horrible pall sank upon their souls and imparted a novel appearance to the old familiar world.

Those who still felt like talking thus described their impressions.

"All objects visible to the eye and sensible to the touch became empty, light and diaphanous like unto luminous shadows flitting through the gloom."

"A great darkness enveloped the universe; and was not dispelled by the sun, the moon or the stars, but enshrouded the earth with a boundless black pall, embracing it like a mother."

"It penetrated all objects, even iron and stone, and the particles thereof lost their union and became lonely; it penetrated even into the hearts of the particles unto the severing of the very atoms."

"For the great void that surrounds the universe was not filled by things visible, by sun, moon or stars, but shoreless it stretched penetrating all things, severing all things, body from body, particle from particle."

"In emptiness the trees spread out their roots and the very trees seemed empty."

"In emptiness tottering to a phantom ruin, and empty themselves, rose ghostly temples, palaces and houses."

"And in that waste Man moved restlessly, and he too was empty and light like unto a shadow."

"For there was no more time, and the beginning of all things and the end thereof met face to face."

"The sound of the builders' hammers was still heard as they reared the edifice, but its downfall could be seen already, and behold, emptiness soon yawned over the ruins."

"Hardly a man was born, before funeral tapers gleamed at his bier; these barely flickered an instant, and emptiness reigned in the place of the Man, the funeral tapers and the bier."

"In the embrace of Gloom and Waste; Man trembled hopelessly with the dread of the Infinite."

Thus spoke those who had still a desire to speak. But those who would not speak and died in silence could have probably told much more.

CHAPTER IV

At that time there lived in Rome a celebrated sculptor. Out of clay, marble and bronze he fashioned the forms of gods and of men, and such was the beauty of his work that men proclaimed it immortal. But the sculptor himself was dissatisfied with it and claimed that there was something else to strive for, a beauty that was truly supreme, such as he had never yet been able to fix in marble or bronze. "I have not yet garnered the splendor of the moon," he was wont to say. "I have not yet caught the radiance of the sun. My marble lacks soul, my beautiful bronze lacks life." At night, beneath the moonlit sky, he roamed about the highways, crossing the black shadows of cypress trees, his white tunic gleaming in the light of the moon, and friends who chanced to meet him hailed him in jest:

"Art thou gathering moonlight, Aurelius? And where be thy baskets?"

And joining in their laughter he made reply, pointing to his eyes:

"Behold the baskets wherein I gathered the light of the moon and the radiance of the sun."

And he spoke the truth, for the light of the moon gleamed in his eyes, the radiance of the sun glowed in them. But he could not convert them into marble, and this was the radiant sorrow of his life.

He came from an ancient patrician family, had a loving wife and dutiful children, and lacked nothing.

When a dim rumor concerning Lazarus reached his ear, he consulted his wife and friends and undertook the long journey to Judea in order to see him who had so miraculously risen from the dead. The monotony of life weighed heavily upon him in those days and he hoped that the journey would awaken his interest in the world. What he had heard concerning the risen one did not deter him, for he had pondered much upon death, though he had no longing for it. Neither had he patience with those who would confuse death with life. "On this side life and its beauty," he reasoned, "and on the other, death with its mystery. Nothing better could one imagine than to live and enjoy life and the glory of living." And he even entertained a somewhat vain and glorious notion of convincing Lazarus that this was the true view and of bringing him back to life, even as his body had been brought back to life.

This seemed an easy task for him, for the rumors concerning

the risen one, fearsome and strange as they were, failed to convey the whole truth and only vaguely hinted at something dreadful.

Lazarus was rising from his rock for his journey into the desert in the path of the setting sun, when the rich Roman, accompanied by an armed slave, approached him, and in a sonorous voice called to him:

"Lazarus!"

Lazarus beheld a haughty and handsome man, resplendent with fame, clad in white apparel bearing precious gems that sparkled in the sunshine. The radiance of the sun lent to the head and the features a semblance of dull bronze. After his scrutiny Lazarus obediently resumed his seat, and listlessly looked to the ground.

"Truly thou art not fair to look upon, poor Lazarus," calmly observed the Roman, toying with his golden chain. "Thou art even terrifying in appearance, poor fellow; and Death was no sluggard the day thou so carelessly didst fall into its clutches. But thou art as fat as a wine barrel, and the great Caesar says that fat people are harmless. I cannot see why people are so afraid of thee. Thou wilt permit me to stay overnight? It is already late and I have no abode."

Nobody had ever sought permission to pass a night with Lazarus.

"I have no couch to offer thee," said he.

"I am somewhat of a soldier and can sleep sitting," replied the Roman. "We shall light a fire."

"I have no fire."

"In the darkness then like two comrades shall we hold our converse. I suppose thou hast some wine here?"

"I have no wine."

The Roman laughed. "Now I comprehend why thou art so morose and why thou takest no delight in thy second life. Thou hast no wine. Very well. We shall do without. Thou knowest there are words that turn one's head even as Falernian wine."

With a motion of his hand he dismissed the slave and they were left alone. And again the sculptor spoke, but it seemed that with the sinking sun the glow of life had departed from his words, for they lost color and substance. They reeled and slipped and stumbled, as though unsteady of foot of drunken with the wine of anguish and dismay. Yawning chasms appeared between them like distant hints of a vast void and utter darkness.

"I am thy guest now and thou wilt not offend me, Lazarus", he said. "Hospitality is a duty even for those who have been dead three days. For they say that thou didst pass three days in the grave. It must have been very chilly there, and it is thence comes thy bad habit of doing without wine and fire. But I love the fire. It grows dark here so early. The line of thy brow and forehead is quite noteworthy, even as the skyline of palaces ruined by an earthquake and buried beneath ashes. But why is thy apparel so odd and unattractive? I have seen the bridegrooms in thy country arrayed like this, such absurd attire, such repulsive garments! But art thou then a bridegroom?"

The sun had already vanished and gigantic black shadows came hurrying from the east, as though the bare feet of giants came rustling over the sands, and the chill breath of swiftly fleeing wind blew up behind them.

"In the darkness thou seemest even bigger oh Lazarus, as though thou hast grown stouter in these last few minutes. Dost thou perchance feed on darkness? But I should like some fire, just a little blaze the tiniest flame would do.... And I am a trifle cold.... You have here such barbarously chilly nights If it were not pitch dark I should say that thou art looking at me, Lazarus. Yes, methinks thou ART looking at me. I feel it. Now thou art smiling!"

The night had set in and a dense blackness filled the air.

"How good will it be when the sun rises again on the morrow.... Thou knowest I am a great sculptor. My friends call me so. I create, yes I create things, but daylight is needed for that. I impart life unto the cold lifeless marble. In the fire I melt the ringing bronze, in a vivid and glowing fire.... Why touchest thou me with thy hand?"

"Come", said Lazarus, "thou art my guest." And they entered the house. And the shadows of a long night descended upon the earth.

The slave who had grown tired waiting for his master called for him when the sun had already risen high overhead. And he saw under its rays Lazarus and his master huddled closely together. They were gazing upward in silence.

The slave wept aloud and called to his master: "Master, what troubleth thee? Master!"

The same day Aurelius left for Rome. The whole way he was pensive and silent, scrutinizing everything, the people, the ship and the sea, as though struggling to commit something to memory. A fierce tempest overtook them, and all the while Aurelius remained on the deck gazing eagerly on the rising and sinking waves.

At home the change that had taken place in him caused consternation, but he calmed the apprehensions of his household and observed significantly: "I have found it."

In the same raiment that he had worn during the journey without change he went to work, and the marble obediently responded to the resounding blows of his hammer. He worked long and eagerly, refusing to admit any one; at last one morning he announced that his work was ready, and summoned all his friends, the severe critics and experts in art. He attired himself into sumptuous and festive garments that sparkled with gold and shone with the purple of Bysson.

"Behold what I have created", he said musingly.

His friends gazed on the work and the shadow of a deep sorrow clouded their faces. The group was simply hideous to look upon: it possessed none of the forms familiar to the eye, though it was not devoid of a dim suggestion of some novel and fanciful image. Upon a twisted thin little twig, or rather upon the misshapen likeness of one, crouched an unsightly, distorted mass of crude fragments that seemed to be weakly striving to flee in all directions. And casually, under a crude ridge they observed a wondrously wrought butterfly, with diaphanous wings that was all aquiver with the futile longing to soar skyward.

"Why this wondrously wrought butterfly, Aurelius?" someone dubiously inquired.

"I don't know", replied the sculptor.

But the truth has to be told, and one of his friends (the one who loved him best) interposed: "My poor friend, this is a monstrosity. It must be destroyed. Give me the hammer."

And with two blows of the hammer he destroyed the hideous heap, sparing only the wondrous butterfly.

From that time on Aurelius created nothing. He gazed with profound indifference upon marble and bronze and upon his former godlike creations wherein beauty immortal dwelt. In the hope of inspiring him once more with his old zeal for work and of reviving his moribund soul, his friends led him to view the beautiful work of others, but he maintained the same lack of interest, and no warming smile ever parted again his tightly drawn lips. Only when they ventured to hold lengthy speeches on love and beauty he wearily and listlessly replied:

"But all this is a lie."

And in the daytime when the sun was shining he strolled into his luxurious garden, and seeking out some spot undimmed by the shade he yielded up his uncovered head and lacklustre eyes to radiance and warmth. Red and white butterflies flitted about the garden, from the contorted lips of a blissfully drunken Satyr the water splashed coursing down into the marble cistern, but he sat unmoved like a faint shadow of him who in a distant land sat as immobile at the very gates of the desert beneath the arid rays of the midday sun.

CHAPTER V

And now Augustus himself, the great, the divine, summoned Lazarus to appear before him.

They attired him in sumptuous wedding garment, for time and usage seemed to have prescribed these as befitting him as though he had remained until his death the betrothed of some unknown bride. It was as though an old, decaying and decrepit coffin were regilded and adorned with fresh gaudy tinsel. And he was conducted by a sumptuously garbed and gay cortege, as though in truth it were a bridal procession, and the heralds loudly sounded their trumpets clearing the way for the messengers of the emperor. But the path of Lazarus was deserted. His native land had learned to execrate the odious name of the miraculously risen one, and the mere news of his dread approach was sufficient to scatter the people. The blasts of the brass horns fell on the solitude and only the desert air responded with a melancholy echo.

Then they took him across the sea. And it was the most gorgeous and the saddest ship that was ever mirrored against the azure waves of the Mediterranean There were many people aboard, but the vessel was as mute and silent as the grave and the very waves seemed to sob hopelessly as they laved the beautifully curved and lofty prow. Lazarus sat alone, holding his bared head to the sun, listening in silence to the murmur of the waters, and afar off the sailors and the messengers lounged around feebly and listlessly huddled together like a cluster of despondent shadows. If a clap of thunder had rent the air, if a sudden gale had torn the gaudy sails, the ship would have doubtlessly perished for there was none on board with strength or zeal enough to struggle for life. With a last weak effort some stepped to the rail and eagerly gazed into the blue and transparent abyss waiting perhaps for a mermaid's pink shoulder to flash from the deep or for some drunken and joy maddened centaur to gallop by splashing the foam of the sea with his hoofs.

With stolid indifference Lazarus set foot on the streets of the Eternal City, as though all its wealth, the majesty of its structures that seemed to have been reared by giants, the splendor, the beauty, the music of its elegance were simply the echo of the desert wind, the reflex of Palestine's arid sands. Chariots sped by, crowds of handsome, sturdy, haughty men passed on, the builders of the Eternal City, the proud participants of her bustling life; the air filled with the notes of songs, the murmur of fountains, the pearly cadences of women's laughter! drunkards held pompous speeches and the sober listened smilingly; and the horseshoes clattered and clatterer upon the pavements. Caught all around by the whirlpool of noisy merriment there moved through the city like a blot of icy silence one fat and clumsy creature sowing in his path annoyance, wrath and a vaguely cankering grief. Who dare be sad in Rome? The citizens were indignant and frowned, and two days later the whole ready tongued Rome knew of the miraculously resurrected one and timidly avoided him.

But there were in Rome many brave people eager to test their prowess, and to their thoughtless challenge Lazarus readily responded. Busy with the affairs of state the Emperor delayed receiving him and the miraculously risen one for seven days in succession paid visits to those who would see him.

A merry winebibber met Lazarus and hailed him with carefree laughter on his ruddy lips.

"Drink, Lazarus, drink!" he shouted. "How Augustus would laugh to see thee drunk!"

And drunken women laughed at the sally, while they showered rose leaves on the blue-streaked hands of Lazarus. But the winebibber looked into his eyes—and his joy was forever ended. He remained drunken for life: he drank no more, yet he remained drunken but in the place of joyous reveries which the wine yields, horrible dreams haunted his ill-fated soul. Horrible dreams became the sole nourishment of his stricken spirit. Horrible dreams held him day and night in the spell of their hideous fancies, and death itself was less terrible than appeared his ferocious precursors.

Lazarus called on a youth and a maiden, lovers and fair to look on in their love. Proudly and firmly grasping the woman he loved the youth remarked with gentle compassion:

"Look on us, Lazarus, and rejoice with us. Is there aught stronger than love?"

And Lazarus looked. And they ceased not from loving all their life long, but their love became gloomy and somber, like the cypress trees that grow above tombs, feeding their roots on the dissolution within the grave and seeking vainly in the evening hour to reach heaven with their dusky and pointed tops. Thrown by the unfathomable force of life into each other's arms they mingled their kisses with tears, their joy with pain, and realized their twofold bondage: the humble slaves of inexorable life and the helpless bondsmen of ominous and mute Nothingness. Ever united, ever parted, they flashed upwards like sparks and like sparks faded in shoreless gloom.

Then came Lazarus to a haughty sage and the sage told him:

94

"I know all the terrors that thou canst relate to me, Lazarus. Wherewith wilt thou terrify me?"

But it was not long before the sage realized that the knowledge of the horrible is not the horrible, and that the vision of death is not death itself. And he realized that wisdom and folly are the equals in the sight of the Infinite, for the Infinite knows them not. And the boundaries between knowledge and ignorance, between truth and falsehood, between height and depth vanished, and his formless thoughts were suspended in emptiness. Then he seized his grey head in his hands and cried out in agony:

"I cannot think! I cannot think!"

Thus succumbed to the stolid gaze of the miraculously risen one all things that served to affirm life, its meaning and its joys. And it was said that it would be dangerous to allow him to face the Emperor, that it would be safer to put him to death and burying him secretly to spread the rumor that he had disappeared without leaving a trace. Swords were already sharpened and some youths devoted to the welfare of the nation volunteered to be his slayers, when suddenly Augustus demanded to have Lazarus brought before him on the morrow and upset their cruel plans.

Though it was impossible to remove Lazarus, it was thought best to soften somewhat the dreary impression produced by his appearance. For this reason skilled artists were summoned, also hair arrangers and masters of make-up and they labored all night over the head of Lazarus. They trimmed his beard, curled it and made it appear neat and attractive. The livid coloring of his face and hands was removed by means of paint: his hands were bleached and his cheeks touched up with red. The repulsive wrinkles of suffering that furrowed his senile features were patched up, painted and smoothed over, and lines of goodnatured laughter and pleasant cheerful good humor were skillfully drawn in their place.

Lazarus submitted stolidly to all they did with him and soon was transformed into a naturally corpulent handsome old man, who looked like a harmless grandfather with numerous descendants. One could almost see the trace of a smile on his lips with which he might have related to them laughable stories, one almost detected in the corner of his eyes the calm tenderness of old age,—such was his quiet and reassuring appearance. But they had not dared to take off his wedding attire, nor could they change his eyes,—dark and dreadful glasses through which there peered upon the world the unfathomable Beyond.

CHAPTER VI

The magnificence of the Imperial palace failed to impress Lazarus. There might have been no difference between his ramshackle but at the threshold of the desert and the splendid and massive palace of stone, so stolidly indifferent was his unobserving glance. Under his feet the solid marble slabs seemed to turn to the sinking sand of the desert, and the throngs of gaily attired and haughty Romans might have been thin air. They avoided looking into his face as he passed, fearing to succumb to the baneful spell of his eyes; but when they judged from the sound of his footsteps that he had passed on, they paused and raising their heads with a little fearsome curiosity watched the departing figure of the tall, corpulent, slightly stooping old man who was slowly wending his way into the heart of the Imperial palace. If Death itself had passed by they would not have glanced after it with greater awe. For until then Death had been known unto the dead only and life unto the living and there had been no bridge between the twain. But this strange being knew Death, and awful, ominous, accursed was his knowledge. "He will be the death of our great and divine Augustus", mused some of them anxiously and muttered curses in his wake as he slowly and stolidly made his way more and more deeply into the palace.

Caesar had already learned the story of Lazarus and nerved himself to meet him. He was a man of daring and courage and thoroughly conscious of his own invincible power. In this fateful encounter with the risen one he chose not to lean upon the feeble aid of men. Face to face, man to man he met Lazarus.

"Do not lift up thine eyes to me, Lazarus," he commanded him as the stranger entered. "I have heard that thy head is like Medusa's turning to stone him who ventures to look upon thee. But I desire to talk with thee and to examine thee before I am turned to stone", he added with an Imperial attempt at a jest that was not unmixed with a little awe.

Approaching him he examined attentively the face and the queer apparel of Lazarus, and though he prided himself on his sharp and observant eye he was deceived by the skill of the artists.

"Well, thou art not so terrible, worthy patriarch. But it is all the worse for people if the terrible assumes such a dignified and agreeable guise. Now let us converse."

Augustus sat down and with a glance that was as searching as his words he commenced to question him.

"Why didst thou not salute me as thou earnest in?"

Lazarus replied:

"I did not know that it was necessary."

"Art thou a Christian?"

"No."

Augustus nodded approvingly.

"Good. I dislike these Christians. They shake the tree of life before it yields its full fruitage and scatter to the wind its blossoming fragrance. But what art thou?"

With an effort Lazarus replied:

"Once I was dead."

"So I have heard. But what art thou now?"

Lazarus hesitated and again replied listlessly, stolidly:

"Once I was dead."

"Listen to me, thou enigma", resumed the Emperor, in measured and severe words voicing the thoughts which had been in his mind before. "My empire is the empire of the living, my people is a living people and not dead. Thou art out of place here. I do not know thee, I do not know what thou hast seen There. But whether thou liest—I abhor thy lying, and if thou be telling the truth I abhor thy truth. In my bosom I feel the throbbing of life. I feel vigor in my hands, and my proud thoughts soar like eagles through space. And there, behind me, under the protection of my dominion, in the shadow of laws created by me, people live and labor and rejoice. Hearest thou this wondrous harmony of life? Hearest thou this warlike challenge which men fling into the face of the future summoning it to a combat?"

Augustus reverently raised his hands and solemnly exclaimed:

"Blessed be Thou Great and Divine Life!"

But Lazarus was silent and with added severity the Emperor continued:

"Thou art out of place here. Thou art a pitiful remnant, a half-eaten scrap from the table of Death, thou breathest into people melancholy and hatred of life. Thou art like the locust that eateth the full ear of grain knitting the slime of despair and despondency. Thy truth is like unto the rusty sword in the hands of a murderous night prowler, and I shall put thee to death like an assassin. But ere I do this I will gaze into thine eyes. Perhaps only the cowards fear them, perhaps they will wake the thirst of conflict and longing for victory in the brave. If that be so thou meritest a reward, not death. Look then upon me, Lazarus."

And at first Augustus fancied as though a friend were looking upon him, so gentle, so caressing, so tenderly soothing was the gaze of Lazarus. It boded no terrors but calm and repose, it was the gaze of a tender lover, of a compassionate sister: through his eyes Infinity gazed even as a mother. But the embrace grew stronger and stronger until his breath was stopped by lips that seemed to crave for kisses. And in the next instant he felt the iron fingers plowing through the tender tissues of his flesh, and cruel claws sank slowly into his heart.

"I am in pain", moaned Divus Augustus with blanching cheek. "Yet, look on me still, Lazarus, look on."

As though through slowly opening gates that had been shut for aeons the horror of the Infinite poured coldly and calmly out of the growing breach. Fathomless waste and fathomless darkness entered like twin shadows quenching the light of the sun, removing the ground underfoot, obliterating all overhead. And pain left the benumbed heart of Augustus.

"Look, look still, Lazarus", commanded he reeling.

Time ceased and the beginning of things faced the end thereof in an ominous meeting. The throne of Augustus, so recently reared, was overthrown; a barren waste reigned in the place of Augustus and of his throne. Rome herself had gone to a silent doom, and a new city rose in her place, only in her turn to be swallowed up by nothingness. Like phantom giants cities and states and empires swiftly fell and vanished into emptiness, swallowed up in the insatiable maw of the Infinite.

"Stop", commanded Caesar, and already a note of indifference sounded in his voice. His arms hung limply from his shoulders, and his eagle eyes now flashed, now grew dim in a futile struggle against the darkness that threatened to overwhelm him.

"Thou hast slain me, Lazarus", he stammered listlessly.

And these words of hopelessness saved him. He remembered his people whose shield he was called to be, and his moribund heart was pierced with a sharp and redeeming pang. He thought of them bitterly as he pictured them doomed to ruin. He thought of his people with anguish in his soul as he saw them like luminous shadows flitting through the gloom of the Infinite. Tenderly he thought of them as of brittle vessels throbbing with life blood and endowed with hearts that know both sorrow and joy.

Thus reasoning and feeling, with the balance now favoring life, now inclined towards death, he slowly fought his way back to life, to find in its sufferings and joys a shield against the emptiness and the terror of the Infinite.

"No, thou hast not slain me, Lazarus", he exclaimed, with firmness, "but I shall slay thee, Go!"

That night Divus Augustus partook of food and drink with a keen delight. But there were moments when the uplifted arm paused in mid-air and a shadow dimmed the lustre of his shining aquiline eyes,—it was like a wave of icy horror beating against his feet. Downed, but not utterly destroyed, coldly awaiting the appointed hour, the spirit of Fear cast its shadow into the Emperor's life, standing guard at the head of his bed as he slumbered at night and meekly yielding the sunny days to the joys and the sorrows of life.

Next day, by the Emperor's command, they burned out the eyes of Lazarus with hot irons and sent him back to his native land. Divus Augustus dared not put him to death.

Lazarus returned to the desert, and the desert received him with the breath of the hissing wind and the arid welcome of the consuming sun. Once again he sat on the rock, raising aloft his shaggy neglected beard. In the place of the two burned-out eyes twin black sockets peered dull and gruesome at the sky. In the distance surged the restless roar of the Holy City, but near him all was deserted and dumb. No one came near the place where the miraculously risen one was passing the end of his days, and his neighbors had long since forsaken their abodes. His accursed knowledge, banished by the searing irons into the depths of his head, lay there concealed as though in ambush; as though from ambush it assailed the beholder with a myriad invisible eyes, and no one dared now look at Lazarus.

And in the evening, when the sun, ruddy and swollen, was sinking in the west, sightless Lazarus slowly groped after it. He stumbled over stones and fell, fat and weak as he was, then he rose heavily and walked on. And against the crimson canvas of the sunset his dark form and outstretched arms gave him a monstrous resemblance to the cross.

And it happened one day that he went and never returned. Thus apparently ended the second life of Lazarus, who had been three days under the dominion of Death and miraculously rose from the dead.

LIFE OF FATHER VASSILY

I

A strange and mysterious fate pursued Vassily Feeveysky all through his life. As though damned by some unfathomable curse, from his youth on he staggered under a heavy burden of sadness, sickness and sorrow, and the bleeding wounds of his heart refused to heal. Among men he stood aloof, like a planet among planets, and a peculiar atmosphere, baneful and blighting, seemed to enshroud him like an invisible, diaphanous cloud.

The son of a meek and patient parish priest, he was meek and patient himself, and for a long time failed to observe the ominous and mysterious deliberation with which misfortunes persistently broke over his unattractive shaggy head.

Swiftly he fell, and slowly rose to his feet; fell again, and slowly rose once more, and laboriously, speck by speck, grain by grain, set to work restoring his frail anthill by the side of the great highway of life.

But when he was ordained priest and married a good woman, begetting by her a son and a daughter, he commenced to feel that all was now well and safe with him, just as with other people, and would so remain for ever. And he blessed God, for he believed in Him solemnly and simply, as a priest and as a man in whose soul there was no guile.

And it happened in the seventh year of his happiness, in the noon hour of a sultry day in July, that the village children went to the river to swim, and with them went Father Vassily's son, like his father Vassily by name, and like him swarthy of face and meek in manner. And little Vassily was drowned. His young mother, the Popadya,[1] came running to the river bank with the crowd, and the plain and appalling picture of human death engraved itself indelibly on her memory: the dull and ponderous thumping of her own heart, as though each heart beat threatened to be her last; and the odd transparence of the atmosphere in which moved hither and thither the humdrum familiar figures of people, though now they seemed so strangely aloof, as if severed from the earth; and the disconnected, confused hubbub of voices, with each word rounding in the air and slowly melting away as new sounds come into being.

---

[1] Popadya, the wife of a Russian village priest or "pope," is a distinct type in the social world of the Russian village.

And she conceived a lifelong fear of bright and sunny days. For at such times she saw again the barricade of muscular backs gleaming white in the light of the sun, and the bare feet planted firmly among the trampled cabbage heads, and the rhythmic swing of something bright and white in the trough of which freely rolled a light little body, so gruesomely near, so gruesomely far, and for ever estranged. And long after little Vassya[2] had been buried, and the grass had grown over his grave, the Popadya kept repeating that prayer of all bereaved mothers: "Lord, take my life, but give me back my child."

Soon Father Vassily's whole household learned to dread the bright days of summer time, when the sun shines too glaringly and sets ablaze the treacherous river until the eyes cannot bear the sight of it. On such days, when the people, the beasts and the fields all around were radiant with gladness, the members of Father Vassily's household were wont to watch his wife with awestricken eyes, engaging purposely in loud conversation and laughter, while she, sluggish and indolent, rose to her feet, eyeing the others so fixedly and queerly that they were forced to avert their gaze, and languidly lolled through the house, as though hunting for some needless article, a key, or a spoon or a glass. Whatever she needed was carefully placed in her path, but she continued to seek, and her search increased in intentness and agitation in the measure that the bright and merry orb of the sun rose higher in the firmament. And she approached her husband, placing her lifeless hand on his shoulder and kept repeating in a pleading voice.

"Vassya! Vassya! I say!"

"What is it, dear?" meekly and hopelessly responded Father Vassily, trying to smooth her dishevcled hair with trembling fingers that were sunburnt and black with the soil and were badly in want of trimming. She was still young and pretty, and her arm rested upon the shabby cassock of her husband as though carved of marble, white and heavy.

"What is it, dear? Will you have some tea now? You have not had any yet."

"Vassya! Vassya, I say!" she repeated pleadingly, removing her arm from his shoulder like some needless, superfluous object, and returned to her searching, only still more restlessly and excitedly. Walking all through the house, not a room of which had been tidied, she passed into the garden, from the garden into the court yard, and again into the house, while the sun rose higher and higher, and through the trees could be seen a flash of the warm sluggish river.

---

[2] Pet name for Vassily.

And step after step, clinging tightly to her mother's skirt, Nastya[3], the Popadya's daughter, shambled after her, morose and sullen, as though the black shadow of impending doom had lodged itself even over her little six-year-old heart. She anxiously hurried her little steps to keep pace with the distracted big stride of her mother, casting furtively yearning glances upon the familiar, but ever mysterious and enticing garden, and she longingly stretched out her disengaged hand towards a bush of sour gooseberries, and stealthily plucked a few, though the sharp thorns cruelly scratched her. And the prick of these thorns that were sharp as needles, and the acid taste of the berries, intensified the scowl on her face, and she longed to whimper like an abandoned pup.

When the sun reached the zenith, the Popadya closed tightly the shutters in the windows of her room, and in the darkness gave herself up to liquor until she was drunken, drawing from each drained glassful fresh pangs of agony and searching memories of her perished child. She shed bitter tears, and in the awkward drone of an ignorant person trying to read aloud out of a book, she kept telling over and over again the story of a meek and swarthy little boy who had lived, laughed and died; and with this bookish singsong she resurrected his eyes and his smile and his oldfashioned manner of speech.

"'Vassya', I say to him, 'why do you tease kitty? Don't tease her, dear. God told us to be merciful to all—to the little horsies, and to the kittens and to the little chicks'. And he lifts up his sweet eyes to me, the darling, and says: 'And why isn't kittie merciful to little birdies? See the pigeons have raised their little ones, and kittie eats up the pigeons, and the little birdies are calling, calling for their mamma.'"

And Father Vassily listened meekly and hopelessly, while outside, under the closed shutters, amid burdocks, nettles and thistles, little Nastya sat sprawling on the ground, and played sulkily with her doll. And always her play was this: dollie refused to mind and was punished and she twisted dollie's arms till she thought they hurt and whipped her with a twig of nettles.

When Father Vassily had first found his wife in a state of inebriety, and from her rebelliously agitated, bitterly exulting face had realized that this thing had come to stay, he shriveled up and the next moment burst cut in a fit of subdued, senseless laughter, rubbing his hot dry hands. And a long time he laughed, a long time he kept rubbing his hands; he strove to restrain this desire to laugh, which was so obviously out of place, and turning aside from his

---

[3] Diminutive of Anastasia.

sobbing wife, he snickered softly into his fist like a naughty school boy. Then just as abruptly he turned serious, his jaws snapped like metal; but not a word of comfort could he utter to the hysterical woman, not a caressing word could he find for her. But when she had fallen asleep, the priest bent down, making three times the sign of the cross over her. Then he went out and found little Nastya in the garden, coldly patted her on the head and stalked out into the fields.

For a long time he followed a little path through the rye which was standing fairly high in the field and looked down into the soft white dust which here and there retained the impress of heels and the outline of someone's bare feet. The sheaves nearest to the path were crushed to the ground, some lying across the path, and the grain was crushed, blackened and flattened.

Where the path turned, Father Vassily stopped. Ahead of him and all around him swayed the full grain on slender stalks, overhead was the shoreless blazing sky of July grown white with the heat, and nothing more: not a tree, not a hut, not a man. Alone he stood, lost in the dense field of grain, alone before the face of Heaven—set high above him and blazing.

Father Vassily lifted up his eyes—they were little eyes, sunken and black as coal; they were aglow with the bright reflection of the heavenly flame, and he pressed his hands to his breast and tried to say something. The iron jaws quivered, but did not yield. Gnashing his teeth the priest forced them apart, and with this movement of his lips that resembled a convulsive yawn, loud and distinct came the words:

"I—believe!"

Unechoed in the wilderness of sky and of fields was lost this wailing orison that so madly resembled a challenge. And as though contradicting some one, as though passionately pleading with some one and warning him, he repeated once more:

"I—believe."

And returning home, once more, speck by speck, grain by grain, he fell to the work of restoring his wrecked anthill: he watched the milking of cows, with his own hands he combed Nastya's long and coarse hair, and despite the late hour he drove ten versts into the country for the district physician in order to seek his advice with regard to his wife's ailment. And the doctor prescribed her some drops.

II

No one liked Father Vassily, neither his parishioners, nor the vestry of the church. He intoned the service awkwardly, without decorum: his voice was dry and indistinct, and he either hurried so that the deacon had a hard time to keep up with him, or he fell behind without rime or reason. He was not covetous, but he accepted money and donations so clumsily that all believed him to be greedy and scoffed at him behind his back. And everybody knew that he was unlucky in his private life and avoided him, considering it a poor omen to meet him or to talk with him. His Saint's Day[4] was celebrated on November the twenty-eighth. He had invited many to dinner, and in compliance with his ceremonious invitation every one promised to come, but only the vestrymen made their appearance, and of the better parishioners not a soul attended. And he was humiliated before the vestrymen, but the Popadya felt the insult most keenly, for the delicacies and wines which she had ordered from the city had to go to waste.

"No one even cares to come and see us," she said, sober and downcast, when the last of their few guests had departed, noisy and drunken, after a senseless gorging, having paid no regard to the rare vintage of wines or to the quality of the food.

But it was the head of the vestry, Ivan Porfyritch Koprov, who treated the priest worse than the rest of the parishioners. He openly exhibited his contempt for the luckless man, and when the Popadya's periodical lapses into appalling inebriety had become a public scandal, he refused to kiss the priest's hand. And the good-natured deacon tried vainly to reason with him.

"Shame on thee. It is not the man, but his holy office that must be respected."

But Ivan Porfyritch stubbornly refused to dissociate the office from the man, and replied:

"He is a worthless man. He can neither keep himself in order, nor his wife. Is it right for a spiritual adviser's wife to persist in drunkenness, without shame or conscience? Let my wife try and go on a spree, I'd stop her quickly."

The deacon shook his head reproachfully and mentioned the long-suffering of Job, how God had loved him, but turned him over to Satan to be tried, but later rewarded him an hundredfold for all his sufferings. But Ivan Porfyritch smiled scornfully into his beard

---

[4] The day in the church calendar dedicated to the saint for whom a Russian child is named. It is celebrated with more solemnity than the birthday.

and without the slightest compunction cut short the disagreeable admonition.

"Don't tell me, I know. Job, so to speak, was a righteous man, a holy man, but what is this one? Where is his righteousness? Rather remember, deacon, the old proverb: God marks a rogue. There is sound sense in that proverb."

"Wait, the priest will get even with thee, for refusing to kiss his hand. He'll drive thee out of the church."

"We'll see about that."

"All right, we'll see."

And they bet a gallon of cherry brandy whether the priest would expel him or not. The vestry man won; next Sunday he turned his back on the priest with an insolent air, and the hand which the priest had extended to be kissed, burnt brown it was from the sun—remained desolately suspended in midair, and Father Vassily flushed a deep purple, but did not say a word.

And after this incident which was much talked about in the village, Ivan Porfyritch became still more firmly convinced that the priest was a bad and an unworthy man and began to incite the villagers to complain to the bishop and to ask for another parish priest.

Ivan Porfyritch himself was a man of wealth, very fortunate in all things, and enjoyed general esteem. He had an impressive face, with firm round cheeks and an immense black beard, and his whole body was covered with a growth of dense black hair, particularly his legs and his chest, and he believed that hairiness was a sign of great good luck. He believed in his luck as firmly as he believed in God, and considered himself an elect among the people; he was proud, self-reliant and invariably in good spirits. In a terrible railroad wreck in which a multitude of people had perished, he merely lost a cap which had been trampled into the mire.

"And it was an old one at that!" he was wont to add with much self-satisfaction, evidently considering this incident an eloquent proof of his merits.

He regarded all men as rogues and fools, and knew no mercy towards either variety. It was his habit with his own hands to strangle the pups, of whom his black setter Gipsy presented him yearly a generous litter; only the strongest one among them he suffered to live for breeding purposes, though he willingly distributed some of the others to those who wanted a dog, for he considered dogs to be useful animals. In forming opinions Ivan Porfyritch was rash and unreasonable, but he easily departed from them, without noticing his inconsistencies; yet his actions were uniformly firm and resolute and only rarely erroneous.

105

And all this made the head of the vestry a terrible and an extraordinary personage in the eyes of the hunted priest. When they met, he was the first to raise his broad-rimmed hat, which he did with indecorous haste, and as he walked away, he felt that his gait grew faster and more shuffling, revealing itself as the gait of a man who was scared and ashamed, and his scrawny legs were tangled in the folds of his cassock. It seemed as though his very fate, cruel and enigmatic, was personified in that immense black beard, in those hairy hands, and in that resolute, straight stride, and if he did not crumple up and slink away and hide behind his four walls, this menacing monster would crush him like an ant.

And whatever pertained to Ivan Porfyritch or belonged to him, aroused the eager interest of the priest, so that some times for days at a stretch he could think of nothing else but of the churchwarden, his wife, his children, his wealth. Working with the peasants in the fields, (in his coarse, tarred boots and in his cheap working blouse he greatly resembled an humble peasant) Father Vassily would often turn his face to the village, and the first sight that greeted his eyes alongside of the church, was the red iron roof of the churchwarden's two-story house. Then behind the greying green of wind-wrecked willows he traced with difficulty the outline of the weather-beaten shingle roof of his own little home; and the sight of these two so contrasting roofs filled the heart of the priest with the anguish of hopelessness.

One feast day the Popadya returned from the church in tears and told her husband that Ivan Porfyritch had grossly insulted her. As she was making her way to her place, he remarked from behind the lectern, loudly enough for the whole congregation to hear:

"This drunken wench ought not to be allowed in the church at all. She's a disgrace!"

As the Popadya sobbingly related this incident to her husband, Father Vassily observed with horrible and merciless clearness how she had aged and come down in the four years which had passed since Vassya's death. She was still young, but silver threads were running through her hair, the teeth once so white had turned black, and her eyes were baggy.

She was now a confirmed smoker, and it was painful to watch her puffing a cigarette which she held in a clumsy, feminine fashion between two rigidly extended fingers. She smoked and wept and the cigarette trembled between her lips that were swollen with sobbing.

"Why, oh why, oh Lord?" she kept repeating in anguish, and with the intentness of stupor she gazed through the window against which pattered the chill drops of a September rainstorm. The panes were dim with water, and the birch outside, heavy with rain drops,

106

seemed to sway back and forth with the shadowy deliquescence of a specter. In their efforts to save fuel, they had not yet started heating the house, and the air in the room was damp and chilly and almost as uncomfortable as outdoors.

"What can you do with him, Nastenka?"[5] retorted the priest rubbing his dry warm hands. "We must bear it."

"Lord, Lord, is there not a soul to take my part?" wailed the Popadya, and in the corner gazed dry and immobile the wolfish eyes of skulking little Nastya through a hedge of coarse and unkempt hair.

The Popadya was drunk before bedtime, and then ensued that appalling, abominable, piteous scene which Father Vassily could never thereafter recall without a sense of chaste horror and of consuming, unbearable shame. In the morbid gloom of tightly closed shutters, amid the monstrous visions born of alcohol, in the wake of obstinate wails for her lost first-born, his wife had conceived the insane notion of bringing a new son into the world. To resurrect his sweet smile, to resurrect those eyes that once had sparkled with benign radiance, to bring back his calm and sensible speech: to resurrect the lad himself, as he had lived in the glory of his sinless childhood, as he had appeared on that horrible day in July when the sun blazed so brightly and the treacherous river glistened so blindingly. And consumed with a frenzy of hope, all beauteous and hideous with the flames that had enwrapped her, the Popadya stormily demanded her husband's caresses, pleaded for them with piteous humility. She coyly primped herself, she coquetted with him, but the expression of horror never passed from his face. She strove with the energy of passionate anguish to become again as tender and desirable as she had been ten years back, and she tried to assume a shy, maidenly look, whispering coy, girlish words, but her liquor-lamed tongue refused to obey her, and through her shyly lowered eyelashes ever more luridly and obviously flashed the flame of passionate desire, while the swarthy face of her husband remained transfixed with horror. He had covered his burning head with his hands, weakly whispering:

"Don't! Don't!"

And she sank to her knees and hoarsely pleaded:

"Have pity on me! Give me back my Vassya! Give him back to me, priest! I say, give him back to me, curse you!"

And the autumnal rain gusts beat fiercely against the tightly closed shutters, and the stormy night heaved deep and painful sighs.

---

[5] Diminutive of Anastasia.

Cut off from world and life by the walls and the curtain of night, they seemed to be whirling in the throes of a frenzied labyrinthic nightmare, and around them swirled wails and curses that would not die. Madness stood guard at the door; the searing air was its breath; and its eyes the lurid glare of the oil lamp stifling in the maw of a soot-grimed globe.

"You will not? You will not?" cried the Popadya, and with maniacal yearning for motherhood she tore off her raiment, shamelessly baring her body, ardent and terrible like a Bacchante, piteous and pathetic like a mother mourning for her child. "You will not? Then before God I tell you I'll go out into the street. I will throw myself on the neck of the first man I meet. Give me back my Vassya, curse you!"

And her passion vanquished the chaste-hearted priest. To the weird moaning of the autumnal storm, to the sound of her frenzied babble, life itself, the eternal liar, seemed to bare her dark and mysterious loins, and through his darkening consciousness flashed like a gleam of distant lightning a monstrous conception: of a miraculous resurrection, of some far-off miraculously hazardous chance. And to the demoniac passion of the Popadya, heart-chaste and shamefaced, he responded with a passion as frenzied, wherein all things blended: the glory of hope, and the fervor of prayer, and the boundless despair of a great malefactor.

In the dead of night, when the Popadya had fallen into a heavy sleep, Father Vassily took his hat and his stick, and without stopping to dress, in a shabby nainsook cassock went out into the fields. The storm had subsided. The vapory drizzle had spread a moist and chilly film over the rainsoaked earth. The sky was as black as the earth, and the night of autumn breathed utter desolation. Within its gloomy maw the man had vanished, leaving no trace. Once his stick knocked against a boulder that chanced to lie in its path, then all was still, and a lasting silence ensued. A lifeless vapory mist stifled each timid sound in its icy embrace. The moribund foliage did not stir, not a voice, not a cry, not a groan was heard. Long lasted the silence—and it was the silence of death.

And far beyond the village, away from any human habitation, an invisible voice pierced the gloom. It was a voice that was broken, choking and hoarse, like the moaning of infinite loneliness. But the words it spoke were as clear as celestial fire:

"I—believe!" said the invisible voice. And in it were mingled menace and prayer, warning and hope.

III

In the spring the Popadya knew that she would be a mother; all through the summer she abstained from liquor, and a peace, serene and joyous, was enthroned in Father Vassily's household. But the invisible foe still dealt his blows: now the twelve-pood[6] hog which they had fattened for the market took sick and died; now little Nastya broke out all over her body in a malignant rash and refused to respond to treatment. But all these blows were borne lightly, and in the innermost recesses of her heart the Popadya even secretly rejoiced thereat: she was still doubtful of her great good fortune, and all these calamities seemed to be a premium which she was glad to pay for its assurance. She felt that if the prize hog fattened at such expense had died on her hands, if Nastya ailed so persistently, if anything else went wrong and caused repining, then no one would dare to lay a finger on her coming son or to harm him. But as for him, why, she would give up not only the whole household and her little daughter Nastya, but even her own body and soul would she gladly yield to that relentless unseen one who clamored for continual sacrifices.

She had improved in looks and ceased even to fear Ivan Porfyritch himself, and as she walked to her accustomed place in church she proudly paraded her rounded form and looked about with daring and self-reliant glances. And lest she should harm the babe in her womb, she had stopped all housework and was passing daily long hours in the neighboring fiscal forest, amusing herself by picking mushrooms. She was in mortal terror of the ordeal of birth, and resorted to fortune telling with mushrooms, trying to forecast whether the birth would pass off favorably or not; and mostly the answer was favorable. Sometimes under the impenetrable green dome of lofty branches, in some dark and fragrant bed of last season's leaves, she gathered a small family of little white mushrooms, all huddled together, darkheaded and naive, and resembling a brood of little children, and their appearance evoked in her keen pangs of tenderness and affection. With that saintly smile peculiar to people who in solitude yield themselves up to truly pure and noble meditation, she cautiously dug the fibrous ashen-gray soil around the roots, and seating herself on the ground beside her mushrooms, gazed at them for a long time caressingly, a little pale from the greenish shadows of the forest, but fair to look upon,

---

[6] 1 pood = 36 lbs.

gentle and serene. And then she rose and walked on with the cautious waddling gait of a woman on the eve of childbirth, and the ancient forest, the hiding place of numberless little mushrooms, seemed to her a thing of life, wisdom and goodness. Once she took Nastya along for company, but the child capered, frolicked and raced through the bushes like a boisterous wolf-pup and interfered with her mother's thoughts; and she never took her again.

And the winter was passing quietly and happily. She spent her evenings busily sewing a multitude of tiny shirts and swaddling cloths, or pensively stroking the linen with her white fingers upon which the oil lamp threw its bright glow.

She smoothed the soft fabric and stroked it with her hand, as though caressing it, thinking the while intimate thoughts of her own, the wonderful thoughts of motherhood, and in the blue reflection of the lampshade her beautiful face seemed to the priest as though illumined by some sweet and gentle radiance that came from within. Fearing by some incautious movement to disturb her beautiful and happy dreams, Father Vassily softly paced about the room, and his feet, clad in felt slippers, touched the floor gently and noiselessly. He let his gaze dwell now on the living room, cozy and agreeable like the face of a cherished friend, now on the figure of his wife, and all seemed well, just like in other people's homes, and everything about him breathed peace, profound and serene. And his soul was peaceful and smiling, for he neither saw, nor felt that from somewhere there had fallen the diaphanous shadow of great grief and was now silently resting on his forehead, somewhere between his eyebrows. For even in these days of rest and peace a stern and mysterious fate was hovering over his life.

On the eve of Epiphany, the Popadya gave birth to a boy and he was named Vassily. His head was large and his legs were thin and little, and there was something strangely vacant and insensate in the immobile stare of his globe-shaped eyes. For the space of three years after the child's birth the priest and his wife lived 'twixt fears, doubts and hopes, but when three years had passed it became evident that little Vassya had been born an idiot.

Conceived in madness, he had come into the world a madman.

IV

Another year passed in the benumbed stupefaction of grief, but when they emerged from this comatose state and began to look about, they discovered that above their thoughts and their lives sat enthroned the monstrous image of the idiot. The household routine went on as in olden days; they built their fires, they discussed their daily affairs, but something new and dreadful had come into their lives: no one had any real interest in life, and all things were going to pieces. The farm hands loafed, refused to obey orders, and frequently gave notice without any apparent cause, and those who were hired in their place soon fell into the same queer state of indifference and restlessness and commenced to be insolent. Dinner was served either too late or too early, and someone was always missing from the table: either the Popadya, or little Nastya, or Father Vassily himself. From some unfathomable sources there appeared an abundance of tattered garments: the Popadya kept saying that she must darn her husband's socks, and she even fussed with them, but the socks remained unmended and Father Vassily was footsore. And at night everyone in the house tossed about restlessly, tormented by vermin which came crawling from all crevices, and shamelessly paraded upon the walls, and try as they might, nothing seemed able to stop their loathsome invasion.

And wherever they went, whatever they undertook, they could not for a moment forget, that there in the darkened room sat one, unexpected and monstrous, the child of madness. When they left the house to go outdoors, they tried hard to keep from turning around or from glancing back, but something compelled them to glance back, and then it seemed to them that the framehouse itself in which they dwelt was conscious of some terrible change within: it stood there squat and huddled, as though in an attitude of listening, listening to that misshapen and dreadful thing that was contained within its depths, and all its bulging windows, its tightly shut doors seemed barely able to suppress an outcry of mortal anguish.

The Popadya went frequently visiting and spent hours at a stretch in the house of the deacon's wife, but even there she failed to find rest, as though from the idiot's side came forth threads of cobweb thinness—and stretched out towards her, binding her to him indissolubly and for all eternity. And though she were to flee to the ends of the earth, though she were to hide behind the high walls of a nunnery, even though she were to seek escape in death, then into the very gloom of her grave those weblike threads would pursue her and enmesh her with fears and anguish.

And even their nights lacked peace: the faces of the sleepers seemed stolid, but within their skulls, in their dreams and waking nightmares the monstrous world of madness returned to life, and its lord was this same mysterious and dreadful image, half-child and half-brute.

He was four years old but had not yet learned to walk and could utter but one word: "give"; he was spiteful and obstinate, and if anything was denied him he screamed with piercing, ferocious animal cries and stretched out his hands with fingers that were rapaciously curved. And in his habits he was as filthy as an animal, performing his bodily functions wherever he chanced to be, and it was agonizing to attend to him: with the cunning of malice he awaited the moment when his mother's or sister's hair came within his reach, and then he tenaciously clutched at it, tearing it out by the roots in handfuls. Once he bit Nastya, but she flung him back on the bed and beat him long and mercilessly, as though he were not human, not a child, but a mere piece of spiteful flesh, and after this beating he developed a fondness for biting and snapped menacingly, showing his teeth like a dog.

It was also a difficult task to feed him: greedy and impatient, he could not gauge his movements, and would upset the dish, choking as he tried to swallow and wrathfully stretching his curving fingers towards the feeder's hair. And his appearance was repulsive and horrible: on a pair of narrow, almost baby-like shoulders rested a small skull with an immense, immobile, broad face, the size of an adult's. There was something disquieting and terrifying in this monstrous incongruity between face and body, and it seemed as though a child had for some reason put on an immense and repulsive mask.

And the tortured Popadya commenced to drink as in the days of old. She drank heavily, to unconsciousness and delirium, but even mighty alcohol could not release her from the iron circle in the centre of which reigned the horrible and monstrous image of the semichild, semi-beast. And as of yore she sought to find in liquor burning sorrowful memories of the perished firstborn, but the memories refused to come, and the lifeless insensate void yielded neither image nor sound. With every fibre of her inflamed brain she strove to resurrect the sweet face of the little gentle lad; she sang his favorite ditties; she imitated his smile; she pictured to herself his agony as he was choking and strangling in the turbid waters; and she felt his nearness, felt the flames of the great and passionately desired grief blaze up within her heart, but with abrupt swiftness—unperceived by eye or ear—the conjured vision, the longed for grief, vanished into nothingness, and out of the chilling lifeless void the

112

monstrous, motionless mask of the idiot was staring into her eyes. And she felt as though she had just buried her little Vassya, buried him anew, interring him deeply in the bowels of the earth, and she longed to shatter her faithless head in the inmost depths of which so insolently reigned an alien and abominable image.

Terror-stricken she tossed about the room, calling her husband:

"Vassily! Vassily! Come—quick!"

Father Vassily came and without opening his mouth sat down in a far corner of the room; and he was unconcerned and still, as though there had been no outcry, no madness, no terror. And his eyes were invisible; but under the heavy arch of his eyebrows yawned the immobile black of two sunken spots, and his haggard face resembled a skeleton's skull. Leaning his chin on his scrawny arm, he seemed congealed in torpid silence and immobility, and remained in this attitude until the Popadya quieted down by degrees. Then with the intense care of a maniac she painstakingly barricaded the door which led into the idiot's room. She dragged in front of it every table and chair she could find, piling cushions and clothing upon them, and still the barricade seemed too frail to suit her. And with the strength of drunkenness she wrenched a ponderous antique chest of drawers from its accustomed place, and scratching the floor in so doing she dragged it towards the door.

"Move the chair aside," she called to her husband all out of breath, and he rose in silence, cleared the place for her and once more resumed his seat in the corner.

For a moment the Popadya appeared to regain her composure and sank into a chair, breathing heavily and holding her hand to her breast, but in the next instant she sprang to her feet again, and flinging back her disheveled hair to release her ears she listened in terror to the sounds which her morbid imagination seemed to conjure up beyond the wall:

"Hear it, Vassily? Hear it?"

The two black spots gazed upon her unmoved and a stolid distant voice answered:

"There's nothing there. He is sleeping. Calm yourself, Nastya."

The Popadya smiled the glad and radiant smile of a comforted child, and irresolutely sat down on the edge of the chair.

"Do you mean it? Is he sleeping? Did you see it yourself? Don't lie, it's a sin to tell lies."

"I saw him. He is asleep."

"But who is talking back there?"

"There is no one there. You only imagine it."

And the Popadya was so pleased that she laughed out loud,

shaking her head in amusement and warding off something with an uncertain movement of her hand: as though some ill-disposed joker out of deviltry had tried to frighten her and she had seen through the joke and was now laughing at him. But like a stone that falls into a fathomless abyss her laughter fell into space without evoking an echo and died right there in loneliness, and her lips were still curved in a smile while the chill of new terror appeared in her eyes. And such stillness reigned in the room that it seemed as though no one had ever uttered a laugh there; from the scattered pillows, from the overturned chairs, so queer to look upon in their upset state, from the ponderous chest of drawers so clumsily skulking in its unwonted position, from all sides there stared upon her the greedy expectancy of some dire misfortune, of some unknown horrors which no human had ever gone through before. She turned to her husband—in the dark corner she saw a dimly grey figure, lanky, erect and shadowy like a spectre; she leaned over: and a face peered at her, but it was not with its eyes that it peered; these were hidden by the dark shadow of the eyebrows; it seemed to peer at her with the white spots of its haggard cheekbones and of the forehead. She was breathing fast—with loud, terrified gasps, and softly she moaned:

"Vassya, I am afraid of you! You're so strange ... Come here, come to the light!"

Father Vassily obediently moved to the table, and the warm glow of the lamp fell upon his face, but failed to evoke a responsive warmth. Yet his face was calm and was free from fear, and this sufficed her. Bringing her lips close to his ear, she whispered:

"Priest, do you hear me, priest? Do you remember Vassya— that other Vassya?"

"No."

"Ah!" joyously exclaimed the Popadya. "You don't? I don't either. Are you scared, priest? Are you? Scared?"

"No."

"Then why do you groan when you sleep? Why do you groan?"

"Just so. I suppose I am sick."

The Popadya laughed angrily.

"You? Sick? You—sick?" with her finger she prodded his bony, but broad and solid chest. "Why do you lie?"

Father Vassily was silent. The Popadya looked wrathfully into his cold face, with a beard that had long known no contact with the trimming shear and protruded from his sunken cheeks in transparent clumps, and she shrugged her shoulders with loathing.

"Ugh! What a fright you have become! Hateful, mean, clammy like a frog. Ugh! Am I to blame that he was born like that? Tell me.

114

What are you thinking about? Why are you forever thinking, thinking, thinking?"

Father Vassily maintained silence, and with an attentive, irritating gaze studied the bloodless and distorted features of his wife. And when the last sounds of her incoherent speech died away, gruesome, unbroken stillness gripped her head and breast as though with iron clamps and seemed to squeeze from her occasional hurried and unexpected gasps:

"And I know ... I know ... I know, priest...."

"What do you know?"

"I know what are you thinking about." The Popadya paused and shrunk from her husband in terror. "You—don't believe ... in God. That's what!"

And having uttered this she realized how dreadful was what she had said, and a pitiful pleading smile parted her lips that were swollen and scarred with biting, burnt with liquor and red as blood. And she looked up gladly, when the priest, with blanching cheeks, sharply and didactically replied:

"That is not true. I believe in God. Think before you speak."

And silence once more, stillness once more, but now there was in this silence something soothing, something that seemed to envelop her like a wave of warm water. And lowering her eyes, she shyly pleaded:

"May I have a little drink, Vassya? It will help me to go to sleep, it's getting late," and she poured out a quarter of a glassful of liquor, adding irresolutely more and more to it, and draining the glass to the bottom with little, continuous gulps, with which women drink liquor. And the glow of warmth returned to her breast, she now longed for gaiety, noise, lights and for the sound of loud, human voices.

"Do you know what we'll do, Vassya? Let's play cards, let's play 'Fools'[7]. Call Nastya. That will be nice. I love to play 'Fools'. Call her, Vassya, dear. I'll give you a kiss for it."

"It is late. She is sleeping."

The Popadya stamped the floor with her foot. "Wake her. Go!"

Nastya came in, slender and tall like her father, with large clumsy hands, that had grown coarse with toil. Shivering with the cold, she had wrapped a short shawl about her shoulders and was counting the greasy deck of cards without emitting a sound.

Then silently they sat down to a boisterously funny card game—amid the chaos of overturned furniture, in the dead of night, when all the world had long sought the oblivion of sleep—men, and

---

[7] A Russian card game, similar to "Old Maid."

beasts and fields. The Popadya joked and laughed and pilfered trumps out of the deck, and it seemed to her that the whole world was laughing and jesting, but the moment the last sound of her words died in the air, the same threatening and unbroken stillness closed over her, stifling her. And it was terrible to look upon the two pairs of mute and scrawny arms that moved slowly and silently over the table, as though these arms alone were alive and the people who owned them did not exist. Then shivering, as though with a crazedly drunken expectation of something supernatural, she looked up above the table—two cold—pallid—sullen faces loomed desolately in the darkness and swayed back and forth in a queer and wordless whirl—two cold, two sullen faces. Mumbling something, the Popadya gulped down another glassful of liquor, and once more the scrawny hands moved noiselessly, and the stillness began to hum, and someone else, a fourth one made his appearance behind the table. Someone's rapaciously curved fingers were shuffling the cards, then they shifted to her body, running over her knees like spiders, crawling up towards her throat.

"Who's here?" she cried out leaping to her feet and surprised to find the others standing up and watching her with terrified glances. Yes there were only two of them: her husband and Nastya.

"Calm yourself, Nastya. We're here. There's no one else here."

"And he?"

"He is sleeping."

The Popadya sat down and for a moment everything stopped rocking and slipped back into place. And Father Vassily's face looked kind.

"Vassya! And what will happen to us when he starts to walk?"

It was little Nastya who replied:

"I was giving him his supper to-night and he was moving his legs."

"It's not so," said the priest, but his words sounded dead and distant, and all at once everything started to circle in a frenzied whirl, lights and gloom began to dance, and eyeless spectres nodded to her from every side. They rocked to and fro, blindly they crept upon her, tapping her with curved fingers, tearing her garments, strangling her by the throat, plucking her hair and dragging her somewhere away. But she clutched the floor with broken finger nails and screamed out loud.

The Popadya was beating her head against the floor, striving impetuously to flee somewhere and tearing her clothes. And so powerful was she in the raging frenzy which seized her that Father Vassily and Nastya could not handle her unaided, and they were forced to summon the cook and a laborer. It required the combined

116

efforts of all four to overpower her; then they tied her arms and legs with towels and laid her on the bed, and Father Vassily remained with her alone. He stood motionless by the bedside and watched the convulsive writhings and twitchings of her body and the tears that were flowing from beneath the tightly shut eyelids. In a voice that was hoarse with screaming she pleaded:

"Help! Help!"

Wildly piteous and terrible was this desolate cry for help, and there was no response. Darkness, dull and dispassionate, enveloped it like a shroud, and in this garment of the dead the cry was dead. The overturned stools were kicking up their legs absurdly, and their bottoms blushed with shame. The ancient chest of drawers stood awry and distracted, and the night was silent. And ever fainter, ever more pitiful sounded this lonely cry for help:

"Help! I suffer! Help! Vassya, my darling Vassya...."

Father Vassily never stirred from the spot, but with a cool and oddly calm gesture, he raised up his hands and clasped his head even as his wife had done a half hour before, and as calmly and deliberately he brought them down again, and between his fingers trembled threads of black and greying hair.

V

Among people, mid their affairs and conversations, Father Vassily was so evidently a man apart, so unfathomably alien to all, that he did not seem human at all, but a moving cerement. He did whatever others did, he talked, he worked, he ate and drank, but it seemed at times as though he merely imitated others, while he personally lived in a different world that was inaccessible to any. And all who saw him asked themselves: what is this man thinking about? so manifest on his every movement was the impress of deep thought. It was seen in his ponderous gait, in the deliberateness of his halting speech, when between two spoken words yawned black chasms of hidden and distant thought; it hung like a heavy film over his eyes, and nebulous was his distant gaze that faintly glowed beneath his shaggy overhanging eyebrows. Sometimes it was necessary to speak to him twice before he heard and responded. And sometimes he neglected to greet others, and because of this some accounted him haughty. Thus once he failed to greet Ivan Porfyritch. The churchwarden was astounded for a moment, then hurried back and overtook the priest who was walking slowly.

"You've grown proud, Father! Won't even greet a man!" he said mockingly. Father Vassily looked up at him in surprise, blushed a little and apologized:

"Pardon me, Ivan Porfyritch, I did not notice you." The churchwarden attempted to look down upon him, measuring him with a look of censure, but for the first time he realized that the priest was the taller of the two, although the churchwarden was reputed to be the tallest man in the parish. And the churchwarden found something agreeable in this discovery, for unexpectedly to himself he invited the priest to call on him:

"Come and see me some day, Father."

And several times he glanced back, in order to size up the receding figure of the priest. Even Father Vassily was pleased, but only for a moment. He had hardly taken two steps, when the burden of persistent thought, heavy and hard like a millstone, succeeded in stifling the memory of the churchwarden's kindly words and crushed the quiet and bashful smile that was on its way to his lips. And he lapsed again into thought—thinking of God and of people and of the mysterious fate of human life.

And it happened during confession; fettered by his immovable thoughts Father Vassily was coldly putting the customary queries to some old woman, when he was suddenly struck by an odd thing which he had never noticed before: there he stood calmly prying into the innermost secret thoughts and feelings of another, and that other looked up to him with awe and told him the truth—that truth which it is not given to anyone else to know. And the wrinkled countenance of the old woman assumed a peculiar expression, it became brightly radiant, as though the darkness of night reigned all around, but the light of day was falling on that face alone. And suddenly he interrupted her and asked:

"Art thou telling the truth, woman?"

But what the old woman answered he heard not. The mist had departed from before his face, with flushing eyes—as though a bandage had fallen from them—he was gazing in amazement upon the face of the woman, and it seemed to him to bear a peculiar expression: clearly outlined upon it was some mysterious truth of God and of life. On the old woman's head, beneath an openwork kerchief, Father Vassily noticed a parting line, a narrow grey strip of skin running through hair that was carefully combed on either side of it. And this parting line, this absurd care for an ugly, aged head that nobody else had any use for, was likewise a truth: the sorrowful

118

truth of the ever lonely, ever sorrowful human existence. And it was then, for the first time in his life of forty years, that Father Vassily became aware with his eyes and with his hearing and with every one of his senses that beside him there were other creatures on earth—creatures that were like him, having their own lives, their own sorrows, their own fates.

"And hast thou children?" hurriedly he inquired, interrupting the old woman again.

"They're all dead, Father!"

"All dead?" inquired the priest in surprise.

"All dead," she repeated and her eyes became bloodshot.

"And how dost thou live?" inquired Father Vassily in amazement.

"How should I live?" cried the woman. "I live by alms."

Stretching out his neck, Father Vassily from the height of his immense stature riveted his gaze upon the old woman but did not utter a sound. And his long, scraggy face, fringed by his disheveled hair, seemed so strange and terrible to the woman that she was chilled to the tips of the fingers which she was holding clasped before her breast.

"Go now," sounded a stern voice above her.

Strange days commenced now for Father Vassily, and something unwonted was going on in his mind; hitherto only this had been; there had existed a tiny earth whereon lived only the enormous figure of Father Vassily. Other people did not seem to exist. But now the earth had grown, had become unfathomably big, peopled all over with creatures like Father Vassily. There was a multitude of them, each living an individual existence, suffering individual sufferings, hoping and doubting individually, and among them Father Vassily felt like a lonely tree in a field about which suddenly an immense and trackless forest had grown. Gone was the solitude; and with it the sun and the bright desert distances, and the gloom of the night had grown in intensity.

All the people gave him truth. When he did not hear their truthful utterances, he saw their homes and their faces: and upon homes and faces was engraved the inexorable truth of life. He sensed this truth, but he was unable to grasp and name it and he eagerly sought new faces and new words. Few came to confession during the fast days of Advent, but he kept them in the confessional for hours at a time, examining each one searchingly, insistently, stealing himself into the most intimate nooks of the soul where man himself looks in but rarely and with awe. He did not know what he was searching for and he mercilessly plowed up everything—that the soul rests on and lives by. In his questions he was pitiless and shameless, and each thought which he conceived was a stranger to fear. But it did not take him long to realize that all these people who were telling him the whole truth, as though he were God, were themselves ignorant of the truth of life. Back of their myriads of trifling, severed, hostile truths he dimly saw the shadowy outlines of the one great and all-solving truth. Everyone was conscious of it, everyone longed for it, yet none could define it with a human word— that overwhelming truth of God and of people, and of the mysterious fates of human life.

And Father Vassily himself began to sense it, and he sensed it now a despair and frenzied fear, now as pity, wrath and hope. And as heretofore, he was stern and cold to look upon, while his, mind and his heart were already melting in the fire of unknown truth and a new life was entering his old body.

On the Tuesday of the week preceding Christmas, Father Vassily had returned from the church rather late. In the dark cold vestibule someone's hand arrested him and a hoarse voice whispered:

"Vassily, don't go inside."

By the note of terror in her voice he recognized his wife and stopped.

"I've been waiting an hour for you, I'm all frozen," and her teeth chattered with the cold.

"What has happened? Come."

"No. No. Listen, Nastya! I came in and found her standing before the mirror, making faces just like him, waving her hands like him."

"Come."

By main force he dragged the resisting Popadya into the living room, and there, looking around in fear, she told him more. While on her way into the living room to water the plants she had found Nastya, standing still before the mirror, and in the mirror she had seen the reflection of her face, not as it always looked, but oddly idiotic, with a savagely contorted mouth and squinting eyes. Then, still in silence, Nastya raised up her hands, and curving her fingers convulsively like the idiot, she stretched them out towards her own reflection in the mirror—and everything was so still, and all this was so terrible and unreal that the Popadya screamed and dropped her water pot. And Nastya ran away. And row she did not know whether it had really happened or her own imagination had been playing a trick on her.

"Call Nastya and step out!" ordered the priest.

Nastya came and stopped on the threshold. Her face was long and scraggy like her father's, and when she was talking she copied his posture: her neck extended, inclined a little to one side, looking sullenly askance from beneath her eyebrows. And she held her hands behind her back just as he was in the habit of doing.

"Nastya, why do you do these things?" firmly, but calmly inquired Father Vassily.

"What things?"

"Mother saw you near the mirror. Why did you do that? He is sick."

"No, he is not sick, he pulls my hair."

"Why do you imitate him? Do you like a face like his?"

Nastya stood sullenly with downcast eyes.

"I don't know," she answered. And then with a queer look of candor she looked into her father's eyes and resolutely added: "Yes, I like it."

Father Vassily looked at her searchingly but did not say a word.

"Don't you like it?" semi-affirmatively inquired Nastya.

"No."

"Then why do you keep thinking about him? I would kill him if I were you."

And it seemed to Father Vassily that even then she was making a face like the idiot: something dull and brutish flitted over her cheeks and drew her eyes together.

"Go!" he sternly commanded. But Nastya did not move and with the same queerly candid expression she kept on gazing straight into her father's eyes. And her face no longer resembled the repulsive mask of the idiot.

"But you never think of me," she observed simply, as though expressing an abstract truth.

And then, in the gathering gloom of the wintry dusk, there occurred between these two—who were so like, yet so unlike one another—a brief and curious dialog:

"You are my daughter. Why did I know nothing about it? Do you know?"

"No."

"Come and kiss me."

"I don't want to."

"Don't you love me?"

"No, I love nobody."

"Even as I," and the priest's nostrils extended with repressed laughter.

"Don't you love anybody either? And how about mama? She drinks so much. I'd kill her too."

"And me?"

"No, not you. You talk to me at least. I feel sorry for you sometimes. It must be very hard, don't you know, when your son is a silly. He is terribly mean."

"You don't begin to know how mean he is. He eats cockroaches alive. I gave him a dozen and he ate them all up."

Without moving away from the door she sat down on the corner of a chair, cautiously, like a scullery maid, folded her hands on her knees and waited.

"It's a weary life, Nastya," pensively said the priest.

Unhurriedly and importantly she agreed with him:

"It certainly is."

"And do you pray to God?"

"Of course I do. Only at night, in the morning there is too much work, I have no time. I must sweep, make up beds, put things in order, wash the dishes, get tea for Vasska[8], serve it to him, you know yourself how much work that is."

"Just like a servant maid," said Father Vassily indefinitely.

"What did you say?" said Nastya uncomprehendingly.

Father Vassily bowed low his head and maintained silence. Immense and black he loomed against the dull white background of the window, and his words seemed to Nastya round and shiny like glass beads. She waited long, but her father was silent and she called out timidly:

"Papa!"

Without raising his head Father Vassily commandingly waived his hand, once, then the second time. Nastya sighed and rose, but hardly had she turned in the doorway when something rustled behind her and two powerful, sinewy arms raised her up in the air and a mocking voice whispered in her very ear:

"Put your arms around my neck. I'll carry you."

"Why? I am big."

"No matter. Hold fast."

It was hard work breathing in the embrace of two arms that were holding her like hoops of iron, and she had to duck her head in the doorway in order not to knock against the transom; she did not know whether she was pleased or merely surprised. And she did not know whether she merely imagined it or her father had really whispered into her ear:

"You must be sorry for mama."

But after she had said her prayers and was getting ready for bed, Nastya sat for a long while on her bed, lost in musing. Her slim little back with the pointed shoulder blades and the distinctly

_____

[8] Contemptuous diminutive for Vassily.

122

marked vertebrae was almost humped; the soiled nightshirt had slipped from the angular shoulder; folding her hands about her knees and rocking back and forth, she resembled a ruffled bird that was overtaken in the field by the frost. She was staring straight ahead with unblinking eyes that were plain and enigmatic like the eyes of a beast. And with pensive obstinacy she whispered:

"And still I'd kill her."

Late at night, when everyone was asleep, Father Vassily silently stole into the room, and his face was cold and austere. Without casting a glance at Nastya, he set the lamp down on the table and bent over the calmly sleeping idiot. He was lying on his back, his misshapen chest stretched out, his arms spread out; his little shriveled head had fallen back, and its receding chin gleamed white. As he lay sleeping, under the pale reflected light which was falling upon him from the ceiling, his face, with the closed eyelids hiding his witless eyes, did not seem as horrible as in the daytime. It seemed wearied, like the face of an actor exhausted after playing a difficult part, and around his tightly shut enormous mouth lay the shadow of stern grief. It was as though there were in him two souls, and while one was sleeping, the other was wakeful—all-knowing and sorrowful.

Father Vassily straightened up slowly, and maintaining an austere and stolid expression, walked out and proceeded to his room without casting a glance at Nastya. He was walking slowly and calmly, with the ponderous and lifeless stride of profound meditation, and the darkness scattered before him, hiding behind him in deep shadows and cunningly pursuing him at his heels. His face was shining brightly in the light of the lamp and his eyes were gazing fixedly into the distance, far ahead, into the very depths of fathomless space, while his feet slowly and clumsily pursued their automatic march.

It was late at night and the second cocks had crowed.

VI

Lent had arrived. The muffled church-bell commenced its monotonous tinkle, but its wan, melancholy, modest sounds of summons could not dispel the wintry stillness which was lying over snow-covered fields. Timidly they leaped from the belfry into the misty air below, and sank and died, and for a long time nobody came to the little church in response to its appeal—faint at first, but persistent and growing more imperious every day.

Towards the end of the first week of Lent two old women came to church—hoary they were, hazy and deaf like the very air of the dying winter, and for a long time they mumbled with toothless mouths, repeating, forever over and over repeating their dull, uncouth plaints which had no beginning and knew no end. Their very words and tears seemed to have grown aged in service and ready for rest. They had received absolution, but they failed to realize it, and were still praying for something, deaf and hazy like fragments of a vapid dream. But in their wake came a throng of people, and many youthful, fervid tears, many youthful words, pointed and gleaming, cut their way into Father Vassily's heart.

When Semen Mossyagin, a peasant, had thrice bowed to the ground, and cautiously advanced towards the priest, the latter gazed upon him sharply and fixedly, but the pose which he maintained did not seem to befit the occasion.

With his neck extended, his hands folded across his chest, he was tugging at the end of his beard with the fingers of one hand. Mossyagin walked up to the priest and was astounded: the priest was watching him and smiling softly with nostrils distended like a horse.

"I have been waiting for thee for a long time," said the priest with a snicker. "Why hast thou come, Mossyagin?"

"For confession," quickly and eagerly replied Mossyagin and with a friendly grin exposed his white teeth—they were white and even like a string of pearls.

"Wilt thou feel better after confession?" continued the priest, smiling, as it seemed to the peasant, in a merry and friendly fashion.

"Of course I will."

"And is it true that thou hast sold thy horse and the last sheep and mortgaged thy wagon?"

Mossyagin looked at the priest seriously and with a show of annoyance: the priest's face was stolid, his eyes were downcast. Neither broke the silence. Father Vassily turned slowly towards the lectern and commanded:

"Tell thy sins."

Mossyagin coughed, assumed a devotional expression, and cautiously inclining his head and his chest towards the priest began to speak in a loud whisper. And while he spoke, the priest's face became more and more forbidding and solemn, as though it had turned to stone under the hail of the peasant's painful and constraining words. His breath came fast and heavy as though choking in that senseless, dull and savage something which was called the life of Semen Mossyagin and which seemed to grip him as though in the black coils of some mysterious serpent. It was as though the stern law of causality had no dominion over this humble but phantastic existence: so unexpectedly, with such clownish absurdity there were linked in it trivial transgressions and unmeasured suffering, a mighty, an elemental will to a mighty elemental creativeness and a monstrously vegetating existence somewhere in No-man's land between life and death. Endowed with a fine mind that slightly inclined to sarcasm, strong in body like a ferocious beast, enduring as though fully three hearts beat in his breast, so that when one of the three died, the ethers gave life to a new one,—he seemed capable of overturning the very earth upon which firmly, though clumsily were planted his feet. But in reality what happened? He was forever on the verge of starvation, as were his wife, his children, his cattle; and his bedimmed mind reeled drunkenly as though unable to find the door of its own abode. Desperately straining every effort in an endeavor to build up something, to create something, he merely fell sprawling into the dust, and his work collapsed and disintegrated, rewarding him with a mock and a sneer. He was a man of compassion, and had adopted an orphan, and everybody scolded him; and the orphan lived awhile and died of constant malnutrition and illness, and then he began to scold himself and ceased to understand whether it was the right thing to be compassionate or not. It seemed as though the tears should never dry in the eyes of so unfortunate a man, or that the outcries of wrath and resentment should never die upon his lips, but strange to say he was always goodnatured and cheerful, and even his beard seemed somehow absurdly gay; blazing red it was, with each hair seemingly awhirl and agog in an interminable whimsical dance. And he even took part in the village choral dances with the young lads and lassies, singing the melancholy folksongs with a high tremolo voice that brought tears to the eyes of the hearers, while on his own lips played a smile of gentle sarcasm.

And his sins were so trivial and formal: a surveyor whom he had driven to the nearest village—Petrovki—had offered him a meatpie on a fast day, and he had eaten of it; and in confessing he dwelt as long upon this transgression as though he had committed a murder; and the year before, just before communion, he had smoked a cigarette and this too he described at great length and with agonized anguish.

"That's all!" finally said Mossyagin, in a cheery voice, and wiped the perspiration from his brow.

Father Vassily slowly turned his haggard face to him:

"And who helpeth thee?"

"Who helps me?" repeated Mossyagin. "Nobody. It's a scant fare for us villagers, you know that yourself. Still Ivan Porfyritch helped me out once," the peasant winked slyly at the priest: "he gave me three poods of flour, and promised four more towards fall."

"And God?"

Semen sighed and his face grew sad.

"God? I daresay I'm undeserving."

The priest's superfluous questions were beginning to annoy Mossyagin. He glanced back over his shoulder at the empty church, carefully counted the hairs in the priest's sparse beard, surveyed his half-rotted teeth and it occurred to him that the priest might have spoilt them by eating too much sugar. And he heaved a sigh.

"What art thou waiting for?"

"What I am waiting for? What should I be waiting for?"

And silence again. It was dark and cold in the church, and the chilly air was stealing under the peasant's blouse.

"And must it go on like this always?" asked the priest, and his words sounded listless and distant like the thud of the earth thrown into the grave upon the lowered coffin.

"And must it go on like this always?" repeated Mossyagin listening to the sound of his own words. And all that had passed in his life rose before him again: the hungry faces of the children, the reproaches, the killing toil, the dull heartache that makes one long to drink and fight; and so it must go on, for a long time, all through life—until death steps in. Blinking his white eyelashes, Mossyagin cast a teardimmed misty glance upon the priest and met his sharp and blazing gaze—and in this exchange of glances they recognized an intimate sorrowful kinship. An instinctive movement drew them together, and Father Vassily laid his hand on the peasant's shoulder: lightly and gently it rested upon it like a cobweb in autumn time. Mossyagin's shoulder quivered affectionately, he lifted up his eyes trustingly, and pitifully smiling with a corner of his mouth he said:

"But like as not it may ease up!"

The priest removed his hand imperceptibly and was silent. The peasant's white eyelashes blinked faster and faster, the little hairs in the blazing red beard danced ever more merrily, while his tongue babbled something unintelligible and incoherent:

"No. I dare say it won't ease up. You're right."

But the priest did not suffer him to finish. He stamped his foot with repressed emotion, scared the peasant with a wrathful, hostile glance, and hissed at him like an angry adder:

"Don't weep! Don't dare to weep. Oh, why do they blubber like

126

senseless calves? What can I do?" he prodded his chest with his finger. "What can I do? Am I God, am I? Ask HIM! Ask HIM! Ask HIM! I tell thee."

He pushed the peasant's shoulder.

"Down on thy knees."

Mossyagin knelt.

"Pray."

Behind him loomed the walls of the deserted and gloomy church, above him rang the angered voice of the priest: "Pray! Pray!", and without rendering account to himself of his actions, Mossyagin commenced to cross himself swiftly, touching the ground with his forehead. And the swift and monotonous movements of his head, the extraordinary nature of the penance, the consciousness of being at that very instant subject to some powerful and mysterious will—filled the mind of the peasant with awe and at the same time with a peculiar sense of relief.

For in this very awe before something mighty and austere was born the hope of intercession and mercy. And ever more frantically he was pressing his brow to the cold floor, when the priest abruptly commanded:

"Arise!"

Mossyagin arose, made his obeisance to the nearest images, and the fiery-red hairs of his beard whirled and danced willingly and cheerfully when he again approached the priest. Now he was sure that he would find relief and he calmly awaited further commands.

But Father Vassily merely measured him with a sternly curious glance and pronounced the absolution. On his way out of the church Mossyagin looked back: still in the same spot stood the nebulous figure of the priest, the faint glimmer of a wax taper could not fully outline it, and it loomed black and immense as though it had no definite contours and limits but was merely a particle of the gloom which was filling the church.

Communicants were now flocking daily in increasing numbers to the confessional and numberless faces, both wrinkled and youthful, alternated before Father Vassily in wearisome procession. He quizzed them all insistently and severely, and timid, incoherent speeches were poured into his ears by the hour, and the purport of each speech was suffering, terror and a great expectation. All united in condemning life, but none seemed anxious to die, and everybody appeared to be waiting for something, and this expectation seemed to have been handed down as an inheritance from the father of the race. It had passed through minds and hearts long since vanished from the world, and for this reason it was so imperious and potent.

And it had become bitter, for on its way it had absorbed all the grief of hope unrealized, all the bitterness of faith deceived, all the consuming anguish of infinite desolation. The blood of all hearts, living and dead, had nourished its roots, and it had branched out over the whole of life like a great and mighty tree. And losing himself among these souls like a wanderer in the forest primeval, he was also forgetting his own pent-up sufferings which had crowned his head with a stern sorrow, and he too began to wait for something with a stern impatience.

He did not wish now for human tears, but they were flowing irrepressibly, overruling his will, and every tear was a demand, and they all penetrated his heart like poisoned arrows. And with the dim sense of approaching horror he began to comprehend that he was not the master of men, not even their neighbor, but their servant, their slave, that the eyes of a great expectation were seeking him, were commanding him, were summoning him. And ever oftener he admonished, them with repressed wrath:

"Ask HIM! Ask HIM!"

And he turned his back upon them.

But at night the living people took on the guise of diaphanous shadows and walked by his side in a silent throng, invading his very thoughts, and they made a transparency of the walls of his house and a mock of the locks and the bars on its doors. And agonized, weirdly phantastic were the dreams that unrolled like a flaming band beneath his skull.

It was in the fifth week of Lent, when the breath of spring wafted its fragrance over the fields and the dusk was blue and diaphanous, that the Popadya had started on another drunken debauch. She had been drinking heavily for four days at a stretch, screaming with terror and struggling, and on the fifth day—it was Saturday—towards evening, she put out the little oil lamp before the saint's image in her room, twisted a towel into a noose and tried to strangle herself. But the moment the noose had begun to stifle her she became frightened and cried out, and Father Vassily came running with little Nastya and released her. It all ended in mere fright. Nor, indeed, had there been any danger, for the noose was clumsily tied and it was impossible to be strangled in it. But more frightened than all was the Popadya herself. She wept and pleaded to be forgiven; her arms and legs were trembling, her head shook as with palsy; the whole evening she kept her husband by her side and clung closely to him. The extinguished oil lamp in her room was lighted again at her own request, and other oil lamps before each holy image, and it looked like the eve of some great church festival. After the first moment of excitement Father Vassily had regained his composure and was now coldly amiable, even jocular. He related a very amusing incident of his seminary days, and then his memory strolled back into the dim past of his early boyhood and he told about his escapades in stealing apples in company with other youngsters. And it was so difficult to imagine a watchman leading him away by the ear, that Nastya refused to believe or laugh, although Father Vassily himself was laughing with a gentle, childlike laughter and his face looked truthful and good.

Little by little the Popadya also regained her composure and ceased to look askance into obscure nooks, and when Nastya had been sent to bed, she smiled gently at her husband and inquired:

"Were you scared?"

Father Vassily's face lost its truthful and kindly expression, and only his lips were smiling as he replied:

"Of course. What had come into your head anyway?"

The Popadya trembled as though chilled by a sudden draught, and picking with shaking fingers at the fringe of her warm shawl she said irresolutely:

"I don't know, Vassya. My heart is so heavy. And I'm so afraid of everything. Afraid of everything. Things go on and I can't make out how and why. There we have spring, and summer will follow. Then again the fall and the winter. And we shall still sit as we are sitting now, you in your corner and I in mine. Don't be angry with me, Vassya. I realize that it can't be different. And yet...."

She sighed and continued without taking her eyes off the shawl.

"There was a time when I did not fear death, I thought when things went very badly with me, I should die. And now I even fear death. What's to become of me, Vassya, dear? Must it be—drink again."

Perplexed she raised her sorrowful eyes to his face, and in them he read the pangs of mortal anguish and of boundless despair, and a dull and humble plea for mercy. In the town where Feeveysky spent his student days, he had seen on one occasion a greasy Tartar leading a horse to the flaying yeard: it had broken its hoof which was hanging by a shred and the horse was stepping up on the pavement with the mutilated stump of the crippled foot; it was a cold day and a cloud of white steam enveloped the horse, but it walked on staring ahead with an immobile gaze, and its eyes were horrible in their meekness. Even such were the eyes of the Popadya. And he thought that if someone were to dig a grave, and fling this woman into its depths burying her alive, he would be committing a kindly deed.

129

The Popadya with trembling lips tried to puff into life the cigarette which had long since gone out and continued:

"And then again he. You know whom I mean. Of course he's a child, and I feel sorry for him. But soon he'll commence to walk and he will be the death for me. And not a soul to help. Now I've complained to you, but what good is it? I don't know what to do?"

She heaved a sigh and threw up her hands in despair. And in unison with her the low squat room itself seemed to sigh, and the shades of night whose silent throng surrounded Father Vassily whirled about him in agony. They were sobbing in frenzied anguish, they were extending their nerveless hands, they were pleading for mercy, for pardon, for truth.

"Ah!" responded a hoarse groan from the depths of the priest's bony chest. He jumped to his feet, upsetting the chair with an abrupt movement, and began to pace the floor with a swift stride, shaking his folded hands, mumbling something, stumbling like a blind or an insane man against chairs and against walls. And when colliding with a wall, he hastily touched it with his scrawny fingers and turned back in his flight, and so he circled in the narrow cage of the room's mute walls like a phantastic shade that had assumed a gruesome and weird materialization. But in an odd contrast to the frantic mobility of his body, immobile like the eyes of a blind man were his eyes, and in them glistened tears, the first tears which he had shed since Vassya's death.

Forgetting her own self, the Popadya's awestricken eyes followed the priest and she cried:

"Vassya, what's the matter with you? What is the matter?"

Father Vassily turned around abruptly, hastily gained his wife's side, as though rushing over to trample upon her, and he laid his heavy and shaking hand on her head. And for a long, long time he silently held his hand above her head, as though in benediction, as though warding off the powers of evil. And he spoke and each resonant sound that composed his words was a ringing metallic tear:

"Poor little woman; poor little woman."

And once more he resumed his pacing, towering and awe-inspiring in his despair, like a tigress who had been robbed of her young one. His face was frantically convulsed, and his shaking lips jerked out half-formed, fragmentary, infinitely sorrowing words:

"Poor woman. Poor woman.... Poor people all. All weeping.... No help ... Oh-oh-oh!"

He stopped and raising aloft his immobile eyes, with his gaze transfixing the ceiling and the misty gloom of the vernal night beyond it, he cried out in a piercing, frenzied voice:

"And THOU sufferest it! THOU sufferest it! Then take...." and he clenched his fist and shook it aloft, but at his feet, with her hands wrapt about her knees, the Popadya lay writhing in hysterics, and mumbled, choking mid tears and laughter:

"Don't! Don't! Darling, precious! I'll never do it again!"

The idiot woke up and was howling; Nastya came running into the room in wild affright and the jaws of the priest set with a metallic snap.

Silently, and with seeming indifference, he tended his wife, laying her down on her bed, and when she had fallen asleep he was still holding her hand between his two palms, and thus he sat until morning by her bedside.. And all through the night, until morning, oil lamps were burning before each image, as though on the eve of a great and glorious festival.

The next day Father Vassily was the same as usual—cool and calm, nor did he by a word recall the incidents of the day before. But in his voice, whenever he exchanged words with his wife, in the glance with which he regarded her was a gentle tenderness which only her own tormented heart could appreciate. And so mighty was this manly, silent tenderness that the tormented heart smiled a timid smile in return and retained the memory of this smile in its depths like a cherished treasure. They conversed but little, and their sparing speech was simple and commonplace; they were rarely together—torn asunder by life's vicissitudes—but with hearts full of suffering they were constantly seeking one another; nor could any human being, nor cruel fate itself divine with what hopeless anguish and tenderness they loved one another. Long ago, since the birth of the idiot, they had ceased living as man and wife, and they resembled a pair of devoted unhappy lovers deprived even of a hope of happiness, dreaming dreams that dared not assume a definite shape. And shame, once abandoned, returned again into the heart of the wife, and with it a desire to appear attractive; she blushed when her husband saw her bare arms and she did something to her face and her hair that made both look fresh and youthful and strangely beautiful in spite of the sadness of her expression. But when the periodic spells of drunkenness came on again, the Popadya disappeared in the seclusion of her darkened room, even as dogs are wont to hide when they feel the approach of madness, and in silence and solitude she fought out her battle with madness and with the monstrous visions born of it.

But every night, when all were asleep, the Popadya stole to the bedside of her husband and made a sign of the cross over his head as though to dispel from his brow all grief and evil thoughts. And she longed to kiss his hand, but dared not, and silently retired to her room, vanishing in the darkness like a dim white vision similar to the nebulous and melancholy apparitions which hover at night over swamps and over the graves of deceased and forgotten people.

VII

The Lenten bell continued to send abroad its monotonous and somber summons, and it seemed as though with each muffled knell it gathered fresh power over the consciences of the village folk. In ever increasing numbers silent figures, somber as the sound of the tolling church bell, wended their way to the little church from every direction. Night still reigned over the denuded fields and a thin crust of ice still spanned the murmuring brook, when from every road and side path human figures appeared marching one by one, but united by some common bond into one solemnly chastened procession moving to the same invisible goal.

And every day, from early morn until late in the evening, Father Vassily was confronted with a succession of human faces, some with every wrinkle brightly outlined by the yellow glow of wax tapers, others dimly emerging out of obscure nooks as though the very atmosphere of the church had taken on the shape of a human being thirsting for mercy and truth. The people crowded and pushed, clumsily elbowing one another; they shuffled their feet heavily as they dropped to their knees with discordant and asymmetric movements; and heaving deep sighs, with relentless insistence they laid their sins and their sorrows before the priest.

Each one had enough suffering and grief for a dozen human existences, and it seemed to the overwhelmed and distracted priest, as though the entire living world had brought its tears and its pangs before him seeking his aid, meekly pleading for it, imperiously clamoring for it. Once he had been searching for truth, but now he was drowning in it, in this merciless truth of suffering; in the agonized consciousness of impotence he longed to die,—merely in order to escape seeing, hearing and knowing. He had summoned the woe of humanity and lo! it came to him. His soul was afire like the sacrificial altar, and he longed to put his arms about every one of them with a fraternal embrace, saying: "poor friend, let us struggle on side by side, let us together weep and seek. For there is no help for man from anywhere."

But this was not what the people, worn out with the struggle of life, were expecting from him, and with anguish, with wrath, with despair he kept repeating:

"Ask of HIM! Ask of HIM!"

Sorrowing they believed him and departed, and in their place came others in fresh and serried ranks, and again he frantically repeated the terrible and relentless words:

"Ask of HIM! Ask of HIM!"

And the hours in the course of which he listened to truth seemed to him as years, and that which had passed in the morning before the confession, appeared dim and faint like all images of a distant past. When finally he came out of the church, being the last to leave, darkness had already set in, the stars sparkled sweetly, and the silent air of the vernal night seemed like a tender caress. But he had no faith in the peace of the stars; he fancied that even from these distant worlds, groans and cries and broken pleas for mercy descended upon him. And he felt crushed with a sense of personal shame as though he himself had perpetrated all the wickedness that reigned in the world, as though he himself had caused all these tears to flow, had mangled and torn into shreds all these human hearts. He was overwhelmed with shame because of these downtrodden homes which he passed on his way, he was ashamed to enter his own house where by virtue of sin and of madness the dreadful image of the semi-idiot, semi-beast, held its autocratic insolent sway.

And in the mornings he walked to the church as men walk to the scaffold to meet a shameful and agonizing death, with the whole world as executioners: the dispassionate sky, the hurrying, thoughtlessly laughing mob and his own relentless inner thoughts. Every suffering person was his executioner, a helpless tool of an all-powerful God, and there were as many hangmen as there were people, and as many lashes as there were trusting and expectant hearts. They were all inexorably insistent. No man thought of ridiculing the priest, but at any moment he tremblingly expected the outburst of some horrible satanic laughter and he feared to turn his back upon the people. All that is brutal and evil is born behind a man's back, but while he is looking, no one dare attack him face to face. And that is why he looked at them, worrying them with his glance, and frequently turned his eyes to the place behind the lectern occupied by Ivan Porfyritch Koprov, the churchwarden.

The latter alone talked loudly in the church as he calmly sold his tapers; and twice during the service he sent up the verger and some boys to take up collections. Then noisily rattling his copper coins, he piled them up in little heaps, and frequently clicked the lock of his cash box; when others knelt, he merely inclined his head and crossed himself. And it was obvious that he regarded himself as a man needful to God, knowing that without him God would be at no small difficulty to arrange things as well as they were going and to keep them in proper order.

Since the beginning of Lent he had been very angry with Father Vassily because of the interminable time he took up in the confessional. He could not understand what great and interesting sins these people could have that could make it worth while to devote so much time to them. It was all due, he claimed, to the fact that Father Vassily knew neither how to live himself nor how to handle people.

"Dost thou think they appreciate it?" he said to the good-natured deacon who like the rest of the church officials was worn out with the heavy burden of Lenten duties. "Not a bit of it. They will only laugh at him."

Father Vassily's stern demeanor, on the contrary, pleased him, just as he had been pleasantly impressed when he had first observed his towering height. A genuine priest and a servant of God seemed to him akin to an honest and efficient steward who requires an exact and accurate accounting from those with whom he deals. Ivan Porfyritch himself went to confession the last week in Lent, and he made long preparations for it, trying to remember and to classify all his small transgressions. And he was inordinately proud to know that he kept his sins in the same good order as his business affairs.

On Wednesday of Holy week, when Father Vassily was fast losing his physical strength, an unusually numerous throng had gathered to confess. The last man in the confessional was a worthless scamp named Trifon, a cripple, who hobbled on crutches from village to village in the vicinity. Instead of legs which he had lost in some factory accident and which had been trimmed down to his loins, he had a pair of short little stumps around which a bag of skin had formed. His shoulders, raised up through the constant use of crutches supported a filthy head that seemed to be covered with a growth of coarse hemp, and he had an equally filthy and neglected beard; his eyes were the insolent eyes of a mendicant, drunkard and thief. He was repulsive and dirty, groveling in filth and dust like a reptile, and his soul was as dark and mysterious as the soul of a savage beast. It was difficult to understand how he managed to live and yet he lived and even had women, as phantastic and unreal and as unlike a human being as himself.

Father Vassily was forced to bend down low in order to hear the cripple's confession. The impudently serene stench of his body, the parasites crawling about his head and neck—even as he himself crawled over the face of the earth—revealed to the priest in a flash the utter destitution of his crippled soul—horrible, shameful, unfathomable to conscience. And with a terrible clearness he realized how dreadfully, how irrevocably this man had been deprived of all the human characteristics, of all the things to which he was as fully entitled as the kings in their palaces, as the saints in their cloistered cells, and he shuddered.

"Go. God absolveth thee of thy sins," he said.

"Wait. I have more to confess," hoarsely croaked the beggar, raising up his purpling face. And he related how ten years back he had in a forest violated a little girl, giving her three copper coins when she cried, and how later begrudging her this money, he strangled her to death and buried her in the woods. And there no one ever found her. A dozen times, to a dozen different priests he had related the same story, and because of this repetition it appeared to him simple and ordinary and unrelated to himself, as though it were a mere fairy tale which he had learned by heart. Sometimes he varied this story: instead of summer time he pictured the event as having occurred late in the fall; now the little girl was a blonde, now darkhaired; but the three copper coins never varied. Some priests refused to believe him and laughed at him, pointing out that for ten years past not one little girl had been killed or missed in the entire region; he was caught in numberless and crude contradictions, and it was demonstrated to him that the whole story was an obvious fabrication, born of his diseased brain while he drunkenly roamed through the woods. And this aroused him to frenzy: he shouted, he swore by the name of God, calling as frequently upon the devil as upon God to bear him witness, and began to recite such repulsive and obscene details that the oldest priests were made to blush with indignation. Now he was waiting to see if this priest of the Snamenskoye village would believe him or not, and he was content to note that the priest believed him: for the priest had shrunk back, with bloodless cheeks and raised his hand as though to strike him:

"Is this true?" hoarsely asked Father Vassily.

The beggar began to cross himself energetically.

"I swear by God it is true. Let me sink into the ground if it ain't...."

"But that means HELL!" cried the priest. "Dost thou grasp it: HELL?"

"God is merciful," mumbled the beggar, with a sullen and injured tone. But from his wicked and frightened eyes it was plainly

135

seen that he expected to go to hell and had become accustomed to that thought even as to his queer tale of the strangled little girl.

"Hell on earth, hell beyond. Where is thy paradise? Wert thou a worm, I would crush thee with my foot, but thou art a man. A man? Or art thou truly a worm? What art thou, speak?" cried the priest and his hair shook as though fanned by a breeze. "And where is thy God? Why has He left thee?"

"I made him believe it," gleefully thought the beggar, feeling the words of the priest strike his head like a hail of molten metal.

Father Vassily sat down on his haunches and drawing from the degradingly unusual pose a strange and an agonizing store of pride, he passionately whispered:

"Listen. Don't be afraid. There will be no hell. I am telling thee truly. I too have killed a human being. A little girl. Her name is Nastya. And there will be no hell. Thou wilt be in paradise. Understand? With the saints, with the righteous! Higher than all.... Higher than all, I tell thee."

That evening Father Vassily returned home very late, after his family had finished supper. He was very tired and haggard, wet to his knees and covered with dirt, as though he had tramped for a long time over pathless and rainsodden fields. In the household preparations were being made for the Easter festival. Though very busy, the Popadya from time to time ran in for a moment out of the kitchen, anxiously scanning her husband's features. And she tried to appear gay and to conceal her anxiety.

But at night, when according to her custom she came into his bedroom on tiptoe and having made a threefold sign of the cross over his head, was about to depart, she was stopped by a gentle and timid voice—so unlike the voice of the austere Father Vassily:

"Nastya, I cannot go to church."

There was terror in that voice, and also something pleading and childlike. As though unhappiness was so immense that it was no longer any use to put on the mask of pride and of slippery, lying words behind which people are wont to conceal their feelings. The Popadya fell to her knees by the bedside of her husband and peered into his face: in the faint bluish light of the oil lamp it seemed as pale as the face of a corpse and as immobile, and only his black eyes were open and squinted in her direction. He lay still and flat on his back like a man stricken with a painful disease, or like a child frightened by an evil dream and afraid to move.

"Pray, Vassya!" whispered the Popadya, stroking his clammy hands which were crossed upon his breast like the hands of a corpse.

"I cannot. I am afraid. Light the lamp, Nastya."

136

While she was lighting the lamp, Father Vassily began to dress, slowly and awkwardly, like an invalid who had been long chained to his bed. He could not unaided fasten the hooks of his cassock, and he asked his wife:

"Hook the cassock."

"Where are you going?" inquired the Popadya in surprise.

"Nowhere. Just so."

And he began to pace the floor slowly and diffidently with faint and shaking limbs. His head was trembling with a measured and hardly perceptible palpitation, and his lower jaw had dropped impotently. With an effort he attempted to draw it up into its proper place, licking his dry and flabby lips, but in the next moment it dropped back again; exposing the dark gap of his mouth. Something vast, something inexpressibly horrible seemed to be impending—like boundless waste and boundless silence. And there was neither earth nor people nor any world beyond the walls of the house, there was only the yawning bottomless abyss and eternal silence.

"Vassya, is it really true?" asked the Popadya, her heart sinking with the fear within her.

Father Vassily looked at her with dim, lack-lustre eyes, and with a momentary access of energy waved his hand:

"Don't. Don't. Be silent."

And once more he fell to pacing the floor, and once more dropped the strengthless jaw. And thus he paced the room, with the slow deliberateness of Time itself, while the pale-cheeked woman sat terror-stricken on the bed, only with the slow deliberateness of Time itself her eyes moved and followed him in his walk. And something vast was impending. There it came and stood still and gripped them with a vacant and all-embracing stare—vast as the boundless waste, terrible as the eternal silence.

Father Vassily stopped in front of his wife, regarding her with unseeing eyes and said:

"It is dark. Light another light."

"He is dying," thought the Popadya and with shaking hands, scattering matches on the floor, she lighted a candle. And once more he begged:

"Light still another."

And she kept lighting and lighting them. Many candles and lamps were now ablaze. Like a tiny faintly bluish star the little oil lamp before the holy image lost itself in the vivid and daring glare of the many lights, and it seemed as though the great and glorious festival had already set in. Meanwhile, with the deliberateness of Time itself he softly paced through the brilliant waste. Now, when the waste was ablaze with lights, the Popadya saw, and for one brief, terrible instant realized how lone he was, for he neither belonged to her nor to anyone else; she realized that she could never alter the fact. If all the good and strong people had gathered from the ends of the world, putting their arms about him, with words of caress and comfort, still he would stand in solitude.

And once more, with sinking heart, she thought: "He is dying."

Thus passed the night. And as it neared its end, the stride of Father Vassily grew firm, he straightened himself, looked at the Popadya several times and said:

"Why so many lights? Put them out."

The Popadya put out the candles and the lamps and diffidently commenced:

"Vassya!"

"We'll talk to-morrow. Go to your room. Time for you to go to sleep."

But the Popadya did not go, and her eyes seemed to be pleading for something. And once again strong and stalwart he walked over to her and patted her head as though she were a child.

"So, Popadya!" he said with a smile. His face was pallid with the diaphanous pallor of death, and black circles had gathered about his eyes: as though night itself had lodged there and refused to depart.

In the morning Father Vassily announced to his wife that he would resign from the priesthood, that he meant to get together some money in the fall and then to go away with her, somewhere afar off, he knew not yet where. But the idiot they would leave behind, they would give him to someone to bring up. And the Popadya wept and laughed and for the first time after the birth of the idiot she kissed her husband full upon his lips, blushing in confusion.

And at that time Vassily Feeveysky was forty years old, and his wife was thirty four.

VIII

For the three months that followed their souls were resting; gladness and hope, long strangers to their hearts, returned to their home once again. Strong through suffering endured was the

Popadya's faith in the new life to come,—in an altogether novel and different life elsewhere, unlike the life that anybody else had lived or could live. She sensed but vaguely what was going on in her husband's heart, though she saw that he bore himself with a peculiar cheeriness, serene even like the flame of the candle. She saw the strange glow in his eyes such as he had lacked before, and she had an abiding faith in his power. Father Vassily attempted to talk to her at times with regard to his plans for the future, whither they would go and how they would live, but she refused to listen: words, exact and positive, seemed to frighten away her vague and formless vision and to drag the future with a strangely horrible perverseness into the power of a cruel past. Only one thing she craved: that it might be far away, far beyond the bounds of that familiar world which was still so terrible to her. As heretofore, periodically she succumbed to attacks of drunkenness, but these passed quickly and she no longer feared them: she believed that she would soon cease to drink altogether. "It will be different there, I shall have no need of liquor," she thought all transfigured with the radiance of an indefinite and glorious vision.

With the coming of summer she once more began to stroll for days at a time through the fields and the woods; coming back at dusk she waited at the gate for Father Vassily's return from haying. Softly and slowly gathered the shadows of the brief summer night; and it seemed as though night would never come to blot out the light of day; only when she glanced upon the dim outlines of her hands which she held folded upon her lap she felt that there was something between those hands and herself and that it was night with the diaphanous and mysterious dusk. And before vague fears had time to fill her heart, Father Vassily was back—stalwart, vigorous, cheery, bringing with him the acrid and pleasant fragrance of grassy fields. His face was dark with the dusk of night, but his eyes were shining brightly, and in his suppressed voice seemed to lurk the vast expanse of the fields and the fragrance of grass and the joy of persistent toil.

"It is beautiful out in the fields," he said with laughter that sounded subdued, enigmatic and somber, as though he derided some one, perhaps himself.

"Of course, Vassya, of course. Of course, it's beautiful," retorted the Popadya with conviction and they went in to supper. After the vastness of the fields Father Vassily felt crowded in the tiny living room; with embarrassment he became conscious of the length of his arms and of his legs and moved them about so clumsily and ridiculously that the Popadya teased him:

"You ought to be made to write a sermon right now, why you could hardly hold a pen in your hands," she said.

And they laughed.

But left alone, Father Vassily's face assumed a serious and solemn expression. Alone with his thoughts he dared not laugh or jest. And his eyes gazed forward sternly and with a haughty expectancy—for he felt that even in these days of hope and peace the same inexorably cruel and impenetrable fate was hovering over his head.

On the twenty seventh day of July—it was in the evening—Father Vassily and a laborer were carting sheaves from the field.

From the nearby forest a lengthy shadow had fallen obliquely across the field; other lengthy and oblique shadows were falling all over the field from every side. Suddenly from the direction of the village there came the faint, barely audible sound of a tolling bell, uncanny in its untimeliness. Father Vassily turned around sharply: there where through the willows he had been wont to see the dim outlines of his shingled roof, an immobile column of smoke—black and resinous—had reared itself up in the air, and beneath it writhed, at though crushed down by a gigantic weight, darkly lurid flames. By the time they had cleared the cart of sheaves and had reached the village at a gallop, darkness had set in and the fire had died down: only the black, charred corner posts were glowing their last like dying candles, and faintly gleamed the tiles of the stripped fireplace, while a pall of whitish smoke that resembled a cloud of steam was hanging low over the ruins, wrapping itself about the legs of the peasants who were stamping out the fire, and against the background of the fading glow of sunset it seemed suspended in the air in the shape of flat, dark shadows.

The whole street was thronged with people; the villagers trampled through the liquid mud formed by water that had been spilled in fighting the blaze, they were conversing loudly and in agitation, peering intently into one another's faces, as though failing to recognize immediately their neighbors' familiar faces and voices. The village herd had been meanwhile driven in from the fields, and the animals were straying about forlorn and excited. The cows were lowing, the sheep stared ahead with immobile, glassy, bulging eyes, and distractedly rubbed against the legs of people, or startled into an unreasoning panic madly rushed from place to place pattering with their hoofs over the ground. The village women tried to chase them home, and all over the village was heard their monotonous summons "kit-kit-kit." And these dark figures, with their dark bronze-like faces, this queer and monotonous calling of sheep, the sight of these human beings and helpless animals fused into one mass by a common, primal sense of fear created the impression of something chaotic and primordial.

It had been a windless day, and the priest's house was the only one consumed by the blaze. It was said that the fire had started in a room where the drunken Popadya had lain down to rest, and that it had been caused by a burning cigarette or a carelessly thrown match. All the villagers were in the fields at the time, and the rescuers succeeded in saving the idiot who was badly frightened but unhurt, while the Popadya herself was discovered in a horribly burnt condition and was dragged out unconscious, though still alive. When Father Vassily who had come galloping with his cart received the report of the disaster, the villagers were prepared to witness an outburst of grief and tears, but they were astounded: he had stretched out his neck in the attitude of listening with concentrated attention, his lips were tightly compressed, and to judge from his appearance it seemed as though he had been fully apprized of the happenings and was now merely trying to check up the report; as though in that brief mad hour, while with his locks fluttering in the breeze, with his gaze riveted to the column of smoke and fire, he stood on his cart and urged on his horse to a frenzied gallop, he had divined everything: that it had been ordained that a fire should occur and that his wife and all he owned should perish, while the idiot and the little girl Nastya should be saved and remain alive.

For a moment he stood still with downcast eyes, then he threw back his head and resolutely made his way through the crowd, straight to the deacon's house where the dying Popadya had found shelter.

"Where is she?" he loudly asked of the silent people within. And silently they showed him. He came close to her bedside, bent low over the shapeless feebly groaning mass and seeing one great white blister which had taken the place of the face once cherished and beloved, he shrank back in horror and covered his face with his hands.

The Popadya was in a flutter; doubtless she had regained consciousness and was trying to say something, but instead of words she emitted a hoarse and inarticulate bark. Father Vassily withdrew his hands from his face; not the faintest trace of a tear was to be seen thereon; it was inspired and austere like the countenance of a prophet. And when he spoke, with the loud articulation of one addressing a deaf person, his voice rang with an unshakeable and terrible faith. There was in it nothing human, vacillating or based on self-strength; thus could speak only he who had felt the unfathomable and awful nearness of God.

"In the name of God—hearest thou me?" he exclaimed. "I am

141

here, Nastya, I am near thee. And the children are here. Here is Vassily. Here is Nastya."

From the immobile and terrible face of the Popadya it could not be gathered whether she had heard or not. And raising his voice to a higher pitch Father Vassily once more addressed himself to the shapeless mass of charred flesh:

"Forgive me, Nastya. For I have destroyed thee, and thou wast not to blame. Forgive me—my one—and—only love. And bless the children in thy heart. Here they are: here is Nastya, here is Vassily. Bless them and depart in peace. Have no fear of death. God hath pardoned thee. God loveth thee. He will give thee rest. Depart in peace. There wilt thou see Vassya. Depart thou in peace."

Everyone had now withdrawn with tearful eyes, and the idiot who had fallen asleep, was taken away. Father Vassily remained alone with the dying woman, to spend with her that last fleeting summer night the coming of which she had so dreaded. He knelt down, pillowed his head near the dying woman, and with the faint and dreadful odor of burnt human flesh in his nostrils, he shed profuse soft tears of infinite compassion. He wept for her in her youth and beauty, trustingly longing for joy and caresses; he wept for her in the loss of her son; frenzied and pitiful, a plaything of fears, haunted by visions; he wept for her in those latter clays, awaiting his coming in the dusk of the summer eve, humble and radiant. It was her body—that tender body so thirsting for caresses that the flames had devoured, and now it reeked with the odor of burning. Had she been crying? struggling? calling for her husband?

With tear dimmed eyes Father Vassily looked about wildly and rose to his feet. All was still with a stillness such as reigns only in the presence of death. He looked at his wife. She was motionless with that peculiar immobility of a corpse, when every fold of garment and bedding seems to be carved of lifeless stone, when the glowing tints of life have faded from raiment, yielding to shades that seem drab and unnatural. The Popadya was dead.

Through the opened window poured the warm breath of the summer night and from somewhere in the distance, accentuating the stillness in the room, came the harmonious chirping of crickets. About the lamp noiselessly circled the moths of the night which had come flying through the window; striking the light some fell, others with sickly spiral movements strove anew towards the light, and either lost themselves in the darkness or gleamed white about the flame like little flakes of whirling snow. The Popadya was dead.

"No! No!" shouted the priest in a loud and frightened voice. "No! No! I believe! Thou art right! I believe."

He fell to his knees, and pressed his face to the drenched

142

floor, amid fragments of soiled cotton and dripping bandages, as though thirsting to be changed into dust and to mingle with dust; and with the rapture of boundless humility he eliminated from his outcry the very pronoun "I" and added brokenly: "... believe!"

Once more he prayed, without words, without thoughts, but straining taut every fibre of his mortal body that in fire and death had realized the inexplicable nearness of God. He had ceased to sense his own life as such,—as though the intimate bond between body and spirit has been cut, and freed from all that is earthy, freed from itself, the spirit had soared to unfathomed and mysterious heights. The terrors of doubt and of tempting thoughts, the passionate wrath and the bold outcries of resentful human pride—all had crumbled into dust with the abasement of the body; only the spirit alone, having torn the hampering fetters of its "I" was living the mysterious life of contemplation.

When Father Vassily had risen to his feet it was already light, and a ray of sunshine, long and ruddy, clung like a bright colored blotch to the petrified raiment of the deceased. And this surprised him, for the last thing that he remembered was the darkened window and the moths that circled about the light. A number of these frail creatures were scattered in charred clusters about the base of the lamp, which was still burning with an invisible yellowish flame; one grey and shaggy moth, with a big misshapen head, was still alive, but had no strength to fly away and was helplessly crawling about the table. The moth was doubtless in great pain, and was groping for the shelter of night and of darkness, but the merciless light of day streamed upon it from everywhere burning its tiny ugly body that was created for darkness. Despairingly it attempted to shake into activity its pair of short and singed wings, but it failed to rise up in the air, and once more, with oblique and angular movements, it fell over on its side and continued to crawl and grope.

Father Vassily put out the lamp and threw the palpitating moth out of the window; then vigorously fresh, as though after a long and refreshing sleep, filled with the sense of strength of restoration and of a supernatural peace, he made his way into the deacon's garden. There for a long time he paced up and down the straight foot path, with his hands behind his back, his head brushing against the lower branches of apple and cherry trees; and he walked and he thought. Finding a path between the branches the sun had commenced to warm his head, and as he turned back it beat down upon him like a current of fire and blinded his eyes; here and there a worm eaten apple fell to the ground with a dull thud, and under a cherry tree, in the loose, dry earth a hen was fussing around, cackling and tending her brood of a dozen downy yellow chicks; but he was oblivious to the light of the sun and to the falling apples and kept on thinking. And wondrous were his thoughts—clear and pure they were as the air of the early morn, and strangely new; such thoughts had never before flashed through his head where sad and painful thoughts were wont to dwell. He was thinking that where he had seen chaos and the absurdity of malice, there a mighty hand had traced out a true and straight path. Through the furnace of calamity, violently snatching him from home and family and from the vain cares of life, a mighty hand was leading him to a mighty martyrdom, a great sacrifice. God had transformed his life into a desert, but only so that he might cease to stray over old and beaten paths, over winding and deceitful roads where people err, but might seek a new and daring way in the trackless waste. The column of smoke which he had seen the night before, was it not that pillar of fire which had marked for the Hebrews a path through the pathless desert? He thought: "Lord, will my feeble strength be equal to the task?" but the answer came in the flames that illumined his soul like a new sun.

He had been chosen.

For an unknown martyrdom, for an unknown sacrifice he had been chosen by God, he, Vassily Feeveysky, who so blasphemously and madly had cried out in bitter complaint against his fate. He had been chosen. Let the earth open at his feet, let hell itself look at him with its red and cunning eyes, he will disbelieve hell itself. He had been chosen. And was he not standing on solid ground?

Father Vassily stopped and stamped his foot. The frightened hen emitted an anxious cackle and calling her brood together stood on guard. One of the little chicks had strayed afar and hurried to answer his maternal call, but halfway to his goal two hands, hot, strong and bony seized him and raised him up in the air. Smiling, Father Vassily breathed upon the tiny yellowish chick with his hot and moist breath, then gently folding his hands into the semblance of a nest he tenderly pressed him to his breast and continued to pace up and down the long and straight walk.

"What martyrdom? I don't know. But dare I want to know? Didn't I once know my fate? And I called it cruel, and my knowledge was a lie. Did I not think of bringing a son into the world? And a monster, without form or mind, entered into my home. And again I thought to multiply my goods and to leave my house, but it had left me first, consumed by a fire from heaven. That was what my knowledge amounted to. And she—an infinitely unfortunate woman, wronged in her very womb, who had exhausted all tears, who had lived through all horrors. She was waiting for a new life on earth, and this life would have been sorrowful, but now she is reclining in death, and her soul is laughing and is branding the old knowledge a lie. HE knows. He has given me much. He has granted to me to see life and to experience sufferings and with the sharpness of my sorrow to penetrate into the sufferings of other people. He has granted to me to apprehend their great expectation and has given me love towards them. And are they not expecting? And do I not love? Dear brethren! God has shown mercy to us, the hour of the mercy of God has come."

He kissed the downy head of the chick and continued:

"My path? Docs the arrow think of its path when sent forth by a mighty hand? It flies and plunges through to its goal subservient to the will of him who sent it on its way. It is given to me to see, it is given to me to love, but what will come of this vision, of this love, that will be His holy will—my martyrdom, my sacrifice."

Coddled in the hollow of his warm hand the little chick closed his eyes and fell asleep. And the priest smiled.

"There—I need only close my hand and he will die. Yet he is lying in the hollow of my hand, upon my bosom, and sleeping trustingly. And am I not in His hand? And dare I disbelieve the mercy of God when this chick believes in my human kindness, in my human heart?"

He smiled softly, opening his black, half-rotted teeth and over his austere, forbidding face the smile scattered into a thousand radiant wrinkles as though a ray of sunlight suddenly set a-sparkle a pool of deep and dark waters. And the great, grave thoughts fled away scared off by human gladness, and for a long time only gladness, only laughter remained, and the light of the sun and the gently slumbering downy little chick.

But now the wrinkles smoothed, the face became once more austere and grave, and the eyes sparkled with inspiration. The greatest, the most significant arose be< fore him—and its name was Miracle. Thither his still human, all too human thought had not yet dared to stray. There was the boundary line of thought. There in the fathomless solar depths were the dim contours of a new world—and it was no longer the earth. A world of love, a world of divine justice, a world of radiant and fearless countenances, undisgraced by lines of suffering, famine and pain. Like a gigantic, monstrous diamond sparkled this world in the fathomless solar depths, and the human eye could not dwell upon it without blinding pain and awe. And humbly bowing his head Father Vassily exclaimed:

"Thy holy will be done!"

People made their appearance in the garden: the deacon and his wife and many others. They had seen the priest from afar and with cordial nods hastened towards him, but as they approached him they paused and stopped as though transfixed, as people pause before a conflagration, before a turbulent flood, before the calmly enigmatic gaze of a madman.

"Why do you look at me in this manner?" inquired Father Vassily in surprise.

But they never stirred from the spot and continued to look. Before them stood a tall man, entirely unknown to them, an utter stranger, whose very calm made him all the more distant from them. Dark he was and terrible to look upon like a shade from another world, but a sparkling smile played on his face in a myriad radiant wrinkles, as though the sun was sparkling in a deep black pool of stagnant water. And in his large gnarled hands he was holding a downy yellow little chick.

"Why are you looking at me in this manner?" he repeated smiling. "Am I a miracle?"

IX

It was obvious to all that Father Vassily was hastening to sever the last ties that still bound him to the past and to the vain cares of this life. He had written his sister in the city and made hurried arrangements with her concerning Nastya, leaving the girl in her charge, nor did he delay a day in despatching her to her aunt, as though fearing that fatherly love might rise up within him and prevent this arrangement to the detriment of his ministry. Nastya departed without exhibiting either pleasure or disappointment: she was content that her mother had died and merely regretted that the idiot had not also burnt to death. Seated in the wagon, in an oldfashioned dress which had been re-made from an old gown of her mother's, with a child's hat sitting awry on her head, she resembled a queerly attired and homely old maid rather than a girl in her early teens. With her wolfish eyes she coldly watched the fussy deacon and protested in a dry voice that was much like the voice of her father:

"Don't bother, Father Deacon. I am comfortable. Good-bye, papa."

"Good-bye, Nastya dear. Mind your studies, don't be lazy."

146

The wagon started off, shaking up the girl with its jolting, but in the next moment she sat up erect like a stick, swaying no longer from side to side, but merely bobbing up and down. The deacon pulled out a handkerchief in order to wave the little traveler good-bye, but Nastya never turned around; and shaking his head reprovingly the deacon heaved a deep sigh, blew his nose and put the handkerchief back into his pocket. Thus she departed never to return to the village of Snamenskoye.

"Why don't you, Father Vassily, send the little boy away as well? It will be hard on you to take care of him with only the cook to help you. She's a stupid wench and deaf into the bargain," said the deacon when the wagon was out of sight and the dust which it had raised had settled.

Father Vassily eyed him pensively:

"Shirk the consequences of my own sin, and burden others with them? No, deacon, my sin is with me and must remain with me. We'll manage somehow, the old and the young one, what do you think, Father Deacon?"

He smiled a pleasant and cordial smile, as though in stingless raillery at something known to himself alone, and patted the deacon's portly shoulder.

Father Vassily transferred the rights to his land to the vestry, providing a small sum for his support, which he called his "dowry."

"And perhaps I might not take even that," he said enigmatically, smiling pleasantly, with the same stingless raillery that was a riddle to all but himself.

And he made it his business to look after another matter: he induced Ivan Porfyritch to give employment to Mossyagin who had been turning black in the face from slow starvation. When Mossyagin had first called on Ivan Porfyritch asking him for work, the churchwarden drove him away, but after a talk with the priest, he not only gave him employment, but even sent over a load of shingles for Father Vassily's new house. And he said to his wife, a woman who never opened her mouth and was always in the family way:

"Mark my word, this priest will raise ructions."

"What ructions?" coldly inquired the wife.

"Just plain ructions. Only as how in a manner of speaking it is none of my business.... So I keep my mouth shut. Otherwise...." and he looked vaguely through the window in the direction of the capital city of the province.

And no one knew whence, whether as the result of the churchwarden's mysterious words or from other sources, vague and disquieting rumors gained currency in the village and in the vicinity with regard to the priest of Snamenskoye. Like the odor of smoke from a distant forest fire these rumors moved slowly and scattered widely, no one knowing whence and how they had originated, and only as the people exchanged glances and saw the sun grow pallid behind a hazy film they began to realize that something new, unusual and disquieting had come to dwell among them.

Towards the middle of October the new house was ready for occupancy, save that only one wing was all finished and covered with a roof; the other wing still lacked roof beams and rafters, and gaping with empty and frameless window openings, clung to the finished portion like a skeleton strapped to a living person, and at night looked grimly desolate and forbidding. Father Vassily had not troubled to buy new furniture: within the four bare walls of crude logs on which the amber sap had not yet hardened, the sole furniture in the four rooms consisted of two wooden stools, a table and two beds. The deaf and stupid cook was a poor hand at building fires and the rooms were always full of smoke which gave headaches to the inmates and hung like a low grey cloud over the dirty floor with its imprint of muddy boots. And the house was cold. During the severe cold spell of early winter the widow panes had gathered a layer of downy frost on the inside and a bleak chilling twilight reigned within. The window sills had been encrusted since the early frost with a thick coating of ice which constantly dribbling, formed rivulets on the floor. Even the unpretentious peasants who came to the priest for ministrations looked askance, in guilty embarrassment, upon the penurious furnishings of the priestly abode, and the deacon referred to it wrathfully as the "abomination of desolation."

When Father Vassily first entered his new house, he paced for a long time in joyful agitation through rooms that were as cold and barren as a barn and merrily called to the idiot:

"We'll live like lords here, Vassily, hey?"

The idiot licked his lips with his long brutish tongue and loudly barked with jerky, monotonous bellows:

"Huh-huh-huh!"

He was pleased and he laughed. But soon he began to feel the cold and the loneliness and the gloom of the abandoned abode, and this made him angry; he screamed, slapped his own cheeks and tried to slide down on the floor, but he fell from the chair painfully hurting himself. Sometimes he lapsed into a state of heavy stupor not unlike a grotesque pensive day dream. Supporting his head with his thin long fingers he stared into space from beneath his narrow, beastlike eyelids and never stirred. And it seemed at times that he was not an idiot, but some strange creature lost in meditation, thinking peculiar thoughts of his own that were totally unlike the thoughts of other people: as though he knew something that was peculiar, simple and mysterious, something that no one else could know of. And to look at his flattened nose with the widely distended nostrils, at the slanting back of his head which in a brutish slope merged straight into his back—it seemed that if one were only to lend him a pair of swift and sturdy legs he would scurry away into the woods there to live out his mysterious forest life filled with savage play and obscure forest lore.

And side by side with him, always the two together, always alone, now deafened by his impudent and malignant screaming, now haunted by his stony enigmatic stare, Father Vassily lived the equally mysterious life of the spirit, that had renounced the flesh. He longed to purge himself for the great martyrdom and the great sacrifice yet unrevealed, and his days and his nights became one ceaseless prayer, one wordless effusion. Since the death of the Popadya he had imposed upon himself an ascetic regime: he drank no tea, he tasted neither meat nor fish, and on days of abstinence, Wednesday and Friday, his food consisted merely of bread soaked in water. And with a puzzling cruelty that seemed to be akin to vindictiveness he had imposed the same strict abstinence upon the idiot, and the latter suffered like a starving beast. He screamed and scratched and even shed floods of greedy, doglike tears, but he could not procure an additional bite of food. The priest saw but few people, and these only when absolutely compelled to receive them, and he assiduously shortened all interviews, devoting every hour, with brief intervals for rest and sleep, to prayer on bended knee. And when he grew tired he sat down and read the Gospels and the Acts of the Apostles and the Lives of the Saints. It had been the village custom to hold services only on Sundays and holidays, but now he celebrated the early liturgy every morning. The aged deacon had refused to officiate with him, and he was assisted by the lay-reader, a filthy and lonely old man who had been once deposed from the diaconate for drunkenness, and was now acting as verger.

Long before daybreak, shivering with the cold of the early winter morning, Father Vassily wended his way to the church. He did not have far to go, but the walk consumed much time. Frequently a snow drift covered the road at night and his feet sank and stuck fast in the dry grainy snow and each step required the effort of ten ordinary steps. The church was not properly heated and it was bitterly cold inside, with that peculiar penetrating cold which in winter time clings to public places left vacant for days at a time. Human breath turned into dense clouds of vapor, the touch of metal felt like a burn. The lay-reader, who was also the verger, built a

149

small fire in a tiny stove, back of the altar, just for the priest's comfort, and by its opened gate, Father Vassily, squatting on his haunches, warmed his hands before the modest blaze, for otherwise he could not have clasped the cross with his numb and unbending fingers. And during the ten minutes thus spent he joked with the old lay-reader about the cold and the gipsy sweat, and the lay-reader listened to him with sullen condescension; constant drink and cold had colored the lay-reader's nose a deep purple, and his bristling chin (after his deposition he had shaved off his beard) moved rhythmically as though chewing a cud.

Then Father Vassily donned his tattered vestments, once embroidered with gold, of which a few ragged thread ends were the sole remaining trace. A pinch of incense was dropped into the censer and they began to officiate in semi-darkness, barely able to distinguish one another's outlines, like a couple of blind men moving by instinct in a familiar spot. Two stumps of wax tapers, one near the lay-reader, the other on the altar near the image of the Saviour, merely served to intensify the gloom; and their sharp flames slowly swayed from side to side responding to the movements of these unhurrying men.

The service was long, and it was slow and solemn. Every word trembled and deliquesced in its outlines, being caught up by the echo of the deserted church. And there was nothing within but the echo, the darkness and the two men serving God; and little by little something began to glow and blaze in the lay-reader's heart. Pricking up his ears, he cautiously strove to catch every word of the priest and moved his chin in quick succession. And his lonely, filthy decrepit old age seemed to vanish somewhere into distance, and with it the whole of his luckless and weary existence, and that which came in the place thereof was strange and joyous to the verge of tears. Frequently to the lay-reader's allocution there came no response; silence, protracted and solemn, ensued, and the sharp tongues of wax tapers blazed straight up without stirring. Then from the distance came a voice that was sated with tears and with gladness. And once more through the semi-darkness moved sure-footedly the two unhurrying celebrants, and the flames swayed to one side and to the other in response to their deliberate measured movements.

The daylight was commencing to break when the service was finished, and Father Vassily said:

"Look, Nicon, how warm it is getting."

A spiral of steam was issuing from his mouth. The wrinkles on Nicon's cheeks had grown pink, he scanned the priest's face with a severely searching expression and diffidently inquired:

"And to-morrow—again? Or perhaps not?"

"Of course, Nicon, again, of course."

Reverently he conducted the priest to the door and then returned to his watchman's booth. There, yelping and barking, a dozen dogs came running towards him—grown up dogs they were and pups. Surrounded by them as though by a family of children, he fed them and caressed them, with his thoughts dwelling constantly on the priest. And as he thought of the priest he wondered. He thought of the priest—and smiled, without opening his lips, and averting his face from his dogs so that they might not see his smile. And he thought, and he thought until nightfall. But in the morning he waited to see if the priest would not fool him, if the priest would not back down in the face of the darkness and the frost. But the priest came despite the cold and the darkness, shivering, yet cheerful, and once more from the gaping mouth of the little stove into the very depths of the vacant church stretched a ribbon of a ruddy glow and along it the black and melting shadow.

At first hearing of the eccentricities of the priest many people came to the early liturgy just to see him officiate and they marveled. Some of those who came to watch him pronounced him a madman; others were edified and wept, but there were others, too, and these were many, in whose hearts was born a keen and unconquerable disquietude. For in the steady, in the fearlessly frank and luminous glance of the priest they had caught a glimmer of mystery, of the most profound and hidden mystery, full of ineffable threats, full of ominous promises. But soon the merely curious began to drop off, and for a long time the church remained vacant in these early morning hours, none disturbing the peace of the two praying men. But after a lapse of time in response to the words of the priest there had begun to come from the darkness timid, subdued sighs, someone's knees struck the flags of the stone floor with a dull thud; someone's lips were whispering, someone's hands were holding a tiny fresh taper, and between the two stumps it looked like a stately young birch in a forest clearing.

And rumor, dull, disquieting, impersonal, grew apace. It crept everywhere where people assembled, leaving behind some sediment of fear, hope and expectancy. Little was said, and what was said was vague; for the most part it was the wagging of heads, followed by sighs, but in the neighboring province, a hundred miles away, someone, grey and taciturn, began to whisper of a "new faith" and was lost again in silence. And rumor kept spreading, like the wind, like the clouds, like the smoky odor of a distant forest fire.

Last of all the rumors reached the provincial capital, as though they found it hard and painful to make their way through stone walls, through the noisy and populous city streets. And like naked, ragged thieves they finally showed themselves, claiming that someone had burned himself alive, that a new fanatical sect had sprung up in Snamenskoye. And people in uniform made their appearance in the village, but they found nothing, for neither the village houses nor the stolid faces of the villagers revealed anything to them, and they drove back to town tinkling with their sleigh bells.

But after this visit the rumors became still more persistent and malicious, while Father Vassily continued to serve mass every morning as heretofore.

X

The long evenings of winter time Father Vassily passed in solitude with the idiot, imprisoned together with him in the white cage of pine log walls and ceiling, as though locked in a shell.

From the past he had retained a love for bright lights—and on the table, warming the room, blazed a large oil lamp with a big-bellied globe. The window panes frozen outside and frosted within reflected the light of the lamp and sparkled, but were impenetrably opaque like the walls and cut off the people from the greying night outside. Like a boundless sphere the night enveloped the house, crushing it from above, seeking some crevice through which to plunge its greyish claws, but finding none. It raged about the doors, tapped the walls with its lifeless hands, exhaling a murderous cold, wrathfully raised a myriad of dry and spiteful snowflakes, flinging them frenziedly against the windowpanes, and frantically ran back into the fields, cavorting, singing and leaping headlong into snowbanks, clutching the stiffened earth in its crosslike embrace. Then it rose and squatted on its haunches and silently gazed into the illuminated windows gnashing its teeth. And once more shrilly shrieking it flung itself against the house, bellowing into the chimney with a greedy howl of insatiable hatred and longing, and it lied: it had no children, it had devoured them all and buried them out in the field——in the field—in the field.

"A snowstorm," said Father Vassily stopping to listen for a moment and turning his eyes back to his reading.

But it found them. The flame of the big lamp melted a circle in the frosty armor, and the damp window pane glistened and it glued its grey wan eye to the exposed spot. "Two of them—two—two—just two." Rough, bare walls with the shining drops of amber sap, the radiant emptiness of air and the humans—two of them.

With the narrow little skull bending over his work the idiot sat at the table pasting little boxes out of cardboard: he was spreading on the paste, holding the tip of the brush in his long narrow hand, or else he was cutting up the cardboard and the click of the scissors resounded noisily through the barren house. The boxes came out all askew and dirty, with overlapping bands that refused to stick, but the idiot was unconscious of these defects and continued to work. Now and then he raised his head and with a motionless glance from beneath his narrow brutish eyelids he gazed into the radiant emptiness of the room, wherein a riot of sounds was fighting, whirling and circling. Rustling, rattling, crackling, booming, explosive sounds they were, mingling with someone's laughter and long drawn out, protracted sighing. They were hovering over him, running over his face like invisible cobwebs, and penetrating into his head—those rustling, crackling, sighing sounds. And the man on the other side of the table was motionless and silent.

"Bang!" crackled the drying wood, and Father Vassily shivered and tore his eyes from the white page before him. And then he saw the bare rough walls, and the desolate windows and the grey eye of the night, and the idiot frozen in a listening attitude with a pair of shears in his hands. All this flitted past him like a vision, and once more before his lowered eyes spread the unfathomable world of the marvelous, the world of love, the world of gentle compassion and of beautiful sacrifices.

"Pa-pa," the idiot mumbled the word which he had recently learned, and looked at his father askance, angrily, worriedly. But the man heard not and was silent, and his luminous face seemed inspired. He was dreaming the wondrous dreams of a madness that was brilliant as the sun. He believed with the faith of those martyrs who enter upon the stake as upon a couch of joy and die with a doxology on their lips. And he loved with the mighty and unrestrained love of the master who rules life and death and knows not the torture of the tragic impotence of human love. "Glory—glory—glory!"

"Pa-pa, Pa-pa!" once more mumbled the idiot, and receiving no reply took up his shears again. But he soon dropped them again, staring with motionless eyes and pricking up his outstanding ears to catch the sounds as they flitted past him. Hissing and rustling, laughter and whistling. And laughter. The night was in a playful mood. It squatted on the beams of the unfinished framework, rocking on the rafters and tumbling into the snow; it quietly stole into nooks and crannies, and there dug graves for those strangers, those strangers. And joyously it whirled up aloft, spreading its grey, wide wings, peering; then it tumbled again like a rock, or circling whizzed through the darkened window openings of the frosty framework, hissing and screaming. It was chasing the snowflakes—pallid with fear they silently sped onward in headlong flight.

"Pa-pa," the idiot shouted loudly. "Pa-pa!"

The man heard and raised his head with the long, black, greying locks that encircled his face like the night and the snow. For a moment before him rose again the bare, rough walls and the spiteful and frightened face of the idiot and the screaming of the rioting snowstorm, filling his heart with agonized elation. It is done—it is done.

"What is it, Vassily? Paste your boxes."

"Papa!"

"Be calm. The snowstorm? Yes, yes, the snowstorm!"

Father Vassily clung to the window—eye to eye with the greying night. He peered. And he whispered in terrified wonderment:

"Why doesn't he ring the bell?⁹ What if some one is lost in the fields?"

The night is sobbing. In the field—in the field—in the field.

"Wait, Vassily. I'll walk over to Nicon's. I'll return at once."

"Pa-pa!"

The door rattles, letting in a flood of new sounds. They first timidly edge their way near the door—no one is there. It is bright and empty. One by one they steal towards the idiot, groping along the ceiling, along the floor, along the walls. They peer into his brutish eyes, they whisper, they laugh, they commence to play with growing glee, with growing abandon. They chase one another, leaping and stumbling. They are doing something in the adjoining room, fighting and screaming. No one there. Light and emptiness. No one there.

"Boom!" somewhere overhead falls the first heavy note of the church bell scattering the myriad of frightened sounds into flight. "Boom!" goes the bell once more, with a second, muffled, viscid, scattered sound, as though an onrush of wind had caught the broad maw of the bell, and it choked and groaned. And the tiny sounds flee precipitously.

"And here am I again," says Father Vassily. He is all white and shivering. The stiff, red fingers cannot turn the page. He blows on

---

⁹ The village church bell is rung during a snowstorm to guide any team or wanderer that may be seeking the road.

them, rubs them together, and once more the pages rustle and all disappears, the bare rough walls, the repulsive mask of the idiot and the measured knell of the church bell. Once more his face is ablaze with joyous madness. "Glory, glory!"

"Boom!"

The night is playing with the bell. Catching its thickly reverberating notes, weaving about them a network of whizzing and whistling sounds, tearing them to pieces, scattering them abroad, rolling them ponderously over the fields, burying them in the snow, and listening with the head askew. And once more it rushes to meet the new clangor, tireless, spiteful and cunning like Satan.

"Pa-pa!" cried the idiot throwing to the ground the shears with a bang.

"What is it? Be quiet!"

"Pa-pa!"

Silence in the room, the whizzing and wrathful hissing of the snowstorm outside, and the dull, viscid sounds of the bell. The idiot is slowly turning his head, and his thin, lifeless legs, with the curving toes and the tender soles that have never known contact with firm ground stir feebly and impotently strive to flee. And he calls again:

"Pa-pa!"

"All right. Stop. Listen, I will read you something."

Father Vassily turned back the page and began with a grave and severe voice, as though reading in church:

"And as He passed by He saw a man who was blind from birth. He raised his hand and with blanched cheeks looked up at Vassya.

"Understand: BLIND FROM BIRTH. Had never seen the light of the sun, the face of his near ones and dear ones. He had come into the world and darkness had enveloped him. Poor man! Blind man!"

The voice of the priest resounds with the firmness of faith and with the transport of sated compassion. He is silent, he is staring ahead with a softly smiling gaze as though he cannot part with this poor man who was blind from birth and had never seen the face of a friend and had never thought that the grace of God was so nigh. Grace—and mercy—and mercy.

"Boom!"

"But listen, son. 'His disciples asked Him: Master who did sin, this man or his parents that he was born blind? Jesus answered: neither hath this man sinned, nor his parents, but that the works of God should be made manifest in him.'"

The voice of the priest gathers strength and fills the barren

155

room with its reverberations. And its sonorous sounds pierce the soft purring and hissing and whistling and the lingering cracked tolling of the choking church bell. The idiot is filled with glee over the flaming voice and the brilliant eyes and the noise and the whistling and the booming. He slaps his outstanding ears, he hums, and two streams of viscid saliva flow in two dirty currents to his receding chin.

"Pa-pa! Pa-pa!"

"Listen, listen: 'I must work the work of Him that sent me while it is day; the night cometh when no man can work. As long as I am in the world, I am the light of the world.' Forever and ever for ever and ever!" into the teeth of the night and of the snowstorm he flings a passionately ringing challenge. "For ever and ever!" The church-bell is calling to the wanderers, and impotently weeps its aged broken voice. And the night is swinging on its black, blind notes: "Two of them, two of them, two-two-two!"

Dimly Father Vassily hears it and with a stern reproof he turns to the idiot:

"Stop that mumbling!"

But the idiot is silent, and once more eyeing him dubiously Father Vassily continues:

"I am the light of the world. When he had thus spoken, he spat on the ground, and made clay of the spittle, and he anointed the eyes of the blind man with the clay. And said unto him, Go wash in the pool of Siloam. He went his way therefore,—and washed, and came seeing."

"SEEING! Vassya, SEEING!" menacingly cried the priest and leaping from his seat he began to pace the floor swiftly. Then he stopped in the center of the room and loudly cried:

"I believe, O Lord, I believe."

And all was still. But a loud galloping peal of laughter broke the silence, striking the priest's back. And he turned about terrified.

"What sayest thou?" he asked in fear, stepping back. The idiot was laughing. The senseless, ominous laughter had torn his immense immobile mask from ear to ear and out of the wide chasm of his mouth rushed unrestrained, galloping peals of oddly vacant laughter.

"Ha-ha-ha-ha!"

XI

On the eve of Whitsunday, the bright and happy festival of spring time, the peasants were digging sand to strew over the village roadways. The peasants of Snamenskoye had for several years past carted huge supplies of rich red sand from pits located a distance of two versts from their village, in a clearing which they had made in a dense wood of low birch, pine and young oak trees. It was in the beginning of June, but the grass was already waist high, hiding half-way the luxuriant and mighty verdure of the riotous bushes and their humid, green, broad foliage. And there were many flowers that year, with a multitude of bees flitting from blossom to blossom. The bees poured their rhythmical, ardent humming, the flowers shed their sweetly plain fragrance down the crumbling, sliding slopes of the excavation. For several days the air had been heavy with the threat of a storm. It was felt in the heated, windless atmosphere, in the dewless, stifling nights; the anguished cattle called for it, pleadingly lowed for it with stretched-out heads. And the people were gasping for breath, but abnormally elated. The motionless air crushed and depressed them, but something restless was urging them on to movement, to loud, abrupt conversation, to causeless laughter.

Two men were at work in the pits, Nicon, the verger, who was taking sand for the church, and the village elder's laborer, Semen Mossyagin. Ivan Porfyritch loved an abundance of sand both in the street in front of his house and all over his cobblestone yard, and Semen had taken away one cartload in the morning and was now loading another wagon, briskly throwing up shovelfuls of golden, ruddy sand. He rejoiced in the heat and in the humming, in the fragrance and in the pleasure of toil: he looked up with a challenge into the face of the morose verger who was lazily scratching up the surface of the sand with a toothless scraper, and he mocked him:

"Well, old friend, Nicon Ivanytch, we're doomed to blush unseen."

"Say that again," replied the verger with a lazy and indefinite menace, and as he spoke the pipe which he was smoking dropped from his mouth into the grey undergrowth of his beard and threatened to fall.

"Look out, you'll lose your pipe," Semen warned him.

Nicon did not reply, and Semen, unabashed, continued to dig. During the six months which he had spent in the service of Ivan Porfyritch he had grown smooth and round like a cucumber, and his

157

simple tasks came nowhere near exhausting his overabundance of vigor and energy. He alertly attacked the sand, digging in and throwing it up with the agility and swiftness of a hen scratching for grain; he gathered the golden gleaming sand, shaking up the spade like a wide and garrulous tongue. But the pit from which many cartloads had been taken the day before seemed exhausted and Semen resolutely spat out.

"Can't dig much here. Shall I try yonder?" he glanced up at a low little cave which had been dug in the crumbling sloping side of the pit and in which he saw a motley series of red and greenish grey layers, and he determinedly walked towards it.

The verger looked at the little cave and thought: "It might slide," yet he did not say a word. But Semen sensed the peril in the instinctive onrush of a vague anxiety which overcame him like a sudden attack of passing nausea and he stopped:

"Do you think it will slide on me?" he asked as he turned around.

"How should I know?" replied the verger.

In the deep recesses of the cave—which resembled a yawning mouth, there was something treacherous, something traplike, and Semen wavered. But from above, where the leaves of a young oak tree were sharply outlined against the azure sky, he caught the stimulating whiff of fresh foliage and blossoms, and this stimulating fragrance incited to gay and daring deeds. Semen spat out into his palm, seized his shovel, but after the second thrust a faint crunch was heard, and the whole slope of the excavation slid down without a sound and buried him. And only the young tree which barely hung on by its roots feebly moved its leaves, while a round lump of dried sand looking so bland and innocent rolled over to the feet of the verger from whose cheeks all color had fled. Two hours later Semen was taken out dead. His broad open mouth, with the clean and pearly teeth, was stuffed tight with the golden gleaming sand. And all over his face, amid the white eyelashes of his hollow eyes, mingled with his sunny hair and the flaming red beard glistened the gold of the beautiful sand. And still the tangled mass of his auburn hair was whirling and dancing, and the gay absurdity, the daredevil merriment of that dance around the pallid face that had settled into the rigor of death created the impression of a fiendish mockery.

With the curious throng attracted by the news of the accident, Senka, the little son of the perished man, had come on the run. No one thought of giving him a lift, and he had run the whole way in the rear of the village wagons; while his father's body was being released from the slide, he was standing aside on a mound of clay, motionless, breathing heavily, and as immobile were his eyes with which he devoured the melting avalanche of sand.

The dead man was laid on a wagon, atop of the golden load of sand which he himself had thrown upon it; they covered the body with a mat, and drove away at a slow pace over the rutty forest road. In the rear of the funeral wagon stolidly strode the villagers scattering in groups among trees, and their blouses struck by the rays of the sun flashed crimson through the wood. When the cortege passed the two-story house of Ivan Porfyritch the verger suggested that the corpse be taken to his house:

"He was his farmhand, let him bury him."

But not a soul was to be seen either in the windows or about the house and the shop was locked with a ponderous iron padlock. For a long time they knocked against the massive gates decorated with black flatheaded nails, then they rang the sonorous doorbell, and its reverberating echoes resounded sharply and loudly somewhere around the corner, but though the court dogs yelled themselves hoarse, for a long time no one came. Finally an old scullery woman came out and announced that her master ordered the body to be taken to the dead man's home, and promised to donate the sum of ten roubles towards funeral expenses, without deducting the gift from the earnings of the deceased. While she was arguing with the throng outside, Ivan Porfyritch himself, frightened to death and wrathful, was standing behind the curtains, gazing with a shudder upon the mat that covered the corpse and he whispered to his wife:

"Remember, if that priest offers me a million roubles I shall not shake hands with him, I'd sooner see it wither away. He is a terrible man."

And no one knew why, whether because of the churchwarden's mysterious words or from some other source, confused and ominous rumors swiftly appeared in the village and crept back and forth like hissing snakes. The villagers talked of Semen, of his sudden and terrible death, and they thought of the priest, not knowing what they were expecting of him. When Father Vassily started on his way to the requiem mass, pale and burdened by vague musings, but cheery and smiling, the people in his path stepped aside giving him a wide berth, and for a long time wavered before they dared to step upon a spot where his heavy footsteps had burned an invisible trace. They remembered the fire in his house and talked of it at great length. They recalled the Popadya who had burned to death and her son, the crippled idiot, and back of plain, clear words scurried the sharp thorns of fear. Some woman sobbed out aloud with a vague, overwhelming compassion, and went away.

159

Those who stayed back for a long time watched her departing sobshaken back, then in silence, avoiding to look at one another, they dispersed. The youngsters, reflecting the agitation of their elders, gathered at dusk on the threshing floor and were exchanging fanciful tales of the dead man, while their bulging eyes sparkled darkly. Cozily familiar irritated parental voices had been calling them to their homes for a long time, but their bare feet were loth to make a homeward dash through the gruesome diaphanous dusk of evening. And during the two days which preceded the funeral there was a ceaseless stream of villagers wending their way to view the corpse that was puffed-up and rapidly turning blue.

The two nights before the funeral the earth had been exhaling a breath of the most intense torridity, and the dry meadows consumed beneath the merciless heat of the sun were bare of vegetation. The sky was clear and dark, few stars were out and these shone dimly. And above all reigned on all sides the ceaseless chatter of the crickets. When after the memorial vesper service Father Vassily emerged from the hut, it was dark already, and the sleepy street was unlighted. Stifled with the close atmosphere, the priest had taken off his broad-rimmed hat and was walking with a noiseless stride as though over a soft and downy carpet. And it was rather from a vague sense of instinctive anxiety than from the sense of hearing that he realized that someone was following him, evidently suiting his stride to his own deliberate gait. The priest stopped, the pursuer who had not expected this, advanced a few steps and also stopped rather abruptly.

"Who is this?" asked Father Vassily.

The man was silent. Then he suddenly veered around, and swiftly retired without decreasing his pace, and a moment later he was lost in the trackless gloom of the night.

The same thing happened the following night; a tall, dark man followed the priest to the very gate or his house, and something in the bearing and in the stride of the heavily built stranger reminded the priest of Ivan Porfyritch, the churchwarden.

"Ivan Porfyritch, is it you?" he called. But the stranger did not reply and departed. And as Father Vassily was retiring for the night someone tapped softly at his window. The priest looked out, but not a soul was to be seen. "Why is he roaming about like an evil spirit?" thought the priest in annoyance, making ready to kneel down for his protracted devotions. And lost in prayer he forgot the churchwarden and the night that was restlessly spreading over the earth, and himself; he was praying for the deceased, for his wife and children, for the bestowal of the great mercy of God upon the earth and its

160

inhabitants. And in fathomless sunny depths a new world was assuming vague outlines, and this world was earth no more.

While he was praying the idiot had slipped from his bed, noisily shuffling his reviving but still feeble legs. He had learned to crawl in the beginning of the spring, and frequently on returning home Father Vassily found him on the threshold, sitting motionless like a dog before the locked door. Now he had started towards the open window, moving slowly, with much effort, and shaking his head intently. He had reached it, and hooking his powerful prehensile hands in the window sill he raised himself up and peered sullenly, greedily into the darkness. He was listening to something.

Mossyagin was to be buried on Whitmonday, and the day dawned ominous and uncertain, as though the confusion of people had found its counterpart in the formless confusion of nature. It had been oppressively hot since morning, the very grass seemed to curl up and wither before one's eyes as though seared by a merciless fire. And the dense opaque sky impended threateningly ever the earth, and its filmy blue seemed to be zigzagged with thin veins of bloody red, so ruddy it was, so sonorous with metallic nuances and shades. The enormous sun was blazing with heat, and it was so strange to see it shine so brightly, while nowhere the sharply defined and restful shadows of a sunny day were to be found, as though between sun and earth hung some invisible but none the less solid curtain intercepting its rays. And over all reigned a stillness that was mute and ponderous, as though an invalid had lost himself in a labyrinth of musing, and with drooping eyelids had lapsed into silence. Grey rows of young birches with withered leaves, cut down with the roots, stretched through the village in serried ranks, and this aimless procession of young grey trees, perishing from thirst and fire and spectrelike refusing to cast shadows, filled the mind with sadness and vague forebodings. The golden grains of sand that had been scattered over the roadways had long since turned into yellow dust, and the refuse of festive sunflower pips of the day before surprised the eye: it babbled of something peaceful, simple and pleasant, while all that had remained in paralyzed nature seemed so stern, so morbid, so pensive, so menacing.

While Father Vassily was donning his raiments Ivan Porfyritch entered into the altar enclosure. Through the sweat and the purpling flush of heat that covered his face timidly peered a grey earthy pallor. His eyes were swollen, and burning feverishly. His hurriedly combed hair, matted with cider, had dried in spots and stuck out in confused thickets, as though the man had not slept for several nights, wallowing in the throes of superhuman terror. He seemed somehow unkempt and distracted; he had forgotten the

161

niceties of human intercourse, failing to ask the priest's blessing or even to salute him.

"What is the matter with you, Ivan Porfyritch? Are you ill?" Father Vassily inquired sympathetically, adjusting his flowing hair that had caught in the stiff neckpiece of his chasuble; in spite of the heat his face was pale and concentrated.

The churchwarden made an attempt at a smile.

"Just so. Nothing important. I wanted to have a talk with you, Father."

"Was it you—last night?"

"Yes, and the night before, too. Pardon me, I had no intention...."

He heaved a deep sigh and once more oblivious of niceties, he openly blurted out trembling with fear:

"I am scared. I have never been scared before in my life. And now I am scared. I am scared."

"Of what?" asked the priest in amazement.

Ivan Porfyritch looked over the priest's shoulder as though someone, silent and dreadful, were hiding behind him, and continued:

"Death."

They were regarding one another in silence.

"Death. It's got to my household. Without rime or reason it will carry off all of us. All of us! Why in my home not a hen dare die without cause: if I order chicken soup, a hen dies, not otherwise. And what is this now? Is that proper order? Pardon me, but at first I had not even guessed it. Pardon me."

"You mean Semen?"

"Whom else? Sidor or Yevstigney?[10] Say, you listen to me, lad," coarsely continued the churchwarden, out of his mind with terror and wrath. "Leave these tricks be. We're no fools here. Get out of here while the going is good. Away with you."

He swung his head with an energetic nod in the direction of the door and added:

"And be lively about it."

"What's the matter with you? Have you lost your mind?"

"We'll see who's lost his mind, you or I. What devil's tricks is this you carry on here every morning? 'I'm praying! I'm praying!'"— he nasally mimicked the liturgical intonation. "This is no way to pray. Bide your time, bear up patiently, don't come with your 'I'm praying'. You're a pagan, a self-willed rebel, bending things to suit yourself. And now you're bent in return: what's become of Semen?

---

[10] Equivalent to "Tom, Dick and Harry."

162

Where is Semen? I ask. Why have you destroyed him? Where is Semen, tell me."

He roughly rushed towards the priest and heard a curt, stern warning:

"Away form the altar, blasphemer!"

Purple with wrath Ivan Porfyritch looked down upon the priest from his towering height and froze rigid with his mouth wide-open. Upon him gazed abysmally a pair of deep eyes, black and dreadful like the ooze of a sucking swamp, and some strange and abundant life was throbbing behind them, some one's menacing will issued forth from behind them like a sharpened sword. Eyes alone. Neither face nor body saw Ivan Porfyritch, but only eyes, immense like a house wall, high as the altar; gaping, mysterious, commanding eyes were gazing upon him, and as though seared by a consuming flame he unconsciously wrung his hands and fled knocking his massive shoulder against the partition. And in his fear-chilled spine, through the thick masonry of the church walls, he still felt the piercing sting of those black and dreadful eyes.

XII

They were entering the church with cautious steps and took up their stations wherever they chanced to be, not where they usually stood at service, where they liked or where they were accustomed to stand, as though finding it improper or wicked on a day of such awe and anguish to stick to trifling habits or to take thought of trivial comforts. And they took up their stations, hesitating a long time ere daring to turn their heads in order to look around. The church was crowded to suffocation, yet ever fresh rows of silent newcomers pressed from the rear. And all were silent, all were gloomily, anxiously expectant, and the crowded nearness of fellow-creatures gave no sense of security. Elbow was touching upon elbow and yet it seemed to each one that he was standing alone in a boundless waste. Drawn by strange rumors men from distant villages, from strange parishes had come to the little church; these were bolder and spoke at first in loud tones, but they too soon lapsed into silence, with resentful amazement, but impotent like the rest to break through the invisible chains of leaden stillness. Every one of the lofty stained windows was opened to admit air, and through them gazed the threatening coppery sky. It seemed to be sulkily peering from window to window, casting over all a dry, metallic reflection. And in this scattered and depressing, but none the less glaring light the old gilt of the image stand shone with a dull and irresolute lustre, irritating the eye with the chaotic haziness of the saints' features. Back of one of the windows a young maple tree greened motionless and dry, and many eyes were riveted upon its broad leaves that were slightly curled with the heat. They seemed like friends, old, restful friends in this oppressive silence, in this repressed hubbub of feelings, amid these yellow mocking images.

And above all the familiar, restful odors of church, above the sweet fragrance of incense and wax reigned the pronounced, repulsive and terrible smell of corruption. The corpse had been rapidly decomposing, and it was nauseatingly terrible to approach the black coffin which contained the decaying mass of rotting and stinking flesh. It was terrible merely to approach it, but around it four persons stood motionless like the coffin itself: the widow and the three now fatherless children. Perhaps they too smelt the stench, but they refused to believe in it. Or perhaps they smelt nothing and fancied that they were burying their dear one alive, even as most folks think when death swiftly and unexpectedly snatches away one who is near and dear and is so inseparable from their very life. But they were silent, and all was still, and the threatening coppery sky peered from window to window over the heads of the crowd scattering about its dry and distracted glances.

When the requiem mass had begun, with its wonted solemn simplicity, and the portly and kindhearted deacon had swung his censer into the throng—all breathed freely with the relief of elation. Some exchanged whispers; others more resolute heavily shuffled their benumbed feet; still others, who were nearest to the doors slipped out to the church steps for a rest and a smoke. But smoking and calmly exchanging small talk about harvests, the threatening drouth and money matters, they suddenly bethought themselves and fearing lest something momentous and unexpected might occur within while they were away, they flung aside the stubs of their cigarettes and rushed back into the church, using their shoulders as a wedge to break through the crowd. And then they stopped. The service was proceeding with a solemn simplicity; the aged deacon was coughing and clearing his throat before each sentence and warningly shaking a stubby fat forefinger whenever his gaze discovered a whispering pair in the throng. Those who had stepped outside before the close of the requiem mass had observed that over the forest, towards the sun, a hazily blue cloud had risen up in the sky, gradually growing dark under the rays of the sun, and they crossed themselves joyfully. Among them was also Ivan Porfyritch; pale and ailing he looked, but he also made the sign of the cross when he saw the cloud, but immediately lowered his eyes with a sullen air.

In the brief interval between the mass and the allocution to the corpse, while Father Vassily was donning his black velvet cassock, the deacon smacked his lips and said:

"A little ice would come in handy, for he smells rather strong. But where can you get ice? In my opinion it is well to keep a supply in the church for such cases. You might tell the churchwarden."

"He smells?" dully said the priest.

"Don't you notice it? You must have a fine nose! I'm simply done for. It will take a week in this hot spell to get the stench out of the church. Just take notice. I've got the smell in my beard, I swear."

He held the tip of his grey beard to his nose, smelt it and said reproachfully:

"Such people!"

Then commenced the chanting. And once more the leaden silence oppressed the crowd and chained each one to his place, cutting him off from among his fellow-men, surrendering him a prey to agonizing expectancy. The old verger was chanting. He had seen the coming of death to him who was now reposing in the black coffin and frightening the attending throng. He clearly recalled the innocent lump of dried earth and the young oak tree that trembled with its finely carved leaves, and the old, familiar, lugubrious words came to life in his mumbling mouth and hit the mark surely and painfully. And he was thinking of the priest with anxiety and sorrow, for in these impending hours of horror he alone of all other people loved Father Vassily with a shy and tender affection and he was close to his great rebellious soul.

"Verily all is vanity, and life is shadow and dreams; for whoso is born of earth striveth for all things, but the Scripture sayeth that when we gain the world we gain the grave, where together dwelleth the king and the beggar. O Lord Christ, give peace to thy servant, for Thou art a lover of mankind...."

Darkness was falling upon the church, the purpling blue ominous darkness of an eclipse, and all had sensed it long before any eye had discovered it. And only those whose eyes were riveted upon the friendly foliage of the maple tree outside had noticed that something cast-iron grey and shaggy had crept up behind it, peered into the church with lifeless eyes and resumed it climb to the cross of the steeple.

"... where there are worldly passions, where there are the

165

dreams of timeservers, where there is gold and silver, where there is a multitude of slaves and fame, all is dust and ashes and shadows," quivered the bitter words on senile trembling lips.

Everyone had now noticed the gathering gloom and turned to the window. Back of the maple tree the sky was black and the broad leaves looked no longer green. They had grown pale, and in their frightened rigid appearance there was nothing left that was friendly and reassuring. Seeking comfort the people looked into their neighbors' faces, and all faces were ashen-grey, all faces were pale and unfamiliar. And it seemed that the whole of that darkness— pouring through the opened windows in broad and silent streams, had concentrated itself in the blackness of that coffin and in the black-garbed priest: so black was the silent coffin, so black was that man—tall, frigid and stern. Surely and calmly he moved about, and the blackness of his garb seemed like the source of light amid the lack-lustre gilt, the ashen-grey faces and the lofty windows that disseminated gloom. But moment by moment a puzzling hesitancy and irresoluteness seemed to take hold of him; he slowed down his steps and extending his neck regarded the throng in surprise, as though he was startled to find this transfixed multitude in the church where he was wont to worship in solitude; then forgetting the multitude, forgetting that he was the celebrant he made his way distractedly into the altar enclosure; he seemed to be inwardly torn in two; he seemed to be waiting a word, a command or a mighty, all-solving sensation—and neither would come.

"I weep and I sob as I contemplate death and see reclining in coffins our beauty that was created in the image of God and is now become formless, inglorious and unsightly. O marvel! What is this mystery that surroundeth us? How are we surrendered unto corruption? How are we subjugated unto death? Verily by the word of God...."

Brightly gleamed the tapers in the gathering gloom as though in the dusk of eve, casting ruddy reflections upon the faces of the people, and many had noticed this sudden transition from day to night while it was high noon. Father Vassily too had sensed the darkness without comprehending it; the queer notion had entered his head that it was the dark of the early winter morning when he remained alone with God, and one great and mighty feeling had given wings to his soul—like a bird, like an arrow flying unerringly towards its goal. And he trembled, unseeing like a blind man, but on the point of receiving sight. Myriads of fugitive and tangled thoughts, myriads of undefined sensations slowed up their frenzied flight—stopped—died away—a moment of terrible nothingness, precipitous falling, death, and something rose up within his breast, something immense, something undreamt of in its joyous glory, in its wondrous beauty. The heart that had stood still was thumping forth its first beats, painfully, laboriously, but he already knew. It had come! It, the mighty, all-solving sensation, master over life and death, able to command to the mountains: "Move from your place!" and the hoary and cranky mountains must move. Glory, ineffable glory! He is gazing upon the coffin, into the church, upon the faces of people and he comprehends—he comprehends everything with that wonderful penetration into the depth of things which is possible only in dreams and which disappears without a trace at the approach of light. So that was it! That was the great solution! Glory! Glory! Glory!

He laughs out loudly and hoarsely, he sees the frightened expression of the deacon who had warningly raised his finger, he sees the crouching backs of the people who having heard his laughter burrow gangways through the crowd like worms, and he claps his hand over his mouth like a guilty schoolboy.

"I won't any more," he whispers into the deacon's ear, while insane rejoicing is fairly splashing fire from every pore of his face. And he weeps, covering his face with his hands.

"Take some drops, some drops, Father Vassily," the distracted deacon whispers into his ear and desperately exclaims: "Lord, Lord, how out of place! Listen, Father Vassily!"

The priest moves his folded hands an inch or two from his face, and looks from behind their shelter askance at the deacon. The deacon with a shiver, edges away on tiptoe, feels his way to the gate with his belly, and groping for the door emerges out of the altar enclosure.

"Come, let us give our last kiss, brethren, to the departed one, giving thanks unto God...."

A commotion ensues in the church; some depart stealthily without exchanging any words with those who remain, and the darkened church is now only comfortably filled. Only about the black coffin is the surge of a silent throng, people are making the sign of the cross, bending their heads over something dreadful and repulsive and moving away with wry countenances. The widow is parting from her husband. She now believes in his death and she is conscious of the nauseating odor, but her eyes are locked to tears and there is no voice in her throat. And the children are watching her with three pairs of silent eyes.

And while the people watched the deacon plunging worriedly through the congregation, Father Vassily had come out into the chancel and stood eyeing the crowd. And those who saw him in that moment had indelibly engraved in their memory his striking appearance. He was holding on with his hands to the railing so convulsively that the tips of his fingers turned livid; with I neck outstretched, the whole of his body bent over the railing, and pouring himself into one immense glance he riveted it upon the spot where the widow stood beside her children. And it was queer to see him, for it seemed as though he delighted in her boundless anguish, so cheerful, so radiant, so daringly happy was his impetuous glance.

"What partings, O brethren, what weepings, what sobbing in this present hour; come hither, imprint a kiss upon the brow of him who from his early youth hath dwelt among you, for he is now to be consigned to his grave, surmounted by a stone, to take up his dwelling in the darkness, being buried with the dead, parting from his kin and his friends...."

"Stop, thou madman!" an agonized voice came from the chancel. "Canst thou not see there is none dead among us?"

And here occurred that mad and great event for which all had been waiting with such dread and such mystery. Father Vassily flung open the clanging gate, and strode through the crowd cutting its motley array of colors with the solemn black of his attire and made his way to the black, silently waiting coffin. He stopped, raised his right hand commandingly and hurriedly said to the decomposing corpse:

"I say unto thee: Arise."

In the wake of these words came confusion, noise, screams, cries of mortal terror. In a panic of fear the people rushed to the doors, transformed into a herd of frightened beasts. They clutched at one another, threatened one another with gnashing teeth, choking and roaring. And they poured out of the door with the slowness of water trickling out of an overturned bottle. There remained only the verger who had dropped his book, the widow with her children, and Ivan Porfyritch. The latter glanced a moment at the priest and leaping from his place cut his way into the rear of the departing throng, bellowing with wrath and fear.

With the radiant and benign smile of compassion towards their unbelief and fear—all aglow with the might of limitless faith, Father Vassily repeated for the second time with solemn and regal simplicity:

"I say unto thee, Arise!"

But still is the corpse and its tightly locked lips are dispassionately guarding the secret of Eternity. And silence. Not a sound is heard in the deserted church. But now the resonant clatter of scattered frightened footsteps over the flagstones of the church: the widow and the orphans are going. In their wake flees the verger, stopping for an instant in the doorway he wrings his hands, and silence once more.

"It is better so. How can he rise in this state before his wife and children?" swiftly flits through Father Vassily's mind, and for the third and last time he commands, softly and sternly:

"Simeon, I say unto thee: Arise!"

Slowly sinks his hand, he is waiting. Someone's footsteps rustle in the sand just outside of the window and the sound seems so near as though it came from the coffin. He is waiting. The footsteps come nearer and nearer, pass the window and die away. And stillness, and a protracted agonized sigh. Who is sighing? He is bending over the coffin, seeking a movement of life in the puffed up and formless face; he commands to the eyes: "But open ye, I say," bends still lower, closer and closer, clutches the edges of the coffin with his hands, almost touching the livid lips and trying to breathe the breath of life into them, and the shaken corpse replies with the coldly ferocious fetid exhalation of death.

He reels back in silence and for an instant sees and comprehends all. He smells the terrible odor; he realizes that the people had fled in terror, that in the church there are only he and the corpse; he sees the darkness beyond the window, but does not comprehend its nature. A memory of something horribly distant flashes through his mind, of some vernal laughter that had been ringing in a dim past and then died away. He remembers the snowstorm. The church bell and the snowstorm. And the immobile mask of the idiot. Two of them.... Two of them.... Two of them....

And once more all is gone. The lacklustre eyes are once again ablaze with cold and leaping fires, the sinewy body is bursting once more with a sense of power and of iron firmness. Hiding his eyes beneath the stony arch of his brows, he says calmly, calmly, softly, softly as though fearing to wake a sleeper:

"Wouldst thou cheat me?"

And he lapses into silence, with downcast eyes, as though waiting for an answer. And once more he speaks softly, softly, with that ominous distinctness of a storm when all nature has bowed to its power and it is dillydallying, tenderly, regally rocking a tiny flake in the air.

"Then why did I believe?"

"Then why didst Thou give me love towards people and compassion? To mock me?"

"Then why hast Thou kept me all my life in captivity, in servitude, in fetters? Not a free thought! Not a feeling! Not a sigh! THOU alone, all for THEE! THOU only. Come then, I am waiting for Thee!"

169

And in the posture of haughty humility he waits an answer—alone before the black and malignantly triumphant coffin, alone before the menacing face of fathomless and majestic stillness. Alone. The lights of the tapers pierce the darkness like immobile spears, and somewhere in the distance the fleeing storm mockingly chants: "Two of them.. Two of them.." Stillness.

"Thou wilt not?" he asks still softly and humbly, but suddenly cries out with a frenzied scream, rolling his eyes, imparting to his face that candor of expression which is characteristic of insanity or of profound slumber. He cries out, drowning with his cry the menacing stillness and the ultimate horror of the dying human soul:

"Thou must! Give him back his life! Take it from others, but give it back to him! I beg of Thee!" Then he turns to the silent corruption of the corpse and commands it wrathfully, scornfully:

"THOU! THOU ask Him! Ask Him!"

And he cries out blasphemously, madly:

"He needs no paradise. His children are here below. They will call for him: 'Father!' And he will say to Thee: 'Take from my head my heavenly crown, for there below the heads of my children are covered with dust and dirt. Thus he will speak!"

Wrathfully he shakes the heavy black coffin and cries:

"But speak thou, speak, accursed flesh!"

He looks with amazement, intently. And in mute horror he reels backward throwing up his swelling arms in self-defence. Semen is not in the coffin. There is no corpse in the coffin. The idiot is lying there. Clutching with his rapacious fingers at its edges, he has slightly raised his monstrous head, looking askance at the priest with eyes screwed up, and all about the distended nostrils, all about the enormous tightly compressed mouth plays the silent dawn of coming laughter. Not a sound he utters, but keeps gazing and slowly creeping out of the coffin—inexpressibly terrible in the incomprehensible fusion of eternal life with eternal death.

"Back!" cries Father Vassily and his head swells to enormous proportions as he feels his hair stand on end. "Back!"

And once more the motionless corpse. And again the idiot. And the rotting mass madly alternates this monstrous play and breathes out horrors. And in maniacal anger he shrieks:

"Wouldst scare me? Then take...."

But his words are unheard. Suddenly, all aglow with blinding light, the immobile mask is rent from ear to ear and peals of laughter mighty as the peals of thunder fill the whole silent church. With a loud roar the mad laughter splits the arching masonry, flinging the stones about like chips and engulfing in its reverberations the lone man within.

Father Vassily opens his blinded eyes, raises his head and sees all about him crumble. Slowly and ponderously reel the walls and close together, the vaults slide, the lofty cupola noiselessly collapses, the stone floor sways and bends, the whole world is being wrecked in its foundations and disintegrates.

And then with a shrill scream he rushes to the doors, but failing to find them he whirls and stumbles against walls and sharp corners and shrieks and shrieks. The door suddenly opens, precipitating him on the flags outside, but he leaps to his feet with the joy of relief, only to be caught and held in someone's trembling, prehensile embrace. He struggles and whines, freeing his hand with maniacal strength; he rains savage blows upon the head of the verger who is attempting to hold him, and casting his body aside he rushes into the roadway.

The sky is ablaze with fire. Shaggy clouds are whirling and circling in the firmament and their combined masses fall down upon the shaken earth, the universe is crumbling in its foundations. And then from the fiery whirlpool of chaos the thunderous peals of laughter, the cackle and cries of savage merriment. In the west a tiny ribbon or azure is still to be seen, and towards that rift of blue he is rushing in headlong flight. His legs are caught in the long hairy cassock, he falls and writhes on the ground, bleeding and terrible to look upon, and rises and flees once more. The street is desolate as though at night, not a man, not a creature, neither beast, nor fowl to be seen near house or window.

"They're all dead," flashes through his mind—his last conscious thought. He runs out of the village limits into the broad highway. Over his head the black whirling cloud throws out three lengthy tentacles, like rapaciously curved fingers; behind him something is roaring with a dull and threatening bellow. The universe is collapsing in its foundations.

Ahead in the distance, a peasant and two women who had been to the village church are wending their homeward way on their wagon. They notice the figure of a black-garbed man in precipitous flight; they stop for a moment, but recognizing the priest they whip up their horse and gallop away. The wagon leaps high on its springs, with two wheels up in the air, but the three silently crouching terror-stricken people desperately whip up the horse and gallop and gallop.

Father Vassily fell about three versts away from the village in the center of the broad highway. He fell prone, his haggard face buried in the grey dust which had been ground fine by the wheels of traffic, trampled by the feet of men and beasts. And in his pose he had retained the impetuousness of his flight: the white dead hands outstretched, one leg curled up under the body, the other—clad in an old tattered boot with the sole worn through—long, straight and sinewy, thrown back tense and taut, as though even in death he still continued his flight.

BEN-TOBITH

On that dread day, when the cosmic injustice was perpetrated, and Jesus Christ was crucified in the midst of robbers on Golgotha, Ben-Tobith, a tradesman of Jerusalem, had been suffering since the early hours of the morning the agonies of an excruciating toothache.

It had started the day before, toward evening; at first his right jaw had commenced to ache slightly, and one tooth, the extreme tooth next to the wisdom tooth, seemed to rise a little, and felt painful when coming in contact with the tongue. After the evening meal, however, the pain had entirely subsided; Ben-Tobith had forgotten it altogether and felt no worry about it; that day he had profitably traded his old ass for a young and strong animal, at a profit, and he was in a merry mood and did not attach any significance to an evil omen.

And he had slept well and soundly, but before the dawn of day something commenced to disturb him, as if someone sought to rouse him to attend to an important matter, and when Ben-Tobith woke up wrathfully, his teeth were aching, aching defiantly and fiercely, with the excruciating fury of sharp and throbbing pain. And now it was impossible to tell whether it was still the tooth of the day before, or whether others had joined it as well; his mouth and his head were wholly filled with the dreadful agonizing pain, as though someone forced him to masticate a thousand red-hot sharply pointed nails.

He took in his mouth a swallow of water from an earthern pitcher; for an instant the fury of the pain subsided; the teeth twitched with undulating throbs, and this new sensation seemed even agreeable in comparison with the pain that had preceded it.

Ben-Tobith lay down again; he bethought himself of his newly purchased ass; he mused how happy he would it be if it were not for his teeth, and tried to sleep. But the water was warm; within five minutes the pain returned, with greater fury than ever, and Ben-Tobith sat up in his bed, rocking back and forth like a pendulum.

His face was all wrinkles, and something seemed to draw it toward his huge nose—and from his nose, that had turned livid with agony, hung a drop of cold perspiration. Thus, rocking back and forth, groaning with agony, he faced the first rays of that sun which was fated to see Golgotha with its three crosses and then to be dimmed with horror and grief.

Ben-Tobith was a good and kindly man, who disliked injustice, but when his wife woke up, he said to her many

173

disagreeable things, barely able to open his mouth, and complained that he had been left alone like a jackal to howl and to writhe in pain. His wife bore the undeserved reproaches with patience, for she knew that they came not from an angry heart, and she brought him many good remedies: some purified rat dung to be applied to his cheek, a sharp elixir of scorpion, and a genuine fragment of the tablets of the law broken by Moses.

A little improvement followed the application of rat dung, though it did not last long, and the same happened after the use of the elixir and the stone, but each time the pain returned with added vigor. But in the brief moments of respite Ben-Tobith comforted himself with the thoughts of the ass, and mused about him; and when the pain grew worse, he groaned, scolded his wife and swore that he would dash his brains out against a stone if the pain did not subside. And all the time he walked back and forth upon the flat roof of his house, from one corner to another, ashamed to come close to the edge because his head was all tied up in a kerchief like a woman's.

Several times during the morning his children came to him on the run telling him something with hurried voices about Jesus the Nazarene. Ben-Tobith stopped and listened to them for a moment, with wrinkled face, but then angrily stamped his foot and drove them away. He was a kindly man, fond of children, but now it annoyed him to be pestered with all sorts of trivial things.

It was also annoying to him that the streets and the neighboring roofs were crowded with people who seemed to have nothing to do but gaze curiously upon Ben-Tobith whose head was tied with a kerchief like a woman's. And he was already on the point of going downstairs, when his wife said to him:

"Look, they are leading the robbers. Perhaps this might take your mind away from your pain."

"Leave me alone, please. Don't you see how I suffer?" angrily retorted Ben-Tobith. But the words of his wife held out a vague promise that his toothache might pass, and he reluctantly walked over to the edge of the roof. Inclining his head to one side, he shut one eye, held a hand to his cheek, made a wry, sniveling grimace and looked down.

Up the steep ascent of the narrow street moved a confused and enormous mob of people in a cloud of dust and with a ceaseless uproar. In the midst of it, bowed under the burden of their crosses, marched the evildoers, and over their heads swished the whips of the Roman soldiers like sinuous dark-skinned serpents. One of them, he with the long, light locks, in a torn and blood-stained cloak, stumbled over a stone which someone had thrown before his feet and fell. The shouts increased in loudness, and the crowd closed in about the fallen man like a sea of motley waves.

Ben-Tobith suddenly shuddered with the pain; it seemed as though someone had pierced his tooth with a red-hot needle and twisted it around; he groaned "oo-oo-oo," and walked away from the edge of the roof, wryly indifferent and wrathful.

"How they yell!" he enviously muttered, picturing to himself their wide-opened mouths with strong and pain-free teeth, and thinking how he might yell himself if he were only well. This mental picture added fury to his pain, and he shook his bandaged head vehemently and howled "moo-moo-moo."

"They say that he healed the blind," observed his wife clinging to the edge of the roof and casting a stone at the spot where Jesus was slowly moving onward, having been raised to his feet by the soldiers' whips.

"Or course! Of course! He might have cured my toothache," replied Ben-Tobith sarcastically and with irritation, adding bitterly: "Just look at the dust they are raising Like a herd of cattle. They should be scattered with rods. Lead me downstairs, Sarah!"

The wife was right; the spectacle had diverted him somewhat, or perhaps the rat dung remedy finally proved its efficacy, and he managed to go to sleep. And when he woke up, the pain was almost gone, only a swelling had formed on his right cheek, so slight a swelling, in fact, as to be hardly noticeable. His wife said that it could not be seen at all, but Ben-Tobith smiled craftily, he knew what a good wife he had and how ready she was to say agreeable things. His neighbor, Samuel, the tanner, had come meanwhile, and Ben-Tobith took him to see the new ass; he proudly listened to his neighbor's words of praise for the animal and for its master.

Then, at the suggestion of his curious wife Sarah, the three of them walked over to Golgotha to see the crucified. On the way Ben-Tobith related to Samuel about his toothache from its very beginning, how the day before he had felt a twitch of pain in his right jaw, and how during the night he had been awakened by an agonizing pain. By way of illustration he made a wry face, shutting his eyes, shook his head and groaned, and the grey-bearded Samuel sympathizingly nodded and said:

"Tss-tss-tss, what suffering!"

Ben-Tobith was gratified by this expression of sympathy and he repeated his tale and reverted to that distant past when his first tooth had commenced to turn bad, the left tooth in the lower jaw. In such animated conversation they reached Golgotha. The sun which was fated to shine upon the world on that dread day had meanwhile set behind the distant hillocks, and in the west glowed like a bloody stain a narrow band of ruddy crimson. Against this background dimly darkled the crosses, and kneeling at the foot of the cross in the center some white-garbed figures glistened vaguely in the gathering dusk.

The people had long since dispersed; it was growing cold; casting a fleeting glance upon the crucified figures, Ben-Tobith took Samuel by his arm and cautiously turned him in the direction of their homes. He felt unusually eloquent and he was anxious to tell him more about the toothache. Thus they walked homeward, and Ben-Tobith, to the accompaniment of Samuel's sympathizing nods and exclamations, made once more a wry face, shook his head and moaned artfully, while from the deep crevices and the distant arid plains rose the blackness of night. As though it sought to cover from the sight of heaven the great misdeed of the earth.

THE MARSEILLAISE

He was a nonentity: the spirit of a rabbit and the shameless patience of a beast of burden. When fate, with malicious mockery, had cast him into our somber ranks, we laughed with insane merriment. What ridiculous, absurd mistakes will happen! But he— he, of course, wept. Never in my life have I seen a man who could shed so many tears, and these tears seemed to flow so readily—from the eyes, from the nose, from the mouth, every bit like a water-soaked sponge compressed by a fist. And even in our ranks have I seen weeping men, but their tears were like a consuming flame from which savage beasts flee in terror. These manly tears aged the countenance and rejuvenated the eyes: like lava disgorged from the inflamed bowels of the earth they burned ineradicable traces and buried beneath their flow world upon world of trivial cravings and of petty cares. But he, when he wept, showed only a flushed nose, and a damp handkerchief. He doubtless later dried this handkerchief on a line, for otherwise where could he have procured so many?

And all through the days of his exile he made pilgrimages to the officials, to all the officials that counted, and even to such as he endowed with fancied authority. He bowed, he wept, he swore that he was innocent, he implored them to pity his youth, he promised on his oath never to open his mouth again excepting in prayer and praise. And they laughed at him even as we, and they called him "poor luckless little piggy" and yelled at him:

"Hey there, piggy!"

And he obediently responded to their call; he thought every time that he would hear a summons to return to his home, but they were only mocking him. They knew, even as we that he was innocent, but with his sufferings they meant to intimidate other "piggies," as though they were not sufficiently cowardly.

He used to come among us impelled by the animal terror of solitude, but stern and shut were our lips and in vain he sought the key. In confusion he called us dear comrades and friends, but we shook our heads and said:

"Look out! Someone might hear you!"

And he would permit himself to throw a glance at the door— the little pig that he was. Was it possible to remain serious? And we laughed, with voices that had long been strangers to laughter, while he, encouraged and comforted, sat down near us and spoke, weeping about his dear little books that were left on his table, about his mamma and his brothers, of whom he could not tell whether they were still living or had died with terror and anguish.

In the end we would drive him away.

When the hunger strike had started he was seized with terror, an inexpressibly comical terror. He was very fond of food, poor little piggy, and he was very much afraid of his dear comrades, and he was very much afraid of the authorities. Distractedly he wandered in our midst, and frequently wiped his brow with his handkerchief, and it was hard to tell whether the moisture was perspiration or tears.

And irresolutely he asked me:

"Will you starve a long time?"

"Yes, a long time," I answered sternly.

"And on the sly, will you not eat something?"

"Our mammas will send us cookies," I assented seriously. He looked at me suspiciously, shook his head and departed with a sigh.

The next day he declared, green with fear like a parrot:

"Dear comrades, I, too, will starve with you."

And we replied in unison:

"Starve alone."

And he starved. We did not believe it, even as you would not; we all thought that he was eating something on the sly, and even so thought the jailers. And when towards the end of the hunger strike he fell ill with starvation typhus, we only shrugged our shoulders: "Poor little piggy!" But one of us, he who never laughed, sullenly said:

"He is our comrade! Let us go to him."

He was delirious. And pitiful even as all of his life was this disconnected delirium. He spoke of his beloved books, of his mamma and of his brothers; he asked for cookies, icy cold, tasty cookies, and he swore that he was innocent and pleaded for pardon. And he called for his country, he called for dear France. Cursed be the weak heart of man, he tore our hearts into shreds by this call: dear France.

We were all in the ward as he was breathing his last. Consciousness returned to him before the moment of death. He was lying still, frail and feeble as he was; and still were we too, his comrades, standing by his side. And we, every one of us, heard him say:

"When I die, sing over me the Marseillaise!"

"What are you saying?" we exclaimed shuddering with joy and with gathering frenzy.

"When I die, sing over me the Marseillaise!"

And for the first time it happened that his eyes were dry and

178

we wept; we wept, every one of us, and our tears glowed like the consuming fire before which savage beasts flee in terror.

He died, and we sang over him the Marseillaise. With voices young and mighty we sang the great hymn of freedom, and the ocean chanted a stern accompaniment, upon the crest of his mighty waves bearing back to dear France the pallor of dread and the bloody crimson of hope. And forever he became our guerdon—that nonentity with the body of a rabbit and of a beast of burden and with the great spirit of Man. On your knees before a hero, comrades and friends!

We were singing. Down upon us gazed the barrels of rifles; ominously clicked their triggers; menacingly stretched the points of bayonets towards our hearts—and ever more loudly, ever more joyously rang out the stern hymn, while in the tender hands of fighters gently rocked the black coffin.

We were singing the Marseillaise.

DIES IRAE

CHANT THE FIRST

1

. . . . This free song of the stern days of justice and retribution I have composed myself, as well as I could, I, Geronimo Pascagna, a Sicilian bandit, murderer, highwayman, criminal.

Having composed it to the best of my ability, I meant to sing it loudly, as good songs should be sung, but my jailer would not allow it. My jailer's ear is overgrown with hair; it has a strait and a narrow channel: fit for words that are untruthful, sly, words that can crawl upon their bellies like reptiles. But my words walk erect, they have deep chests, broad backs—ah, how painfully they tore at the tender ear of the jailer which was overgrown with hair!

"If the ear is shut, seek another entrance, Geronimo," I said to myself amicably; and I pondered, and I sought, and finally I succeeded and found it, for Geronimo is no fool, let me tell you. And this is what I found: I found a stone. And this is what I did: I chiseled my song into the stone, and with the blows of my wrath I set aflame its icy heart. And when the stone came to life and glanced at me with the fiery eyes of wrath, I cautiously took it away and placed it at the very edge of the prison wall.

Can you not see what I have in mind? I am wise, I figure that a friendly quake will soon again set the earth aquiver, and once again it will destroy your city; and the walls will crumble, and my stone will drop and shatter the jailer's head. And having shattered it, it will leave upon his soft waxy blood-grey brain the impress of my song of freedom, like the seal of a king, like a new commandment of wrath—and thus will the jailer go down to his grave.

I say, jailer, shut not your ear, for I shall enter through your skull!

2

If I am then alive, I shall laugh with joy; and if I chance to be dead, my bones shall dance in their insecure grave. That will be a merry Tarantella!

Can you say upon your oath that such things can never be? The same quake might cast me back upon the face of the earth: my

180

rotting coffin, my decayed flesh, my whole body, dead and buried for keeps, tightly clamped down. For such things have happened upon great days: the earth opening up about the cemeteries, the still coffins crawling out into the light.

Those still coffins, uninvited guests at the banquet!

3

These be the names of the comrades with whom I made friends in those fleeting hours: Pascale, a professor; Giuseppe, Pincio, Alba. They were shot by firing squads. There was also another one, young, obliging, and so handsome. It was a pity to look at him. I esteemed him as a son, he reverenced me as a father, but I did not know his name. I had not chanced to ask him, or perhaps I have forgotten it. He, too, was shot by the soldiers. There may have been one or two more, also friends, I do not remember them. When the youngster was being put to death, I did not run far away, I hid right here, back of the wall—now crumbled—near the trampled cactus. I saw and heard everything. And when I started to leave, the trampled cactus pierced me with its thorn. Was it not planted near the wall to keep away the thieves? How faithful are the servants of the rich!

4

The firing squad put them to death. Remember the names which I have mentioned; and with regard to those whom I have not mentioned by name, remember merely that they were put to death. But don't go and make a sign of the cross upon your brow, or worse than that—don't go and order a requiem mass—they did not like such things. Honor the dead with the silence of truth, and if you must lie, lie in some merrier fashion, but never by saying mass: they did not like that.

5

That first quake that destroyed the prison and the city had a voice of rare power and of queer, superhuman dignity: it roared from below, from beneath the ground, it was vast and hoarse and menacing; and everything shook and crumbled. And ere I grasped what was going on, I knew that all was over, that it was perhaps the end of the earth. But I was not particularly frightened: why should I be especially frightened even if it were the end of the world? Long did he roar, that deaf subterranean trumpeter.

And all at once politely opened the door.

6

I had sat a long time in prison, without hope. I had tried to flee and failed. Nor could you have managed to escape, for that accursed prison was very well built.

And I had become accustomed to the iron of the bars and to the stone of the walls, and they seemed to me eternal, and he who had built them the strongest in the world. And it was no use to think whether he was just or not, so strong and eternal he was. Even in my dreams I saw no freedom—I did not believe, expect or feel it. And I feared to call it. It is perilous to call freedom; while you keep still, you may live; but call freedom once, ever so softly, you must either gain it or die. This is true, so said Pascale, the professor.

And thus without hope I sat in prison, and suddenly opened the door. Politely and of its own accord. At any rate it was no human hand that opened it.

7

The streets were in ruins, in a terrible chaos. All the material of which people build was resolved to its elements and lay as it had been in the beginning. The houses were crumbling, bursting, reeling like drunken, squatting down upon the ground, on their own crushed legs. Others were sulkily casting themselves down upon the ground, with their heads upon the pavement—crash! And opened were the little boxes in which human beings live—pretty little boxes, all plastered with paper. The pictures still hung on the walls, but the people were no more; they had been thrown out, they were lying beneath masses of stone. And the earth was twitching convulsively—for, you must know that the subterranean trumpeter had started to roar again, that deaf devil who can never have enough noise because he is so deaf. Sweet, painstaking, gigantic devil!

But I was free and I did not understand it yet. I hesitated to walk away from that accursed prison. I was standing there, blinking stupidly at the ruins. And the comrades had also assembled, none attempting to leave, crowding distractedly, like the children about the figure of a dissipated, drunken mother that had fallen to the ground. A fine mother, indeed!

Suddenly Pascale, the professor, said:

"Look!"

One of the walls which we had deemed eternal had burst in two; and the window, with its iron bars, had split in two as well. The iron was twisted and torn like a rotten rag—think of it, the iron! In my hands it had not even rattled, it had pretended to be eternal, the most powerful thing on earth, and now it was not worth to be spat upon,—the iron, think of it!

Then I, and the rest of us, understood that we were free.

8

Free!

9

It is harder for you to bend a grass blade than for him to bend three iron rails one atop the other. Three or a hundred, it is all the same to him. It is more difficult for you to raise a cup of water to your lips than for him to raise a sea of water, to shake it up, to lift the dregs thereof and to cast them out upon the shore; to bring the cold to boiling. It is harder for you to gnaw through a piece of sugar than for him to gnaw through a mountain. It is more difficult for you to tear a thin and rotting thread than for him to break three wire ropes twisted into one braid. You will perspire and flush with exertion before you manage to stir up an anthill with your stick— and he with one push destroys your city. He has picked up an iron steamship as you with your hand pick up a tiny pebble, and has cast it ashore—have you ever seen the like of such strength?

10

All that had been open he has shut; the door of your house has grown into its walls, and together they have choked you: your door, your walls, your ceiling. And he likewise has opened the doors of the prison which you had shut so carefully.

You, rich man, whom I hate!

If I gather from all over the world all the good words which people use, all the tender sayings, all the ringing songs and fling them all into the joyous air;

If I gather all the smiles of children, the laughter of women whom none has yet wronged, the caresses of greyhaired mothers, the faithful handshakes of a friend—and weave of them all an incorruptible wreath for some one beautiful head;

If I pass over the face of the earth and garner all the flowers that grow upon it: in the forests and in the fields, in the meadows and in the gardens of the rich, in the depths of the waters, upon the azure bottom of the ocean; if I gather all the precious sparkling stones, bringing them forth out of hidden crevices, out of the gloomy depths of mines, tearing them from the crowns of kings and from the ears of the rich—and pile them all, the stones and the flowers, into one radiant mountain;

If I gather all the fires that burn in the universe, all the lights, all the rays, all the flashes, flares and silent glows, and in the glare of one mighty conflagration illumine the quaking worlds;

Even then I shall be unable to name thee, to crown thee, to laud thee—O Freedom!

12

Freedom!

13

Over my head was the sky, and the sky is always free, always open to the winds and to the movement of the clouds; under my feet was the road, and the road is always free; it was made to walk on, it was made for the feet to move over its surface, going back and forth, leaving one spot and finding another. The road is the sweetheart of him who is free; you have to kiss it on meeting, to weep over it on parting.

And when my feet began to move upon the road, I thought that a miracle had occurred. I looked, and Pascale's feet were also moving, the professor! I looked, and the youngster was also moving with youthful feet, hurrying, stumbling, and suddenly he ran.

"Whither?"

But Pascale sternly reproved me.

"Don't throw questions at him; you'll break his limbs. For you and I are old, Geronimo."

And we wept. And suddenly the deaf trumpeter roared out anew.

CHANT THE SECOND

1

A long time we walked about the city and saw much that was striking, strange and sinister.

2

Neither can you shut in the fire—I was saying this, I, Geronimo Pascagna. If you would be at peace, put it out altogether, but do not lock it up in stone, in iron or in glass; it will escape, and your strongly built house will come to a bad end. When your mighty house is fallen, and your life is extinct, it alone will burn, retaining the heat and the blazing ruddiness and all the force of the flame. It may lie awhile on the ground, it may pretend even to be dead; then it will lift its head upon a slender neck and look about—to the right and to the left, forward and backward. And it will leap. And it will hide again, and will look again, it will straighten up, throw back its head, and suddenly it will grow terribly stout.

And it will no longer have one head upon one slender neck: it will have thousands. And it will no longer crawl slowly, it will run, it will make gigantic bounds. It had been silent, now it is singing, whistling, yelling, giving orders to stone and to iron, driving all from its path.

And suddenly it will begin to circle.

3

We saw more dead people than living; and the dead were

185

calm; they did not know what had happened to them, and they were calm. But what about the living? Just think what a ridiculous thing was told us by a madman for whom, too, in those days of stern equality the door had opened!

Do you think he was amazed? He looked on attentively and benignly, and the grey stubble on his yellow face bristled with proud joy—as though he had done it all himself. I do not like madmen, and was going to walk past him, but Pascale, the professor, stopped me, and respectfully asked the proud madman:

"What makes you so pleased, signor?"

Pascale was far from being short of stature, but the madman searched for him a long time with his eyes, like for a grain of sand that has suddenly spoken out aloud from amidst of a sand heap, and finally he discovered him. And hardly parting his lips—so proud was he—he repeated the question:

"What makes me so pleased?"

And he waved his hand majestically and said:

"This is perfect order. We have so long craved for order."

He called that order! I laughed out aloud, but just at that moment a corpulent and altogether insane monk came up, and proved even more ridiculous.

4

For a long time they played their comedy among the ruins, the lunatic and the monk, while we sat on a heap of stones, laughing and encouraging them, shouting "bravo."

"Fraud! I have been deceived!" cried the fat monk.

He was so fat, I don't think you've ever seen any one as fat. It was repulsive to watch him, the yellow fat of his cheeks and of his belly quivered and shook so with wrath and fear.

"There's perfect order for you!" cried the lunatic approvingly, hardly deigning to part his lips.

"Fraud!" yelled the monk.

And suddenly he commenced to curse God. The monk! Think of it!

5

....
....

6

He assured us all that God had deceived him and he wept. He swore like a crooked gambler that this was poor recompense for his prayers and his faith. He stamped his feet and he cursed like a mule driver who comes out of a gin mill and suddenly discovers that his mules had scattered to the four winds.

And suddenly Pascale, the professor, lost his temper. He demanded that I give him my knife and said to the monk who had sat down for a rest after his outburst of curses:

"Listen, in a minute I will slit your belly, and if I find there but one drop of wine or one atom of a pullet...."

"And if you don't?" angrily retorted the monk.

"Then we shall count you among the saints. Hold his legs, Geronimo!"

The monk was frightened and departed mumbling:

"And I thought you were Christians! Blasphemy! Blasphemy!"

But the lunatic gazed after him benignly and spoke approvingly:

"This is what I call perfect order. We have been so long waiting for perfect order."

7

And we walked a long time about the city and saw many odd things. But the day was short, and the night fell upon earth earlier than ever before; and when the firing squad was killing Pascale, the soldiers had lighted their torches.

8

When Pascale was put against the wall, against the portion of it which had remained uninjured, and the soldiers raised their rifles, the officer said to him:

"You will die in a moment. Tell me why are you not afraid? That which has happened is terrible, and we are all pale with horror, but you are not. Why is that?"

Pascale was silent; he waited for the officer to ask him more questions so that he might reply to all of them in one.

"And whence comes your boldness: to stoop and to take that which belongs to others at a time when people in terror forget even themselves and their children? And are you not sorry for those women and children who have perished? We have seen cats that have lost their mind through terror, and you are a human being. I will have you shot instantly."

This was well spoken, but our Pascale could speak every bit as well. He has been shot dead. He is dead, but some day when all the dead arise you will hear his speech, and you will shed tears, if by that time all the tears are not exhausted, O Man.

He said:

"I take that which is another's because I have nothing that is my own. I took the raiment off a dead man in order to clothe my living flesh, but you have seen me do it, and so you have stripped me; and now I stand naked in front of your rifles. Soldiers, fire!"

But the officer did not suffer them to fire and asked him to speak further.

9

"Naked I stand in front of your rifles and fear nothing, not even your rifles. But you are pale with fear, and you fear everything, even your own rifles, even my naked body. When the quake was heard, it destroyed and killed your city, your fortunes, your children and wives—but it opened a prison for me. What then shall I fear? I have nothing of my own upon the face of the earth. I am, naked.

10

"And if the whole earth crumbled into ruin, and the very beasts howled with horror, and the fish found a voice to express their grief, and the birds fell to the ground with dread, even then I would not fear. For all others it means the ruin of the earth, for me it opens the doors of a prison. What then shall I fear? I am naked.

11

"And if the universe crumbled, with heaven and hell, and horror were enthroned over the infinity of living creatures, even then I would know no fear. For all it would be the end of the universe, for me the opening of a prison. What then shall I fear? I am naked.

12

"And now, when with one salvo of your rifles you will destroy for me the earth and the universe, even now I know no fear. For all of you it will be the destruction and the fall of a human body, but for me a prison will open its gates. Soldiers, fire! I am naked."

13

The torches blazed. It was the shortest day which I had ever seen. Night fell upon the earth more quickly than ever before.

"It is your turn now," ordered the officer, when Pascale, the professor, had fallen.

True, I had not been caught in any wrongdoing, and there was nothing to kill me for. But can you argue with them? And so I stood up. And I lamented the night. Do you understand me? the night! Here the torches and the fires were ruining it, and there, behind the torches and the fire, it stood out strong, and firm, and dark as the nights of my youth. I love the night, for then I do not see myself and can think what I will. The day reaches my garments, but can go no further. It stops at the darkness of my body and turns blind. But the night reaches my very heart. That is why it is so easy to love at night; anybody will tell you that. Ah, to spend only one hour in the shade of the faithful, of the black and beautiful night, only one hour. But can you argue with them? So I stood up.

But it is well to love also in the day time, when the sun is shining. Love itself is like the night, it reaches the heart, don't you see. And in love you fail to see your own self, even as in the midst of night. And if you only look into its eyes—straight into its black eyes—and look without tearing your gaze away....

Suddenly for some reason the officer shouted angrily at the soldier and snapped at me:

"Get out of here!"

14

Another day passed. And on that day the soldiers shot that youngster who had called me father.

15

Night sank upon the earth and I departed from that city of the dead.

16

Dies irae—the day of wrath, the day of vengeance and of stern retribution, the day of Horror and of Death.

17

. . . . That procession which I had watched from behind the wall was a strange and a terrible sight. They were bearing the statues of their saints, but did not know whether to raise them still higher over their heads or to cast them upon the ground, trampling the fragments underfoot. Some were still cursing, while others were already saying their prayers, but they walked on together, the children of the same father and the same mother, or Horror and of Death. They leaped over the crevices and disappeared in abysses. And the saints reeled like drunkards.

Dies irae.... Some were singing, others were weeping, and still others were laughing. Some howled like lunatics. And they were waving their hands, and all were in a hurry. The fat-bellied monks were running. From whom were they running away? Not a soul was seen behind them. Meekly lolled the ruins in the warm glow of the sun, and the fire was disappearing into the ground, smoking wearily.

18

From whom were they fleeing? There was not a soul behind them.

19

You barely touched a tree, and a ripe orange fell at your feet. First one, then another, a third.... The crop bids fair to be fine. A good orange is like a little sun, and when there is an abundance of them, you feel like smiling, as though the sun shone brightly. And the leaves are so dark, just like the night back of the sun. No, they are green, dark green. Why are you telling untruths, Geronimo?

But how cautious is that deaf devil, that subterranean trumpeter, who is never content because of his deafness: he has destroyed a city, but has left an orange suspended on a branch, to wait for Geronimo. You barely touch the tree, and a ripe orange drops at your feet. First one, then another, then a third.... They will be taken overseas to strange lands. And in those lands, where reign the cold and the fogs, people will look at them and say: "Yes, there is a sun for you!"

20

Pascale, the professor,—we called him "il professore" because he was so wise, he could write verses, and he discoursed so nobly on all sorts of subjects. He is dead.

21

Why am I terrified? Why do I walk faster and faster? I had been afraid there....

22

I never knew that my feet so loved to walk. They love every step which they make. They part so sadly with every step; they seem to want to turn back. And so greedy are they that the longest road seems short to them, that the widest road seems narrow. They regret—fancy!—that they cannot at once walk backward and forward, to the right and to the left. Let them have their will and they will cover the earth with their traces, not leaving a patch: and still they would seek more.

And another thing I did not know: I did not know about my eyes that they can breathe.

Afar off I see the ocean.

23

What else can I tell you? I was seized by the gendarmes.

191

24

Once more thou hast locked the doors of my prison, O Man! When didst thou have time to build it? Still in ruins lies thy house, the bones of thy children are not yet bare in the grave, but thou art already at work, tapping with thy hammer, patching together with cement the obedient stone, rearing before thy face the obedient iron. How fast dost thou build thy prisons, O Man!

Still in ruins are thy churches, bu thy prison is all finished.

Still shaking with terror are thy hands, but already they grasp the key, and rattle the lock, and slip the bolt. Thou art a musician: to the jingle of gold thou requirest the accompanying rattle of fetters— let that be the bass.

Grim death is still in thy blanched nostrils, and already thou art sniffing at something, turning thy nose this way and that way. How fast buildest thou thy prisons, O Man!

25

The iron does not even rattle—so strong it is. And it is cold to the touch like someone's icy heart. Silent is also the stone of the walls—so proud it is, so everlasting and mighty. At the appointed time comes the jailer and flings at me my food like at a savage beast. And I show my teeth—why should I not show my teeth? I am starved and naked. And the clock is striking.

Art thou content, O Man, my master?

26

But I do not believe in thy prison, O Man, my master! I do not believe in thy iron; I do not believe in thy stone, in thy power, O Man, my master! That which I have once seen destroyed, shall never be knit together again.

Thus would have spoken even Pascale, the professor.

27

Set thy clock a-going, it marks well the time until it stops. Rattle thy keys, for even thy paradise thou hast shut with lock and key. Rattle thy keys and shut the door, they shut well while there is a door. And walk around cautiously.

And when all is still, thou wilt say: it is well now, it is quite still now. And thou wilt lie down to sleep. It is quite still now, thou wilt say, but I hear how he is gnawing at the iron with his teeth. But thou wilt say that the iron is too strong for him, and thou wilt lie down to sleep. And when thou hast fallen asleep, holding tight thy keys in thy happy hands, suddenly the subterranean trumpeter will roar out loudly, awaking thee with his thunder, raising thee to thy feet with the force of terror, holding thee erect with a mighty arm: so that dying thou shalt see death. Wide as the day will open thy eyes; terror will tear them wide open. Ears will come to thy heart, so that dying thou shalt hear death.

And thy clock will stop.

28

Freedom!